ANTS 169

Revised, illustrated

Keith Hulse

ISBN-9798412230467

Cover design by: Art Painter
Library of Congress Control Number: 2018675309
Printed in the United States of America

Dedicated to science fiction lovers.
And if aliens are living amongst us, to them also.
To insect life, remember our bees.

CONTENTS

Chapters

82745 words

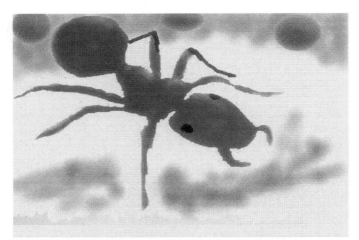

Utna, The good Black Ant, below the three crimson moons

of White Planet World.

ANT RIDER.

Welcome and introduction page

Here the Insects rule and we humans are the farmed cattle farms. Then let us hope we always give grace for what we eat.

Sheep. Cow, chicken, duck, (Farm sounds), snake, (hissing).

Anything you fancy, especially if moving and with four legs; and (table running about escaping chef, has four legs, DNA altered to taste like kangaroo).

A sauce, yes, a sauce just for the dish. More chili the better, humans like to burn inside.

For it says, 'everything is given humans,' and that is why we must say grace; a 'Thank you;' but say, 'we have not been given everything and are guardians only.'

'Whatever pass the salt and pepper.' Remember we eat anything. **Ostrich Eggs so big;** but lions and tigers are almost extinct so farming them is out. But what if your culture does not mind? The we say yes, to farming lions.

Who is right? And **IF a**liens see us as tasty farm animals. **What If** they are not vegetarians? **What IF** they use us as Sunday spreads? **What IF,** they use us as plough animals. Fancy living in a cozy pig pen.

All because their culture says it is right as their god gave them all in space to eat, without saying grace.

Besides whom really said we eat this and that? The dodo is extinct as sailors ate them, not a farming thought, selling them to visitors. Just pass the salt and pepper please.' And suddenly there was no cod left because someone said eat it Fridays. Well, **what IF** someone said eat human; I hear we taste like pork.

'Pass the salt and pepper,' the alien said.

"Mummy, can I cover my human in ketchup?" The alien kid.

"What is wrong with my cooking?" Mummy.

"Where's the toy?" The alien kid trying to change the subject, he knew mummy grew extra arms when angry. Extra hands to catch him running away on his penguin feet.

They were aliens and farming us, animals that tasted like pork; so Melanesian cannibals said. There is nothing like the taste of tomato ketchup unless the watery vinegary type at driver's roadside cafes.

Then aliens did fling cups and demand only the best brands whose names escapes.

Book 1

What Tarves Dallas the silver eyed Vernal deciphered from the Shurrupuk hieroglyphics, and what Ulana his daughter told by her mate Luke.

And Tarves Dallas called his book 'Ant Rider.'

Humans were not meant on White World arriving accidentally, when their silver decked red hulled passenger ship Phoenix went down a black hole.

"We all know black holes eat planets and stars as we see them do it, so, presume disaster waits at the other end.

Nothing of the sort; black holes are gateways to universes, and more black holes so, we who went down that hole know the original universe is one layer of space upon another. Well, imagine a sandwich, the bread being black holes and the filling universes.

And a black hole exists to return us to our own universe. Otherwise, I Luke could never have returned a man."

Lo, Tarves Dallas added, "Vornals were not meant on White World either. It was the place where the dead went, **hell**." And we the living ended up there too

(Color: white sky, red sun, blue grass and little blue, red clouds and a rainbow. Sound: Loud chitin segments clicking.)

I, Luke, was not born when Star Ship Phoenix went down. My ancestors survived in the stern engine sector. Lucky the engineers got the engines to break the land on

World. There were forty thousand humans in that section.

That was in the Time of Myths as we descendants call it, today being year 2000, Day 2000 and Root Day when we remember we are human and not slave. There are now 320,000,000 million of us humans on world as our masters breed us ruthlessly.

And it began: Our nest was idle, Root Day was a festival, tables spread with curried pupae, kebab fly larvae, tubers, current cakes, and lemonade.

Our human musicians' metal musical instruments on the reed platform waiting played, waiting for Elder Peter to release a silver balloon shaped as a ship with sails. **(Cooking essences).**

The meaning behind the balloon was simple, it was Star Ship Phoenix. I stood near the band stand, dead center of the nest, holding the shovel Utna the ant, had given me.

"Utna, you ordered us to work when by law is a slave holiday?" I asked substituting slave for human. When speaking to the giant ants you had to be crafty, remember your place even if Utna was a Black friend.

A black hole was a gateway.

But Utna was always kind to me, as all black ants who would work all day as

(White sky)

their biological clock is set for cleaning fungus off white eggs and carting away litter.

They could not take holidays as were unable to be idle, as we. Born workers and would die such. Their "Little books," Peter Elder, "does not allow them rest." He meant their gene code as I learned later from Phoenix.

And the blacks liked us for we pried red mites off them, we did not mind, we threw them into boiling water, then cracked the shells and ate the meat.

And I knew I was something special to Utna, my shining eyes attracted Utna. My eyes glowed life, sparkled, attracting people, like Peter our elder who said he saw something in me, that I could not, and he did not tell me what? And Nina, the great Noble Insect Queen who ruled us had not listened to our calls, we were not born workers, but to be divergent as her own race. Nobles as they called themselves.

Even now her red wax image stared down at me, from its niche by the band. And Utna replied by sign language that Nina said, "Root Day no more." I had suspected as much watching him go back to work and picked up the white cabbage butterfly caterpillar that was to be our lunch.

Behind Utna, soldier ants and more Black worker ants carrying more caterpillars. The ants would not roast theirs as our mothers would, although the Ant Ghoster humans would imitate our masters in their insect masks and, rip their grubs apart live, stuffing their mask mouths full of dripping white protein.

Me, being a little five feet nine runt looked forward to mine in my mother's sweet and sour sauce.

These Ant Ghosters were the only humans Nina allowed to carry weapons, fire hardened tipped spears, for she trusted Ghosters to a degree for they proved their loyalty by treating us as Nobles did..........ate us.

In front of us in our owner's halls, toasting Queen Nina monthly. Sullenly watch them roll out wheeled spits with charred meat. Watched them baste the limbless headless torso with minted oil, as if it were a whole sheep, but it was not, it was human, pork.

"I made her out of wax," the bee hummed as the morning rays turned the blue grass pink, and since the grey of the night was still lingering, it matched Queen Nina. "

Someone who had offended a Noble Insect by clearing his throat and aiming the green slime at the insect foot, **(Throat clearing sound).**

I could not understand this insanity. How people could vent their frustrations knowing it resulted in death.

Now I do, they had gone insane and saw spit a lethal weapon. A way of worthy defiant expression.

But still the Nobles kept pens for kids reared on milk......human kids, tender meat, veal.

You see Nina was afraid humans would come to dominate World.

Our babies were healthy and a result of the Noble breeding program. Queen Nina had come to realize that she could not have a slice of the cake and whole cake. You breed slaves faster than you breed yourselves, there can only be one mathematical outcome; slaves will outnumber masters.

And Queen Nina feared us for we were different. Just look at me, I did not have yellow wobbly antennae sticking out of my cranium.

Serious, our women are prizes amongst Insect Nobles for they were fair, and Nobles did come riding their giant red ants and emerald dragonflies and pick our women, for their harems, **(Perfume smells).**

Our women's skin was hairless and ninety percent non-chitinous. And for two thousand years Nobles have laid us across their teaching tables, pinned and displayed our organs in the name of Noble science, and now Noble women have smooth legs as our women, for they have our genes inserted into themselves.

Become humanoid insects, well they breed of us.

They have schools and universities with science labs.

And we share the same fate as frogs and pigeons.

They breed us **ruthlessly,** could spare us.

And take handsome teenagers from us and we see them as attendants to Nobles as

(Marching army sounds)

harem attendants and to their women as pet lap dogs.

"I, God Enil, gave you humans for your pleasure," scribes wrote in their holy book. So, why my mum cut my curly brown hair short, made sure I rolled in ant dung, wore rags, and did not bath and rubbed black stuff on my strong white teeth.

"Luke," mother speaking, "they have divine right to use us. Never bring attention to yourself." So far, I have heeded her, I never danced for no one; only to what made my blue eyes glow and at night privately.

Anyway, back to the present: Then the Black soldier ants came to regiment us into our work gangs for Root Day was no more.

"Stay where you are," Peter Elder shouted in the center of our nest, and we stood while Black soldier ants became confused, who did not kill us as saw us as smaller brother Black worker ants.

We smelled as them, **(Insect resin smell).**

Our bare feet trod the soil that was their latrine.

And Peter summoned other elders, and they walked out of our underground nest into the white daylight of World looking towards Shurrupuk the city of our queen. Elders **silhouetted** in their Jacobs multicolored robes, and magician hats against the white horizon and termite towers that the Nobles lived in. "Dung Towers," Elder Peter called them for termites made them.

Luke full of the milk of ants

Now, as I said the black ants became confused and after clicking their complaints fell silent.

And the red sun was hot and the day still, not a mammal stirred in the nest discarded matter pit, **(Yellow umbrella).**

Grey meteorite dust rose from where the blue grass stomped dead by warriors, over the eons that was the road from Shurrupuk to the nest.

And clicking sounds of chitinous armor on that road. Still Peter and the elders stood facing the sounds, our magicians as Nina called them. Magicians nothing, they could not make frogs out of thin air; but did have knowledge like how to draw roads up Nina's termite towers on paper and then build them.

Anyway, our black ants, were excited, and now Black soldiers raised themselves opening massive mandibles. And they came wanting trouble, giant red soldier ants and thirty feet long red and yellow striped centipedes which are the hunting hounds of Nobles.

Behold a black stag beetle bigger than all, and his flanks covered in brass segments with bronze bells that we could hear now that this host had halted. And on the huge beetle grey dust and a wicker cane howdah with a yellow umbrella.

And a great insect Noble Lord in it.

And wore a blue spider silk robe under gold chest armor and on his head a silver crown.

(Army stinks & sounds, sweat, latrines, cooking, drums, pipes)

And was chewing a delicacy held to his mouth by an almost naked human girl.

"We demand to see Nina," Peter waving his carved elder staff at Lord Hupamuk, cousin and lover of Queen Nina, commander of her army. Hupamuk First Advisor to Nina, I saw him smile and for an Insect folk he was handsome, humanoid, stunning in his blue gashed silk robes showing his scarlet limbs, for Nobles have chitin two legs, and arms. And dozens have ant antennae.

Silence except for this Noble: "Peter or should I say Lord Peter," and I saw the corners of Hupamuk's white lips twitch and was afraid,

"Here Lord Peter take my crown," and Lord Hupamuk threw a silver crown at Peter's feet.

"Since you refuse to pick it up you are unworthy to lead your people, to speak to me not alone Nina......slave," and with this he waved his pink gloved right hand gently and his girl slave threw the delicacy at Elder Peter.

And Peter picked it up and tears from his eyes for it was a child's hand covered in hot

*(Shurrup
uk City, Termite Towers)*

peanut sauce. And I saw Peter remove a human crafted ring from one crackling finger. Yes, Peter did more than spit his wrath, he hit the stag beetle's right eye with his staff, so it cracked as he shouted: "My child my child you have eaten my daughter."

And reds and centipedes fell upon Peter and the elders. **Peter screamed** as an orange centipede sixty feet long sank its front claws into his belly squirting venom.

Then chewed him up good.

And Lord Hupamuk who had fallen off his beetle, mounted a giant red battle ant covered in copper sheeting directed the slaughter of our elders.

And saw from my burrow where I had fled seeking my family; reds, blacks, centipedes, humans all running.

Now something big and black fell across the burrow preventing me joining the melee.

Nobles rode latest models.

If I had really wanted to?

And elders and black ants fought back and died. Now Lord Hupamuk had ordered the black ants not to interfere, but how could they obey? The Black Ant nest invaded by hereditary red enemies and so fought.

We were also their workers and had a duty to defend us, so died beside their human friends. And Noble trumpets of dried waxed giant sun flowers sounded so reds and centipedes stopped eating and stood feeling the vibrating ground with their legs, new attack orders.

And our survivors fled to the center of the nest, high ground and a stream of black ants carted eggs and young here.

Humans carted their own young and belongings. And the high ground was a human elder idea, barricaded by stakes and piles of builders ready for pushing on the enemy, a colorful host marching .... onto the fawn sun baked soil of our nest. Queen Nina, her court, men folk Nobles pointing out the interesting bits about human life like the fish smoking houses and the bits of human anatomy that lay about to stupid giggling courtesans, all fanned by deformed Nobles, those whose genetic human cocktail had misfired; entertained by dwarf Noble jugglers, sword swallowers, fire eaters or them that stuck needles through their ears and navels.

And Nina's trumpeters fell silent, **(Blaring fanfare),** wonderful peace.
Nina on her olive sedan chair on the backs of humans on all fours,
her dyed green hair flowing under her gold head band, black chitinous
skin gleaming under our red sun while her small blue eyes emotionless,
insect eyes housed in a cranium that would pass as human.

(Sound of dying fades)

And she was as disturbing as I had last seen her, as shapely as our own women.

Not ashamed to wear only a red robe, soft, made from human baby down and her silver bodice, spider silk.

(Tantalizing woman smell)

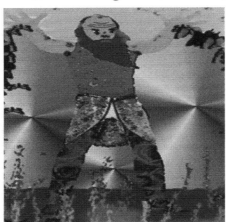

Peter could pull white rabbits out of hats too!

Proud, displaying pointed yellow bosoms, straight backed, "Look at me," she was saying, "desire me, worship," and the Ant Ghosters did, and waving bits of our elders at her while performing acts of bestiality.

"For the soil is life, the mother of all wheats, nourish it, its womb is bountiful," God Enil and the Ant Ghosters did.

And Queen Nina was pleased for she knew they acted their desires for her. Nina the mother of all insects as from her womb came countless eggs and new nests.

And the queen pointed at those who had fled to the high ground now guarded by defiant Black soldier ants.

And I was afraid, (Fear smells).

So, the Ant Ghosters fell upon the high ground with their fire hardened spear tips and berserks died by hundreds, but they did their job, weakening our defenses. And when our resistance collapsed, Queen Nina sent the red ants and centipedes to finish us off.

And I cursed wanting to die with my tribe, Utna breathed life, I survived. So, peace fell upon our nest for all fighting stopped. **And** these sounds drifted to my ears, **(Moaning.)** the sounds of marrow extracted from bones; centipedes feeding. The screams of human families separated, **(crunching's)** and **the loud crack of necks,** snapped as defeated Black soldiers decapitated by reds, executions, **and** the Ant Ghosters wanting similar.

Now these foolish Ghosters, humans believe they go straight to the heavenly world Naja if insects devour them. And blood lust was upon all, and dozens got their wish as they kneeled in front of a centipede that suddenly sunk its venomous claws into a chest.

So much yellow venom that it squirted elsewhere.

And was a painful death as the offerings twitched and loosened their bowels.

And saw the satisfaction on the faces of the Ant Ghosters priests over this unnecessary suffering; now pain is a major part in Insect and Ghosters rituals and I noted no priest offer themselves.

And that day I saw ten Ant Ghosters become dust for new seed to plant root in. But the Ghoster priests were not worried; they would recruit ten that number from amongst the human slave pens with promises of Lordship over other slaves.

(Termite towers)

And I and families of those taken by force would not mourn the ten deceased Ghosters.

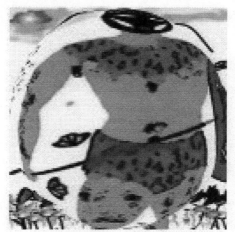

Want to be a weevil? An ant Ghosted did

That day was the end of our existence upon world, for the victorious Insects chained human ankles and necks.

Our nest had boasted twenty thousand humans and a million black ants. Wells, sewers, paths as our elders had knowledge and even amphitheaters for our plays and such made Queen Nina afraid of her human slaves.

By the time the red sun came again on **Day 2001** six thousand men lay drying under the sky. Two thousand left to repopulate the nest and the rest into cages aboard giant transport flies and beetles.

And our women numbered thousands enslaved under these orders, "Let there be pure stock for future Noble needs," Queen Nina's decree before she left for Shurrupuk City.

And the hieroglyphics in Shurrupuk City show on day 2007 the last Black soldier ant kneeling under a red sun. The next picture shows a black head at the feet of the red.

And the lesson repeated throughout the Lands of Shurrupuk in every black ant nest Queen Nina claimed domain.

"And it would take a human slave two calendars to walk Nina's empire from west to east and from north to south at thirteen miles a day," Peter Elder said.

And one calendar month is two hundred Days.

(Insect sounds. <u>Two days later Day 2009,</u> I had fled the nest never wanting to return and now lay by a pink lily covered blue pool dozing with nightmares. Seeing Queen Nina order a centipede to crawl over my baby sister's pink naked body, watching the black sting go in her tongue, heard her scream, saw her vomit, and awoke finding Utna over me, it was only a nightmare.

Shurrupuk City never slept, human slaves treaded mills to keep the lights glowing, one-way street signs illuminated.

Human carved graffiti except the Insect Nobles did not read too well so thought it said "Praise you," when it said, "nasty rotten things?"

*

Ants do not have our eyes so; it is a waste of time seeking their intent there. They give away their feelings by movement and Utna was gentle, offering affection.

I did not refuse it, been round ants to long, knew them as insects who belonged to the master race of World.

Even if Utna was my friend.

To him I was a worker who had escaped the invasion of the nest.

Utna was good.

Nina might be Queen of Shurrupuk, but she did not need to do what she had, send in reds and centipedes that way to exterminate. She was just a vain woman who could not rub two twigs together to make a sunrise.

She could have used bees to strum their wings to send vibrations to the black ants to block our elder's paths, have them picked up and dumped in slave pens till promise of good behavior, but we were different, so killed us, we were humans, were we not we? And the message today sent to Governor Ziusudra of our province, who like Nina belonged to what we called The Insect Noble Folk.

They who no longer looked like legged insects but had bodies as ours, except the eyes, insects, and the skin, mostly chitinous. About a tenth of Insect folks can still fly, Nina cannot. To have wings is lowly, common insect, a worker; if Nina had wings it would be a reversal of society.

World rural peace scene.

See their God Enil did not have wings in the hieroglyphics? A high percentage of Insects are born deformed, become outcast, cannot call themselves Nobles, the performers, jugglers, mutants, Berserkas.

And Ziusudra wanted to come as before and talk with Peter making promises, always promises on our behalf.

Governor Ziusudra never sent a human to the Dust Bowl unless it was for a capital crime, in that he/she had killed Noble or giant insect.

In this respect Red Ziusudra as we called him because of his flowing red hair and knotted beard was good. He allowed us to police our own and was a man of future vision.

"But they share insect programming, look at Ziusudra's red skin, insect chitin," as Peter often said, "operating robots," he insulted and talked to us of hidden books of knowledge whose contents were handed down by word of mouth from elder to elder.

Human writing as writing Peter told us, only the elders taught the secrets of the magic words for Nina and her kind had forbidden that knowledge to humans.

Writing was dangerous..........it enlightened humans.

And no elder had ever become an Ant Ghoster so, Nina would never find our secrets of building and medicine.

So, Peter taught secretly. And he liked my shining eyes, and I had a sneaky suspicion he had watched me dance alone under the three crimson moons of World.

He knew me, knew who my soul danced too but never told me.

I danced when I looked at the moon and felt one with what animates everything, I filled with love, then got too dance and hug trees.

And the elders were correct for the good of humans only the elders should know such secrets for, if caught marched by red ants to Dust Bowls.

(Spiritual bliss)

Meteorite craters covered in soft grey dust which the black ants, and humans clean. Clearing away the chewed remains of them eaten, **(Decay wafts).**

And Dust Bowls were the main entertainment of Queen Nina and her Insect Nobles.

Anyway: Nineteen and alone, Luke the son of Shaun the cheese maker. Well, I had Utna, but it was not the any sort of consolation for my grief. And if I did have remembered my shinning eyes and understand, I would have known I was not alone, but then I was full of youth and nothing else in my conscious mind.

(World's Grass is mostly giant flowers)

Oh yes, my conscious mind before the invasion filled with thoughts of girls.

Anyway, ants are funny creatures, they work hard and make good mothers if you can say a worker, is a mother. So, I guess they must feel grief when the reds and wasps come to collect for Nina....... black ant eggs are a delicacy of the Insect citizens of Nina, so I should not have been surprised when Utna gently touched me making clicking sounds with his mandibles.

And it was hard looking up into his eyes without seeing anything, just a maze of hundreds of eyes staring down.

No tears, no words of sympathy. I had to do that bit and like a mother Utna picked me up and heaves me over his head.

Was not frightened, did not get ideas about Insect Nobles eating me.

Black ants are not like that. "Never known a black kill a human," Peter often as I remembered his face.

He was right, black ants saw us as brothers. It was the reds they feared like we did, those that killed humans and blacks, as did to my family.

So, I was not scared and from habit knew Utna wanted me to ride, a thing I had done often, **(World's air is thick with pollen)**.

Did not know where we were going, simply happy to have privacy to weep allowing someone else to take care of the responsibility of living.' As Elder Peter said, "Utna knows you, will never harm you, will protect you, the ant has light," and never explained as usual which was annoying. **(Honey smell)**.

And was all because my eyes shone. I thought it was just natural intelligence showing.

Day 2011

The planet favored flowering plants that led to insects in top hats and canes to evolve before humans, why not we are just the clay in the potter's hand.

So, became afraid when I realized Utna was rock like, not moving at all at all. So, I sit up and peer out the flowering foliage and look down at our raided nest from our hill position.

Just still letting the midges bite and the yellow pollen in the air stick to my seat like glue.

I see humans all standing waiting orders, and chewed bits carted away by black ants watched over by reds. The nest cleared of debris; Nobles know plague comes from germs and witches.

We humans over eons taught them something.

And healthy human babies and black ant eggs are valuable.

(Hot suffocating pollinated air.)

And ten percent of reds have howdahs with Nina's Insect Nobles in them supervising. Their colored eyes look human from here, but I know that when you get close peering at them, you see are made up of thousands of lenses, insect eyes.

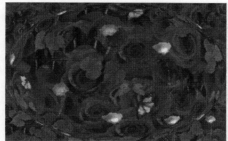

An insect lense saw more than one butterfly or flower.

Even their hair is not soft like a warm-blooded beast, but bristly.

"Insects that learned to walk and walking makes life on a similar pattern," Peter had said but I did not understand, did not want to. Now I did want to know everything about Insects.

"We cannot destroy them because we do not understand them," Peter had said and if that was how I could free my people and the black ants, then I did learn fast. Strange it was me who had to pull Utna away. The sight of Black soldier ants executed by reds dug up programs inside Utna to defend the nest.

And I was nineteen and never lived, a girlfriend, friends, been to battle, painted a picture, baked a cake without any help.

So, saw the chewed dried husks of my parents. World's red sun dries things out quick in our hot part of World.

Yes, that warm wind was blowing the dead about like kites. Sucked dried paper thin and I let the midges bite all they wanted too; I needed to stay alive, be motionless.

As an omen my father Shaun the Cheese maker landed on a fire thorn tree and saw his blue eyes stare at me. Saw his mouth work with the warm wind,

"Vengeance son, vengeance," I heard him scream

as the thorns reduced him to paper *slithers that blew away.* **Wind blows)**

Yes, I was alone on World and promised I would not be a slave, but the man I was born to be. This thought sobered me a bit and pushing grief behind I realized, I was grieving for myself and not my fathe, so thought of all the stories Elder Peter had told about our race.

Stories that we came from another world and knew secrets we had forgot.

"Find Starship Phoenix," *I was told.

This cheered me and saw myself as a deliverer for our race and dismissed it as quick as the thought walked into the right side of my head as egoism.

And was happy and sang words I did not understand and Utna danced so I danced and saw that ant's eyes shine.

So, I Luke set off to find Phoenix that existed in the Time of Myths with Elder Peter's words ringing in my mind,

"On Earth insects are the pests of man,

Mindless.

And we crush them under our feet,

For they are small."

So, I took hold of Utna's left antennae pulling left.

Those insect eyes again, looking down, seeing yourself in a hundred mirrors, hundreds of Luke's staring back, not knowing what feelings are churning behind those lenses.

"We will find a new nest," in hand signs, "come back and free our people."

Then Utna came away with me happy.

I did not want to look back as I heard my kind screaming as those pegged out became centipede

PET FOOD.

Did not want to look back at the departing fawn dust cloud where the elderly, ugly and week walked to Dust Bowls. A lesson and reminder to humans who ruled World.

INSECTS.

"Nina is bad," I said then heard my elder sister scream "Luke." So, ran back and saw Lana. carried like a table with jerking limbs, held fast by Noble Insect warriors. Her brown smock bubbling about her midriff like rolls of fat.

And averted my eyes in case I saw too much and knew her fate; she was not going to Dust Bowl but a Noble's harem.

I will tell you Nobles would have killed me, if Utna, did not stop me running down to Lana. Well, he took hold of me screaming and biffing and he never hit me back. And I was lucky those insect Sunflower Horns were blowing, or they did have heard me, (**Sound hunting horns**).

My sister had been the closest Utna had to a real sister. Utna was good, he saved me that day. I saved him; we were a good team. ....You see Utna was a worker, sexless. I called him a male while my sister called Utna female. It all depends on who was confiding secrets with Utna at the time.

Even my father Shaun spoke more to him complaining of life while feeding him cheese, and my mother also as she tidied up. I think Utna saw us as his/her family, and it must have torn its heart out to see what the reds had done.

And I remembered Elder Peter's words, "We had soldiers once in the Time of Myths, they fought Nobles," and gritting my teeth told myself that was what I would become, World's human soldier, a nightmare to my enemies.

It was as if an intuitive light turned on, in my head and a door opened for me to follow.

But I had forgotten the hieroglyphics in Shurrupuk City, the pictures the mind of Tarves Dallas deciphered later.

Human shaped men with round heads with antennae and sticks that smoked red fire, with packs on their backs which made them fly. And the pictures said, "The children of Enil," and a larger man riding a circle pointing at the slain winged insects under his feet the hieroglyphics said, "God Enil."

The Insect Noble God Enil, but what was his terrible secret?

Planet Red World belonged to Enil.

CHAPTER 2 — DUST BOWL

CH 2: Dust Bowl.

Scenario: Still on Utna's back facing a red horizon.

Day 2020.

The Time of Myth Peter taught orally, was the beginning of human history on World.

Ever since I was old enough my mother had taken me to hear him.

Therefore, I had knowledge of Phoenix, knew it must be more than myth, and would give what I needed to destroy Nina.

My belief was based on hope and refusal to accept that only dark ignorance existed.

All I knew, "Miles behind the Red Mountains lies Phoenix," my father the cheese maker Shaun had said pointing towards mountains on the northern horizon of our nest.

So, I rode Utna towards the Red Mountains with swirling green sulphuric gas clouds decorating their tops and a red glow in their middle.

I was afraid.

But full of the pride of youth.

And something in my spirit connected with an unseen feeling that I belonged to the Vault of Heaven, and this uplifted me and gave purpose.

And found out that a mile was not myth, the term now meant distant. Sure, I had visited Nina's city of Shurrupuk which was ten miles away but then I was a boy slave travelling in a cart, pulled there by Blue Dragonflies who are the fastest insects out.

I remembered: Year 1987 DAY something or rather.

"A day's flight son, to Shurrupuk," dad had said, "and do not bring attention to yourself in The Dance of Insects, we want you home."

And I did not listen as I was too excited. The dance meant I was going to see the bright lights. Did not matter I was going as slave, me, and my friends like Jack thought we could slip away and see 'these lights.'

"They have drinking houses and beautiful women who can make men out of us," Jack would say, and we grew excited and saved harder in scrap metal lying about the mines near the nest.

And we never got a chance to escape.

And flew to Shurrupuk in crowded cages and saw the great city aerially. It was teaming with life and stank. I also saw the main Dust Bowl and was afraid.

When we landed Insect Noble people in Shurrupuk stuffed me and other children in a large mud wasp nest that was a purple gym and common dressing room.

The windows grilled and locked which was worrying for it was obvious we were prisoners.

I was thirteen and stood like the other boys and girls waiting for screens or skins up for segregation. We might just be humans to Nina's Insects, but we were decent.

"Crack."

And a boy's scream filled the gym as whip tore back. It was a chosen deliberately. He was fat which made me wonder why he was here for the dance.

"They always pick the prettiest," dad sadly as he sliced cheese.

Closed the subject after that, he knew about The Dance of Insects, been himself; dad was not a talker.

Made me think dad was not interested in me, just cared about cheeses. But I was wrong, and it took my journey with Utna to see things clearly.

Year 2000 Day 2021:

Me and Utna pass Pha Nest and did not show ourselves. It was obvious the reds had been for the refuge tip at the bottom of a cliff was full of slain black ants.

All nests are on high ground; it makes shuffling litter off a cliff easier.

And the elders of the village pegged out dead except one, a lone centipede over him and the human kids practicing The Dance of the Insects stopped, watching frozen.

They were learning a lesson about disobedience.

The sixteen-foot centipede liked to start on its food from a soft spot. The prey was not going anywhere, pegged as it was; so, the belly went first.

Damn those screams.

I was trying to live again, to forget the details of what had happened to my tribe.

And did not last long unless the centipedes were not hungry, then it will come back and finish supper later.

So, when moved back off to supervise the dancers, it left a living skeleton behind and done insect toilet on the man.

A final degradation to humankind.

I just looked down remembering how I had danced, what had happened to my elder auburn haired sister Lana, friend Jack and the fat boy.

I remembered again:

Year 1987 Day maybe and more flash back.

No segregation, ever try and dress into a flimsy insect costume that was bits of shiny chitin and wobbling rubbery legs, with eyes closed to preserve a sister's

dignity.

I fell and Jack helped me up, could not stop him peeking a look at Lana, as curious boys looking at the girl's little bits that made them different from boys.

And Jack pawed a blond girl,

hit him for it.

And hit back by something dropped from the gym rafters. Wham right on the back, floored me so when I spun round, I looked into the mouth of a hunting spider.

Silence except for the dribble of my hot wee.

I was about to be supper.

I was also scared, and this spider saw it so went back up.

Obedience lesson over.

And Lana touched me gently comforting but being boy, I shrugged her hand away.

I knew they knew I was frightened and would have felt better, if I had realized, they were scared.

Let Jack and every boy one of them see Lana's body; what did I care?

Her gold eyebrows'

Blue eyelashes,

Green eyes,

Red sun world has affected our genes.

So, have the Insect Nobles who use our gene codes cosmetically upon us.

I shamed, a coward and did not have the sense to see we were all cowards

wanting life.

And we were supposed to obey at the first Insect summons. Any who did not found themselves short listed for Dust Bowls.

Like the fat red haired kid but we did not know it then, and I guess myself for when Lord Hupamuk who is scarlet limbed with yellow hair, and green eyes inspected us dancers, it was his party to celebrate Queen Nina's birthday; a red ant picked me up and dangled me in front of Hupamuk.

He said nothing to me.

I got the message; the hunting spider above hovered over my brown curls.

"He is Luke, a good worker, learning to be a cheese maker," it was Governor Ziusudra sticking up for me. Good all Ziusudra, was compassionate and liked

humans.

He liked cheeses too.

Did not guess at the time his own neck was at risk?

Usually humans meant troublesome provinces, meant Queen Nina heard, meant the governor became a star attraction in a Dust Bowl especially if he had wings.

And Ziusudra had wings.

Big gold paper thin ones.

Then the ant drops me, and I do not even dare rub my grazed shins. Just press me face to the red wax floor smelling bees and pollen.

Then they moved on with Lord Hupamuk walking on my head. That hurt and I in my green grasshopper outfit, and my comrades too scared to associate with me in case they went to Dust Bowl.

Except Lana who sent love out of her eyes to me.

That gave me strength, made it worth it.

Also, the blond girl who smiled at me and moved to Lana.

I felt ashamed, strange, two girls just by giving me support made me feel that way.

I was a man, even if I was thirteen and a slave.

I should never have wet myself, accepted my fate with fatalism, and showed them Insects they can do what they want to our bodies but can never kill the human spirit.

Made me see what they are afraid of.

(White sky)

Understand why we spit at them.

So, I took a deep breath smiling back; alive not dead needed.

I got horny, nothing I could do about it, but that blond girl was beautiful, and I was just a spotty kid.

So, I learned the meaning of embarrassment and my first lesson in ignoring it.

There was nothing to be embarrassed about. My arousal I could not control, it was my body's way of saying, "Blond girl I want babies with you."

And Hupamuk he just curls his white lips at me as if watching snakes mating.

But his disgust vanishes as his eyes wonder over the blond girl, then he left the gym. Whether Insect or human the male is the same, affected subconsciously and consciously by the female figure.

And that girl she goes and touches me, our World way of her saying "Make babies for the tribe."

Was I glad I had a cod piece on?

And it was safe to relax now as Lord Hupamuk had gone and as Peter said, "It needs an Insect Noble Lord like Hupamuk to see through the depths of human deceit.

Not the programmed robots the reds and centipedes."

Why rowdies got away with touching up girls. Red ants and Insects liked to see humans' mate as we watch domestic cows, nothing was private, and we were fodder animals making more fodder.

Yes, I did do my dance routine in their stupid rubber costume and Insects would watch. Home I did churn cheeses, cut down giant rape flowers and mash the seeds into a rich soup for Insects to drink, and spared death if my limbs moved the way expected of me in a non-threatening manner.

It needed an Insect Lord to see the murderous intent in my eyes to give reason for my execution.

"I want you to know only fear. Never let me detect hate, hate is dangerous, "Peter had quoted from Lord Hupamuk.

Well, they could have my hate.

So, I went and danced and ignored my shame, only aware of the support of my sister and blond girl.

And here I learned the difference between right and wrong. I was a male grasshopper and expected to gene female May Flies.

It was not right, but I was thirteen at the time and wanted to live. I never enjoyed what I did to that blond girl but noticed Jack my friend grinned from start to finish.

That was wrong, it was not wrong what we were doing but how we were doing it.

Only attractive girls selected to dance the Dance of the May Fly so securing futures.

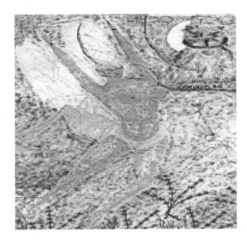

And after the dance Lord Hupamuk came with two reds and a red and yellow centipede and took the fat boy from the gym.

And that boy toileted out of fear as he was only a kid and, shamed for feeling anger towards him because I thought he was reminding everyone what I had done.

And Lord Hupamuk smile told all, the boy was going to a Dust Bowl. I knew then we should love one another, find strength in sharing our slavery.

To the rest of us, "You danced well, for this I will allow you a treat, do not bother to change. Now come with me," and unquestioning we followed like mindless sheep.

But what else could we do?

"I am Alana," the blond girl next to my sister whispered and smiled.

I did not see Lord Hupamuk notice; he was looking at my eyes. I always knew I had strange eyes.

I really was suicidal.

Did see him smile as we walked past and he took Alana aside, "Thank you boy......also......what is your name again?" At first, I could not speak from fear, even

forgot to fall face down at his feet.

And a red mandible closed about my feet tripping me, then a red leg upon my back forcing my face so hard into the red wax floor it made an impression.

"Luke son of Shaun Cheese maker," Lana apologized.

He just stood there, Lord Hupamuk, looking down at me, his solid black eyes a mass of twinkling lenses.

"And what is your name girl?"

"Lana, I am his sister."

"Come," he said to the two girls and left with the red ant.

I would have run after them, but Jack took my arms, "Do not," he hissed as a spider above readied to pounce on us.

Then a centipede barred the way and I allowed Jack to push me out of the gym, and saw Shurrupuk for what it was, a huge night soil cart pulled by dung beetles.

For we were dung, and it was the job of dung beetles to keep Shurrupuk clean. That is how Nobles saw us, walking dung.

Saw an evil place where humans and Noble slaves hustled along crocodile fashion on the grey meteorite roads. And behind Noble supervisors on red ants.

Saw steel cages hanging at crossroads with human remains

Saw humans on leads with their head hair outrageously styled.

Saw above me roads built into the sides of the termite towers.

Saw humans with shovels running after the howdah beetles with Nobles in them.

Saw market centers with cages full of pollen and vegetable produce Nobles loved and slaves for sale as food or entertainment.

Saw Shurrupuk City was not a bright place but gloomy, for the white termite towers discolored through pollen carried there by World's warm winds.

Saw colorful giant flowers dripping nectar for insects and Insect Nobles to drink. I saddened, so my soul tore apart. Also felt something inside me weeping and the light went from my eyes. Sure, they shone but with sadness instead of bright love.

Lo, forgot my father Shaun Cheese maker's advice for I stood and shouted, "Shurrupuk, Shurrupuk, Babylon will become dust and I will make it dust," and shouted again, again, again and added strange words like Zukerman zap alum, not knowing their meaning.

As if I was speaking strange tongues?

They were Elder Peter's words. He spoke to me about things on Earth's origins. I think he might have spoken on a city called Babylon that was an evil place were gods made of gold, worshipped and people burned their precious children to them.

It was because my spirit had been torn that I shouted what I did, who knows?

*

Dust Bowl of Shurrupuk.

A Beast Master terrified humans as was a bad human.

It was large and we slaves had front seats, chained by the ankles to wooden red and white stripped posts where we huddled, fearful smelling the meteorite dust of the bowl.

"It tastes of metal, iron hemoglobin from slave blood," Peter Elder had said and I saw his gentle face. Knew the redness of the grey dust was blood.

And all about us Nobles breathing deeply as if the dust was something heavenly.

"Philistines," I muttered knowing Elder Peter called them that meaning they were vile evil idolatrous creatures.

Reeds blowing......the events had started. First a red and

Black soldier ant fighting with bets on them.

The black one won even if had lost two legs. There was shouting over this, guess he beat the favorite.

Reeds blowing.... a naked fat human comes out, holding a wooden shield and then chased about by a wasp while a human worked clock ticked above the stands. The

Nobles were betting how long he could keep running.

Was not long, his shield got stuck on the wasp's sting till it freed and then The sting caught him panting and stung him dead.

Reeds blowing......chariots entered staffed by Nobles and pulled by forty humans each.

And to make it interesting obstacles erected, like poles of blazing oil, stakes with spikes and pits full of serpents.

That race lasted till only three chariots passed the winning line. Those Nobles who had fought off the lashes, thrown off spears and arrows of their competitors.

Reeds blowing......a small boy released from a wicker cage, and he ran, ran, ran, had too, soldier ants were running after him. The Nobles seemed to be betting on which ant be first to reach him?

Did not find out, some vendor stood in front of me shouting, "Pickled crackling, vinegary sweetmeats, jelly eyeballs, soup entrails and...." Knew he was selling mostly human stuff reared on Noble farms as had health certificates saying free of intestinal worms.

Young ones reared on milk so the meat would be tender, into steaks that sizzled on a hot pan nearby.

And standing took a handful of dust in my hands and blew it with emotionless eyes at my seated peers.

And Lord Hupamuk stared at me.

I do not know how long I stood but when I came out of my dream of seeing this Babylon ash, the fat boy is leaving with Nobles. You see all insects that look like humans are Nobles. No Noble is a commoner; even the lowest has a household of ordinary real insects to command like red ants.

Of course, human slaves to.

The difference between an ordinary insect and a slave is in Nina's Law on Death.

"A Noble must be granted a decree of death to kill giant insect. To kill human.

Whim decides."

Now I looked for Alana and Lana and guessed they did be next to Lord Hupamuk, who due to his elevated position would be next to Nina.

Finding Nina was easy, just look for the most colorful canopy shaped liked rhododendron flowers.

The leaves were her favorite snack.

And were just to my left and Nina was looking at me, trying to see something in my eyes. Always my eyes and I was shocked and averted them till she looked elsewhere.

And saw Lana and Alana were on either side of Hupamuk, resting their heads on his knees while he stroked their soft human hair.

Lap pets.

Hupamuk spoke loudly so we could hear, "The Dance of the Insects will provide us beautiful offspring. The breeding vats will have them adults in five years."

Now I knew why the prettiest always chosen for the dance. My memory also provided feedback and realized the fat boy had only walked with a multicolored large bird fan cooling us during the dance.

Now I knew the fat boy's purpose, he was not for breeding beautiful people for gene shuttling into the Noble breeding pool; but to breed farm animals that

could put on weight quick making it economical to rear for the market.

Then Jack stood agitated, and I looked and saw the fat boy pegged out in the Sand.

Heard his screams as green praying mantis rubbed their legs, blue fat flies their wings and cicadas shook so the din on Dust Bowl was much.

For them, the musicians of Nina had announced the arrival of competing teams. At either end of the bowl was an army of brown soldier ants. One with red ribbons

and the other blue.

Red dust.

Silence.

The armies set off.

The first to reach the fat boy would win his dinner.

The fat boy bred for sporting purposes.

And it was a long ten minutes during which I had time to see Lord Hupamuk fondle my sister, she was a pet hamster, she had no rights: could not object and wanted life so obeyed.

And saw Alana return my stare, void of fear but love *which is strength for it is* divine.

"You will never defeat me Hupamuk," I promised.

And you know he knew I was staring for he grinned back.

And Jack who must have been sixteen broke free and ran forward and stood above the fat boy.

I looked at our Queen Nina who seemed amused.

And like a merciful monarch she allowed two lesser Nobles to approach Jack on dragonflies and hand him steel spear, copper sword and oval bronze shield.

"What use are they against soldier ants, give him fire," I spat.

And Jack knowing his temper had sentenced himself to die threw the spear at the nearest Noble so, it pierced his forehead, splitting his copper helmet in two, and with

the sword he sliced his dragonfly's head twain.

Now the other Noble was motionless, shocked, so Jack leapt and landed beside him on his blue dragon fly.

What happened next?

They flew away and above the Bowl's yellow mud walls the Noble fell, bounced on the dust and fragmented as his chitinous skin shattered.

It was just like what comes out of a squashed bug.

And Jack was gone.

We did not need fire to kill insects but courage.

Hope rose in our hearts if Jack could do this so could we. And the breeze brought the stink of the slain Noble to us.

And for the first time since I entered Shurrupuk City I wanted to dance to the unseen power that made me. I was happy, like nothing the Nobles could throw at me

could take away my humanity.

Rape my sister, cut off my legs, I will still defeat you because I have hope and am human.

And the other soldier ants fought each other to be first at the fat boy, they were insects, humans would have chased Jack and brought back his body as an example.

In Queen Nina's stand.

Jack killed them easily.

"Spare them Nina," Governor Ziusudra begged for us for we had watched how easy it was to kill Nobles and Queen Nina looked at him with blue eyes.

She had heard his arguments before, give the humans freedom, to develop, World needed them.

"Has any insect travelled the stars? No, but humans have, remember great queen the Time of Myth and Phoenix?" And she shuddered; yes, Queen Nina knew more

about the Time of Myth than cared.

Behind stood her religious teacher, Priest Lord Enalusdra, his black chitinous skin gleaming with massaged oils and behind him a solid crystallized wax statue of wingless God of Air, Enil, from which all insect life had originated.

There was no mention of humans created in the works of Enil who had created insects by taking air, mixing it with Nammu, the primordial sea into mud and shaped insects with his fingers, blowing breath into lungs thus giving life.

And Enil did not have wings, the reason Governor Ziusudra and the winged insect Nobles were lower caste.

Too near relatives of the mindless ants, earwigs, and centipedes. Could never mate with Queen Nina in case wings appeared amongst the young.

Or worse, was rumored winged Nobles sired eggs with wing genes, or pupae with wings ready for flight, pupae that wriggled as white maggots amongst the human filth their Noble mothers had squatted on to lay them.

Queen Nina looked at Governor Ziusudra as if he was dung.

Nina was beautiful, all powerful.

Queen Nina represented love, mercy, creativeness, light, progress out of darkness for her Noble race.

Towards what God Enil looked like, wingless. Turning she saw her gold bees wax god's statue, tall bearded with flowing knotted hair. He looked more human than her?

And Queen Nina was afraid that humans were something mysterious, powerful from an unknown universe like God Enil, they had arrived on Phoenix from where?

She knew Governor Ziusudra was correct in one point, humans could offer World much, but from the supremacy of Insects not humans.

There could be no power sharing, or the Nobles would lose dominance. That made Queen Nina afraid, seeing the future, seeing humans not as equals but as superior for she knew anyone who could travel the stars and heavens of their god Enil, were the masters, *not Insects.*

It did not occur to Queen Nina humans might share knowledge, such a hope would rise when all else failed.

Their insect fear led to hate which is equal to love in power. Lo fear justified her Noble folk's cruelty towards humans.

Humans must never find Phoenix.

And she knew whereas Peter told a myth, Phoenix had broken up landing, to protect it from Insect adventurers, that Phoenix had not broken up. It was intact, covered in moss, flowering creepers and the home to insect eating germs.

So, Nobles left it be.

In other words, no stern section had broken away.

Lord Priest's Enalusdra's predecessors had declared the Land of Time of Myth taboo. All Nina knew was that Phoenix was beyond the Red Mountains where the gods

lived.

To go to Phoenix would be death, to bring sickness back that would decimate Nobles.

And Nina deep down wanted Phoenix's knowledge for herself, she could cheat death and become a goddess, immortal.

And she looked at me who had stood cheering and clapping hands. And I did not remember my father's advice not to bring attention upon oneself.

And Nina saw I was handsome, and her spirits lifted for Governor Ziusudra was right, treat humans kindly, but her mercy was false for she had plans for me.

I did not know it at the time, but I had just caused the death of Peter and my parents.

"Governor Ziusudra bring that boy to me in my private chambers," and the winged Noble bowed and left thinking their secret had once again influenced her to his wishes.

That they had been lovers sixty years earlier and produced one hundred lovely white eggs.

Twenty had become winged insects.

The secret that Nina had born winged Nobles.

The children of Ziusudra.

"Yes, we will get the secrets of Phoenix and that boy will bring them," she added to Lord Hupamuk and Enalusdra. Whether Lana my sister or Alana heard was of no consequence, they would not be returning home. But they did hear her ask, "What is Babylon?"

*

And I was before Queen Nina after the Dust Bowl emptied and I saw her alluring appeal. And I became aroused and showed it under my short red leather kilt and shamed she could do this to me for she was Insect.

For Nina lay sprawled on a bed of hard brown wax covered in soft leaf pulp, chewed that way by leaf cutter ants and stitched into a mattress and pillows.

Her dark chitinous skin glowed for she had bathed.

The room smelt of flowers.

And all she wore was a spider's silken white robe.

And caged nightingales sang.

And the three crimson moons off World rose behind the curtain of green silk.

"Come," she said and Noble guards pushed me, and I sprawled on the floor, then they left.

Two male human youths in lion clothes and flowered headdresses fanned with giant paper fans.

"What do you know of the Time of Myths?" And I looked up excited and she saw in my give away human blue eyes that I knew much.

She smiled and patted the bed indicating I should sit beside her.

Here I noticed the fan holders each had a wandering spider sitting on his shoulder in case of treason.

"I have power Luke," and was surprised she knew my name, "I can give death," and then moved her fingers above me and one spider bit so one human fanner fell groaning.

And all the while the other kept fanning while his friend salivated as his head swayed from side to side disorientated.

"Or I can give life," and took from a wooden drawer carved as Death Watch beetles its makers a vial and gave it to the other human to administer.

"Take him and go," she commanded, and I was alone, afraid of crawling hidden horrors. Queen Nina would never be alone with a human.

She knew I had already caused trouble.

Was I brought here to see my new station in life?

Insects are exceptionally good at reading minds by reading body language and secretions.

Smiling, "No, you are too handsome to suffer their fate," and she touched me were she should not.

"Would you like to go to Phoenix?" She asked and ordered me drink, drink, drink, drink, till I emptied a flagon of wine and while I stood with reeling head, she readied herself for bed.

The last thoughts to spin through my head were, "No you are not the giver of life and death," I do not know what was in the wine but after it I was anyone's.

And watched amused as she flipped blue lenses from her eyes and put in others so her eyes were gold and glowed in the crimson light of World's three crimson moons.

(3 Crimson Moons)

Ten hours later:

Now Lord Hupamuk lay semi dressed on his yellow wax bed. Beside him lay the sleeping forms of Lana and Alana.

And Lord Hupamuk slipped into a golden threaded spider robe and visited a secret chamber made by Death Watch beetles. Here to spy on his Queen Nina which he often did.

For he kept a Black Widow as pet and knew the male, him, after coupling was eaten, and **Lord Hupamuk wanted to live.**

He was one of Queen Nina's lovers and she was a black widow spider.

In her genes, one of her founding ancestors one.

Already the boy Luke lay chained to her bed asleep while Nina stared out a window towards the Red Mountains and Phoenix.

A good plan of Nina's to corrupt the boy so he would go to Phoenix and make it safe for Nobles to come and retrieve what he took out.

But it was not her idea but his, Hupamuk's, from a seed of intuition that had sprang out of the dark caves of his mind. His idea to have her notice Luke, there was something special about the boy, his eyes showed it, they shone.

And he gloated? Who could resist Nina's famed beauty? Not this weak human youth?

He would not be the first human girl or boy to come to worship Nina and the privileges she gave. Not the first to betray one's own kind and for what? Lust, mistakenly called love, there was only the weak and strong.

And Lord Hupamuk grew excited and went back to awaken his new human slaves; when he had gone later, rats came out from secret tunnels to eat fallen scraps. Little mammals not insects were the masters of Shurrupuk City, the weak would inherit the city.

*

And a human was a human and an Insect an insect and the Nobles had found human genes mixed with their own and were valuable for we were wingless and fair.

"It is said God Enil took peas and cross bred them and showed the first Noble farmers the value of genes. Enil also gave us humans to work our farms," Priest Enalusdra during one of his religious lessons to Queen Nina.

*

And I Luke spent a year with Queen Nina, so the calendar was 1988 and she pampered me, always coupling, four to five times a day and I like a boy became obsessed with her for she was my beautiful lover.

I would do anything for her, weak not evil, and she broke my soul for she forced me into perversions, so preoccupied with naught else.

Forgot my roots in my soft surroundings

Addicted to her, always listening about Phoenix and how she would hold back future charms if she could not get there.

Living in her perfumed chambers,as Master Slave Master, which means an office of inspectorate to oversee the slave pens. For even my Noble masters knew filthy pens brought disease into Shurrupuk, human diseases that affected Nobles for they were now part human.

And for one hundred days I did my job and my eyes glowed again and was reminded I was human.

If Queen Nina had thought it a lesson, showing me how lucky I was to be different she was wrong.

For after the hundred days I came to my queen, and as I walked royal chambers saw men chisel pictures in the walls. This is not to say I did not visit her anymore, she always called for me, but this summons had arrived by Lord Hupamuk, and warriors and their eyes were full of hate.

And in the new pictures saw a human clothed in fine clothes supervising the breaking of slave pens and was happy for the human was myself.

My happiness was short lived for on my way to Nina, saw Lana and Alana swollen with child and was shocked.

Beside them walked Priest Enalusdra while a human harem attendant held the silver manacles that chained the girls' captive by their necks.

Enalusdra's musicians, green praying mantis made music with their claws as if wooden hollow bamboo beaten.

Saw all by the light of glow worms in lanterns hanging from Nina's termite tower chambers.

And reminded I was human.

It was a mistake on my part for I became moody and when I finally stood in front of Nina, she sensed it, and was easy for her to drag out of me why?

I was only fourteen, **Year 1988 Day something or rather.**

"Go to Phoenix for me?" She asked.

My eyes said it for me, "I am human."

Dismissed, I went back to work but then arrested instead by Lord Hupamuk, stripped of my fine clothes, and beaten on the spot by his warriors with thorn branches.

Fought back, beat me harder for they were afraid of my shinning eyes.

A week later I was in front of Priest Enalusdra, thrown across a splintered wooden table and forced to drink a potion. I fell asleep and awoke and at once looked

down to see if I had become an Insect harem attendant.

What a relief I was not and then they freed me.

I had no idea how long I had been out for?

And put me in rusted chains and knew I was human again. Had returned to Luke who had come here a year ago, slave. I was free and felt like dancing, singing, uttering words I did not know the meaning of?

After that they threw me into an open wagon pulled by black ants. Our escort was Utna whom took away my fear, I was going home.

Then they took out Lana and Alana and put them in the wagon. They were no longer swollen, having served the evil purpose of Priest Enalusdra, and they kept asking why the babies removed?

And the girls were sullen and moody.

Alana was more talkative, and I learned they had not seen their children since snatched away at birth.

"You would not want it?" Lana had said, "I managed to see, just a glimpse of leg......it was chitinous, I had a filthy insect in me."

I did not press the point.

We were going home.

And Nina had done her work well, I thought of nothing, but Phoenix and it grew into an overwhelming urge to find. I missed the ways of Nina and struggled to suppress the longing for her. I think if she had come and asked me to go to Phoenix then I would.

And at the same time cursed the ground she walked over. I was sick, needing healing of mind and spirit.

I had a dual personality, one craving lust, the other the joy of dancing with the animated spirit of the universe around me.

I was fifteen now **Day 1989 something or rather.**

By the time I was nineteen I still wanted Phoenix, but not for Nina but for humans.

And during these years......my work as Master Slave Master had proved that. And thus, did not fit into her plans to go to Phoenix.

So, sent home.

If only she had known my longing for her.

"You are a lucky man to be alive," Peter had said when I came home.

"Why?"

"She is a black widow…...did you see harem humans?"

"Yes."

"They are dead, their minds are in a silken cocoon allowing their numbed bodies to serve her private needs and eventually eaten.

And I knew Peter was right.

Thus, I remembered my youth.

*

This I did not know but told later by Tarves Dallas who deciphered the hieroglyphics of Shurrupuk City. This translation is from the diary of Lord

Priest Enalusdra.

Year 1989 Day 2390

Queen Nina sat on a red wax throne exactly like a human birthing chair, with a hole in the bottom.

Nina was a queen and like all insect queens of a colony it was her job to couple with desirables and lay eggs, pupae or young miniatures of herself or male partners.

To be soldiers.

To be workers.

A fraction as future queens in distant colonies accepting her authority; the rest to be sold off as wives to the Nobles for breeding to increase the number of their stock; see Nobles were not as fertile as they did like to be, too much inbreeding to keep what they owned amongst their wingless kin.

This time she laid one hundred white, slippery eggs, the size of golf balls.

It took her six hours.

And Priest Enalusdra attended with novices and human harem attendants; these eggs were special, they had been fertilized with human Luke's wingless chromosomes.

Royal babies that would fetch the mightiest Insect Noble families to the door of Enalusdra and pay for them, royal babies to strengthen those wingless blood lines and claims to The Bee Wax Throne of Shurrupuk.

And Enalusdra took their payments and kept a tenth.

He was not greedy; a tenth of a hundred sold babies, since he had not done any of the laborious work of giving birth to them.

Enil, their god did not have wings, none of us ever recognized the significance of this.

CHAPTER 3   Enalusdra

The Wilderness

The High Priest Enalusdra

Six feet ten and green with

A mane of yellow bristles

And long brown hair.

The rest was human

Apart from his pink cosmetic lenses

And his diet

Took the eggs in silver bowls, and laid them in special heated niches in a dimly lit chamber where a six-foot green wax statue of God Enil stood, plus other deities like a stuffed baby crocodile whose job was to eat demons and protect the royal young against supernatural horrors.

Once a queen gave birth to eggs, they needed cleaned by bees or ants of fungus and disease. But these were challenging times, World with white sky, red sun, and crimson moons had humans on it. Phoenix had brought germs that ate insects.

Bees were rare these days, Nobles tended to keep them near living quarters for pollinating flowers for nectar. Humans with hay fever their parents hid, or they ended up in a Dust Bowl as hay fever genes introduced into the Insect gene pool was lethal, as Nobles being insects needed pollen to survive.

Now those human harem attendants would tend and clean the eggs for the next nine weeks till they hatched into larvae and then remain in the egg chamber three months.

And Enalusdra ordered pegged a dozen fatted up humans. Ugly ones like the fat boy who had ended up in Dust Bowl; deliberately bred that way by Nobles.

Not dressed because of the heat down here but because Nobles did not want them babies eating leather kilts and trousers.

And the harem ones did help as they did not want to become pegged supper.

And hammered steel tipped wooden pegs into outstretched human limbs.

And the pegged food saw the children of Luke, their limbed human form and sharp teeth under the egg sacks and fainted.

Good clean healthy flesh needed for larvae to gorge for their nine months growing period as pupae. Then to emerge male or female miniatures of the queen and what human characteristics Luke the slave had passed on?

Such the value of winglessness.

And the children would not call Luke daddy so were not his.

And long into the summer night Lord Hupamuk and Queen Nina had discussed taking from humans their superior intellect without them knowing; genetics was one way.

Learnt when Phoenix crashed, that humans contained everything Nobles needed to eat to be healthy.

Protein......calcium......vitamins......minerals.

Nests raided for food on a pretext although Nina now argued no excuse needed. Luke had shown her humans would always remain human and never share knowledge with Insects.

This had led to the abolition of Root Day and the total withdrawal of any rights humans had on World. Now humans exploited ruthlessly without excuses.

And Nina's miniatures taken to a nursery and taught to be Insect Nobles.

The females going to Noble harems as egg laying machines, the men as soldiers. There was always more soldiers and workers needed than females, female rivals Nina was fearful of, _an insect trait?_

Her empire was expanding.

And this way the Nobles would look like their winless god, Enil.

And they would not need Phoenix they hoped, for the new blood would be as intelligent as humans. Not only that, but Luke also passed on genes that made antibodies

against the new viruses that Phoenix brought that ate insects.

A beautiful kid like Luke was valuable and when with Nina his hair was long and perfumed like the rest of him.

And there was something special about Luke that made him noticed, his shining eyes. No one knew when younger, he danced outside the nest at night, swirling, as if possessed by something.

Love possessed him for the unseen love that bathed him and made him one with the universes about him, seen and unseen.

But since coming to Shurrupuk he had stopped dancing. His heart closed to whatever it was that made his eyes shine.

He did not know what it was, did not know its name.

And when Tarves Dallas later deciphered the walled hieroglyphics, he saw pictures of a youth with shinning eyes and Tarves Dallas star traveler knew where Luke came from but kept it secret.

It was also rumored Lord Hupamuk would be a mate for an heir, although Nina wanted to use Luke's chromosomes she had stored within herself, for she was an

insect true and through.

Lord Hupamuk might contain flight genes; _he was an insect._

So, took from Luke while he lay in a drugged sleep. As a human must not suspect Nina would become pregnant from him; it was time for her to lay eggs.

And Enalusdra examining the human gene code through microscopes, selecting the best for his queen's eggs.

Enalusdra would also sell at a profit what Nina did not need. Priest Enalusdra put one person first, himself; and fertilized one egg, a male to be the hidden secret heir.

Secret for he had used his own chromosomes.

And Queen Nina and Lord Hupamuk did not know of this, although Enalusdra suspected she carried flight genes and was afraid to mate with an Insect Noble in case her young were like common insects, and Nina dismissed as queen.

Have Lord Priest Enalusdra strap her on a high place with her subjects watching, and break her chitinous skin so her line would end as she shriveled up under the hot

red sun of World.

Thus, Priest Enalusdra remembered in the egg chamber.

And Enalusdra looked at the wax figure of God Enil and knew why Enil did not have wings? Why has he looked more human than insect? Enalusdra's grandmother was a human slave you know.

They all knew wings were primitive, that meant Nobles carried genes that could give birth to winged hideous monsters that looked more fly than Noble.

And Enalusdra remembered once Nina had given birth to a hundred eggs and ten had wings. Enalusdra had slit the pupae open while Nina watched, then thrown them into the alter fire of God Enil.

All present apart from himself, sealed in the egg chamber.

It was their secret fear the wingless Nobles all carried, that they could produce winged Insects after all these years of careful selective breeding with humans.

. And Enalusdra remembered Phoenix and the excitement it had created, Enil had sent beings like himself to strengthen the line of the Nobles.

In those days there had not been thousands of wingless Nobles until the forced couplings with humans, then the diseases started, and the children of the mating's survived, and it became an obsession to have human chromosomes in you, to survive the plagues Enil had sent down with humans as punishment for having paper thin wings.

And Enalusdra looked at the green wax image of his god and pushed it over. Enil did not exist, humans did, and it was human genes that guaranteed the survival of his Noble clan.

Enalusdra knew the secret of God Enil, *do you?*

And ground the god's face under his feet, then drew a dagger and spun smacking it in the remaining human harem attendants, killing them all.

All would think the humans had defaced god Enil the insect god; and summoned more slaves to clean the gore up for the egg chamber must be clean, or disease would

come, humans had taught them that; besides, one egg was his.

*

Half a calendar later and a calendar was two thousand Days.

And Queen Nina looked towards the nest of Ur where Luke originated and thought of him, for he was handsome for she spied upon him continuously. For the time had come for Luke to go to Phoenix since he had not ventured there himself.

He would be, forced, to find the ship for her.

One reason, Queen Nina ended Root Day, sent in reds and centipedes and drove Luke into the wilderness with Utna.

And Luke's food they laced with a tapeworm egg, for his miles of innards.

A tapeworm that through his droppings would leave a trail for the reds and centipedes that would lead Nina, Lords Hupamuk and Enalusdra to him and Phoenix.

And Nina asked often, "What is Babylon?"

I rode on the back of Utna, black ant full of hate which made me no different than Nina and her race. Wanting to destroy all insects forgetting Utna was one.

Everywhere insects, on the giant flowers and flowering trees. Even the blue, red and yellow grasses flowered. Big and little insects flew about you, darting, investigating, and complaining you had entered their flower kingdoms.

Sometimes Luke saw mammals, small ones sneaking up on food, sunbathing flies and spiders making nests. Big lions escaped from Phoenix, waiting for the noon heat when most big carnivorous insects slept. See, insect wings on World are paper thin, our red sun could burn paper to a crisp at noon.

Then the lions would kill the sleeping giant insects.

And I was happy, World did not belong to insects entirely.

Yes, I was lucky I did not go mad, and it was an insect that saved me, Utna.

I would not hunt, cook or wash; gone remorseful over the events of life.

My eyes had stopped shining like they had during the days of my captivity under Queen Nina after the dance of the Insects.

Selfish wrapped up in revengeful thoughts and all the while Utna cared for me till one day he threw me in a stream. I went mad, but he would not let me out. I

knew he wanted me to wash, knew I smelt bad.

I threw stones at Utna, and he could have killed me in return.

I stood till I chilled and Utna still would not let me out till I washed. And when I did, felt clean like I had performed a religious ritual.

After I sat on the dry black sand thinking what Queen Nina had reduced me too. I was not Luke; it was time to live again. I had to become myself for if we got to Phoenix

I had to be responsible with all that knowledge the ship would give.

I saw the pink clouds of World above fat with rain, saw the infinite whiteness of the sky and danced. I was happy again, what mother often said, "You suffer from too much spring fever," but it wasn't spring fever, the happiness sort of came upon you from outside your body.

Luke rode ant Utna with wild abandon.

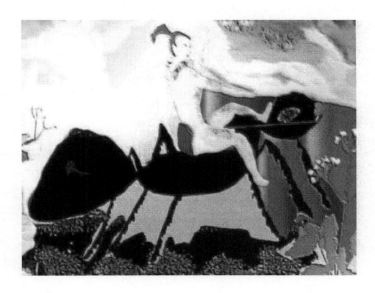

Saw I could not wipe out every insect, why Utna was one was he not? He was good, if I started slaughtering insects Nina would have proven her point why humans needed enslaved.

I had to be wise like Peter who had said, "Earth, our ancestors reduced to waste. That is why humans took to the stars to find new planets."

And my dad Shaun, "We virtually extinguished mammal life till only human and insect remained."

With these somber thoughts I realized I needed a plan.

I would free Lana and Alana and have Alana to mate. Never sharing her or myself at the whim of a Noble Insect. Our union would be more than just a mating to provide beautiful offspring to enhance Noble furniture. Later I would be ashamed of choosing Alana for I did not love her. We were very promiscuous as was the human way. And the Nobles encouraged us to have more than one mate for breeding purposes.

Had not Alana stroked my hair stating she wanted me?

I would face Nina again but as the human Luke son of a cheese maker.

*

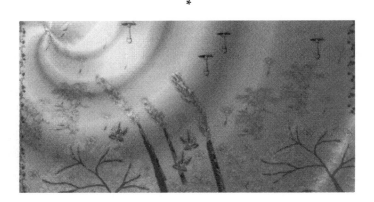

World's wilderness.

Two weeks later:

The Red Mountains after a hard trek seemed no closer and the yellow grass plains about Shurrupuk Nest overgrown with blue flowering shrubs.

.   We seemed to be getting lower and only when I looked behind and saw the white sky as a horizon on the escarpment, did I realize we had entered a vast depression.

And saw a winding yellow river pass me that became a wide flow on the bottom.

Here the banks were thick in cherry trees thirty feet high and flowering purple creepers.

At the bottom heard before I saw and here saved Utna's life. Ants follow chemical trails left by other ants; I Luke a human had other senses.

"Wasps," I use hand language to get Utna to understand and then pulling his four foot left antennae led him from the yellow water's edge.

But he was thirsty, and the moisture made him break away and head back.

"Foolish ant," I shouted running after him, "stupid insect," and threw stones and

(Leech infested pool)

sticks at his disappearing body. Now our ants are the size of rhinos and when they run you say, "Goodbye see you tomorrow."

Then I saw the giant wasp with a Noble rider darting along the cherry tree tops.

So, fell flat in a leech infested poll remaining still.

"Dung head," I cursed Utna.

And did not see the wasp land but felt leeches feeding.

And the leeches are a foot long.

Then heard crashing undergrowth as Utna was surprised and stung, not by this giant wasp but another who was at the yellow water side.

"Utna," I whispered feeling my insides tighten and ran. Words against a wasp as long as three men lying head to toe together.

"Always use your brain son," Shaun my father had said, "or how else do we make cheese and the insects cannot?"

So, running looking for tools I see a fallen tree and help myself to two long splintered branches, and now feel armed.

With Wooden swords?

And stopped behind red flowering creepers whose perfumed smell hid my human stink. Perfectly still knowing insects see movement. But that Noble might smell the unmistakable odor of a slave.

"They boast amongst themselves that we stink of sour milk, at least we don't smell of wax," my father told me.

"But wax has no smell?"

"Then always remember insects can't smell you, only flies who like our milk."

Then I saw: The wasp was crawling over Utna while another sat on a red lion like beast and beside it lay a pale humanoid, but the face was cat like. Never had I have seen the likes on white World.

And another Noble standing beside this man with a steel sword.

The wasp on top of the lion creature was laying an egg with its depository. The egg would hatch and the larvae eat the lion, a ready meal for baby wasp.

"Lucky for us we found you," the Noble said to the cat man, then kneeling began slicing a thin strip of flesh from his back, "you have saved us hunting you."

And peeled leeches off in my hiding position.

Now the other Noble knelt making a fire as he drank watered down beer, for the water in the jungle was full of liver flukes, and the watered beer another human secret and his wasp stood waiting for them to finish with the tied cat man, then I presume it would eat him.

Now had no fighting training and did not know the meaning of fear, but I knew what they were doing was wrong, and remembered how easy Jack had killed Nobles in the red dust of Dust Bowl. Knowing you are doing right

also helps you.

Right from a human point of view.

Not that I am about to become a blood letter, but that I am going to stop blood letting happen.

So, armed with my wooden swords I leap out and drive one into the thorax segment of this wasp, and it died.

Green and yellow ooze splattered my body.

The other wooden stick I drove with all my strength into the Noble who was just about to cut the cat man's tail off, straight through his rising neck and he dropped his iron sword and I picking it saw the egg laying wasp, listless until her egg laid.

But the fire lighter, this Noble now stood and drew his sword and I run wildly smiting the egg laying wasp so, thick yellow ooze gushes out.

And the wasp hummed wings singing its death chant.

Then I found anger does not overcome skill for I kept bashing at the Noble's sword till I drove both into the yellow river, so he slipped and became submerged.

He saved my life doing that for I saw two eyes watching and fled the water.

He must have known I was not running from him when I had the advantage, while he floundered in a hole in the pool bottom. I was running wild with one thought showing, get quickly onto dry land.

And he turns saw the black mouth upon his upper torso. There followed thrashing of water and fountains of blood, then silence as the lower body stood a moment just before it vanished in one bite.

"What was that?" I said trembling needing gulps of air.

"A water wolf, the insects forget they are not masters of everything," the cat man said, "come and free me."

Without thinking would this creature kill me while I did his bidding trusting I had acted out of right, all on my side must be good, and therefore he was good and friend?

Now he was bleeding and bade me fetch his leather pouch from which he found a small box of leaf cutter ants.

When the ant bites, the body twists leaving head and jaws that close the wound. Its blood also acts as an antiseptic.

So, closed the wound with ants.

I also rubbed in venom from a vine snake that congeals blood so, lessened the bleeding.

And found the cat man's skin velvety soft like rich fur.

And his eyes were yellow like cats.

"Young, are you not?" He asked and I replied telling him who I was but not where I was going.

"I am Howal, King of the Veneti and friend to all those who fight Nina." Now this shook me for I never realized my world extended beyond our nest, Shurrupuk City and

the yellow grasslands.

Us, insects, and Nobles, and here I stood speaking to a stranger in the language of Nina. Just when I had come to terms with being alone, I must now grasp the fact I was not and world was indeed HUGE.

After he helped me cut the egg from his lion beast, he spitted it and we ate. Then he

(Can you hear lion paws coming?)

combed cleaning his long yellow hair. Insect eggs are good, sweet, and full of strength. And Utna and the lion devoured the wasps.

And I fell asleep content.

That night his lion devoured the Nobles too.

(Silent paws)

Next day was something; I saw nothing to feel proud of killing my enemies. It needed done to free Utna, but gloating was wrong; I was now becoming a man.

I must have been a sight too, because I had put on the silver skull cap of my slain foe, his leather bronze studded vest and taken his weapons.

An inner insight told me to do that. Also told me to pick up a Noble's discarded sling, a toy they use to shoot down singing birds, not insects.

Howal he just smiles and says, "The boy grows up?" And I ignore and strap on the other folded armor and weapons onto Utna, "Never know when I might need them?"

"Luke Hoarder," Howal grins.

"Yep, that is me, Luke Hoarder, it sounded better than Luke the son of a cheese maker. Nothing wrong with the profession but standing holding a Noble's gold spear

and wooden colored spiraled shield my name just did not sound right. Cheese maker, it did not sound soldier enough, more like an Insect's slave.

Hoarder does? A young man had to change with the times, and I look with squinted eyes at the white universe and think, "I don't want any of this but what can I do? All I want is to wake up each day and thank you for the day."

*

Lords Hupamuk and Enalusdra stood in silver litters on the backs of giant brown dung beetles.

Surveying the Noble remains left by us. Although I had wanted to bury their bones, Howal would not let me, "What made them reason has left them, what you see here is just dust, that part that goes back into World as physical food."

I did not realize it at the time he thought Nobles did not deserve a decent burial so guess he meant they would help life's cycle keep going.

Dust to dust,

Ashes to ashes,

Life is a school, then you graduate, die.

So, the two Nobles Hupamuk and Enalusdra watched army ants marching into the creepers carrying chunks of Noble bone.

A lone purple feather that Howal had stuck next to them in a pile of lion dung bespoke their fate.

I thought this crazy letting the enemy know who was responsible, but he wanted to strike fear into Nobles.

I also had not come to terms at being free. In the nest we hid mistakes for fear the Nobles would beat you for them.

Howal could not understand why I wanted to bury them. Either could I after what the Nobles did to my nest. But it seemed the decent thing to do. When I knew the

Nobles would not bury me.

Remember I was not a hateful person and Howal saw this and seemed amused.

We humans cannot hide our soul, our eyes are too open. Even a basking lizard shows happiness in its eyes. But insects, they do not give anything deeper down away.

*

And she stood there behind Lords Hupamuk and Enalusdra, armed in a silver breast plate, auburn hair trailing down tanned bare shoulders to the end of her green kilt. On her head was a gold skull cap that protected ears, nose, and neck with false antennae.

In one hand she held a bronze circular shield, in the other an aluminum javelin and she was handsome.

Green shoes developed into leggings.

And I never saw her eyes then or I might have been on my guard, solid green and hating life.

To the Insect Nobles she was the face in the moon come pay them a visit the way she looked, mysterious and mythical.

Why then were they so surprised that life existed amongst the stars is crazy? She had come from the stars and was a closely guarded secret *so that even Peter did not*

know of her existence.

And she had not come in Phoenix in the Time of Myth.

"Do you understand what is required of you?" Lord Hupamuk asked.

She just stared at him, and he crawled back inside his soul from all that hate.

A Noble warrior gave her a green dragonfly to mount.

"Follow the army ants who follow the tapeworm trail till you find him who we call Babylon," Hupamuk.

She showed no emotion apart from hate.

And Priest Lord Enalusdra waved his green human chitin arms and the small insects of the land went back to their toils for he had read their lenses and seen what

had occurred here.

Knew King Howal's purple feather was unnecessary. Knew Babylon had done this and spat, "Babylon, hear Luke, we know what Babylon means and you are a dreamer of dreams. It is you who are Babylon, you who will be a nameless mound with weeds growing upon you."

And the green-eyed girl heard him faintly and pondered how one salve could arose so much fear in a nation and knew what Babylon meant. Except that the one slave

referred too did not know.

Her planet still traded with Earth and Vornals' universities offered degrees on Earth subjects. She had also seen Earth movies; they were popular as something new.

*

One month out:

I and Howal were in the middle of the blue grass dry depression watching pink flamingos cover an entire white shallow lake. I had never seen anything like it before.

I must have still been a boy though I was twenty now, it was like I entered a sweet shop. I could have spent a week there, but Howal tells me we must go on.

It was about now I met my second companion.

Howal, he grips my right foot since the lion creature his mount is not as high as Utna.

And I look and there lying next to a smoldering fire and a dead dragonfly a motionless auburn-haired girl.

I knew she was a girl from behind because of the hairless legs and small cheeks behind those green pants that showed from her ruffled green kilt.

I had seen women before you know.

Nina.

No man looks like that.

Now Howal he wants to retreat and scout before doing anything. Well, it made sense, but Luke is different stuff. I was full of victory over my first kills and had changed.

Foolishness might have been the word so Howal went off thinking I was behind him while I was walking over to the girl.

Well, I am Luke and my own master these days.

Anyway, Utna was behind me with his jaws ready to snap anything in two.

And she smelt good, too good like tangerines and

SNAP

I stood on a twig, and she not only turned but had the point of her aluminum javelin in my gut.

I did not show fear thankfully, was too surprised. Annoyed too that she was behaving this way to a total stranger before finding out if I was harmless or deadly.

that is what comes with living with ants.

Well, Utna he towers over me mandibles wide, his two black eyes say to the woman, "Just try it?"

And saw all this hate in her green eyes and felt pity, how could something so pretty hate so?

"I am Luke and mean you no harm."

She just stays the way she is so, does the spear point.

And did not know she knew who I was, Hupamuk had shown her pictures of me; *I* was a targeted person.

Also see real annoyance in those eyes......towards me.

Well, slow so, she can see what I am doing I push her spear down, and she hesitatingly allows me too.

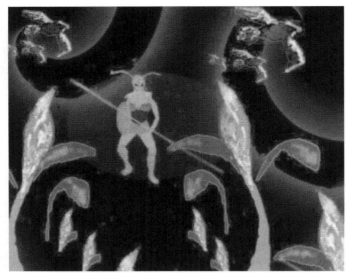

Was she Insect or woman the green-eyed girl?

She was trusting me. *No way, Utna was all too visible.*

That is when Howal took her in a bear hug and she screams something awful at me, **"Liar,"** well at least we all speak Noble Insect.

Liar meaning, she had trusted me and Howal grabs her, so I was a liar!

Makes sense, does it not? Thank you very much Howal.

CH4 Vornalians

Vase fragment of Luke, pottery industry evidence.

The present: Year 2001, second calendar, Day 3002.

Draught: The Nobles blamed the human witches, and blackened stakes with poles and ash and charred femurs started appearing in the fields of the Nobles.

But Priest Enalusdra who along with his astronomers and telescopes had seen a large comet hit World.

And the picture writers went to work with hieroglyphics.

Lo Queen Nina was happy with the burnings for it kept the slaves controlled and rid World of more human magicians......soothsayers.

And Queen Nina sat on the back of a blue green segmented Imperial Dragonfly, the fastest of all dragonflies. Her whole court was with her riding an assembly of bugs, so courtesans eyed Alana and Lana from our nest, as Noble playthings.

Queen Nina might not have allowed them to come if they were ordinary slaves. They like the harem attendants never went anywhere apart from Noble homes and like other girls to provide babies.

And the human Insect Nobel babies had pedigrees for trade and wax papers noted wingless offspring and bore the seal of Enalusdra.

Now one of the families the two girls rented to was Governor Ziusudra's, who had taken a shine towards them. His red son Ziu treated my fair sister as a wife while one of his human men slaves did likewise with Alana.

"This is progressiveness, what was meant to be," Ziusudra defended in front of Queen Nina.

"That we treat humans as equals?"

He did not mention the profitability of breeding your own slaves from rented stock.

So, said nothing, he would be lucky to walk away with his head still intact, but he knew a secret, Enalusdra was a cousin of Nina's and knew they came from the same batch of eggs which meant he was of their clan.

It was the way the governor had stood with that smile when he should have been kissing her feet that made her send everyone away.

"What do you know?" She asked and he told he knew she had winged genes and she wanted to kill him there and then.

Instead, she offered life in return for who told him.

"Enalusdra my cousin," and both smiled for Enalusdra was her kin; and her smile was irony at its best.

"My queen, we all take humans for their winglessness. Even we winged ones wish to look like god Enil," then governor Ziusudra fell to the red dust floor and kissed her feet.

And Queen Nina drummed fingers on chin, he was right, **let his son Ziu with** his long orange hair and blue eyes treat slave Lana as wife, good might come of it.

Also, Alana with the man slave Mac, let them parade like free Nobles. Let the slaves see a sort of equality obtained at a price, by becoming insect as the Ant Ghosters.

Already Lord Priest Enalusdra had inserted insect genes into Mac's back for wings to bud. Alana, her future lay with Noble breeding programmers.

And Queen Nina would pass a new law that would have horrified even Peter.

"Let insect marry human," it would speed up the absorption of human genes into Noble blood, make wings outdated and protect against the diseases that favored

winged Nobles.

(Draught)

And they put wings in his back, and he flew and buzzed as a fly and went to feed on flowers.

An Insect to Peter and my father Shaun the cheese maker was a dirty fly. None would willingly hand over a fair daughter; the thought of grandchildren with wings and those insect eyes just too much.

And why Lana and Alana accompanied Queen Nina.

The other reason was Nina knew these girls were special to me; and never occurred to me, Nina had chosen me before I went to wiggle in the Dance of the Insects.

My mum had wasted time cutting my hair to make me ugly. I had strange eyes did not I? They shined and nothing is private when you live in a nest. Elder Peter was not the only one who had witnessed my night dancing with the universe; but at that time, I was elsewhere upon the blue grass depression. When I heard of this marriage from the auburn girl I asked, "Had they forgotten

the Dance of the Insects?"

For I remembered Alana and Lana learning how to be grownups at the hands of Queen Nina.

She was a woman.

She was an insect.

I know love can conquer these differences.

In this respect I am more infinite than Peter.

It was meant to be and I to take his place?

Peter knew and that is why he taught me things he did not others.

Anyway: Queen Nina looked upon the burnt remains of the star ship from which an auburn green-eyed girl had come from.

Often did the queen come, dream about it under the blazing red sun and know fear that fed hate? Creatures like Luke, and this green-eyed girl encircled their heaven Naja. The Phoenix for her survival needed found, deep down she was the egg layer of her race, a queen insect.

Like a bee or ant queen, the rest could die, if she survived for from her will come future soldiers, workers, egg laying queens and race.

And the survivors of the new star ship lingered in the dungeons below Shurrupuk City her nest, those that had fought Nobles, red ants, centipedes, and were overpowered.

It had been quite a fight.

(Draught)

The offworlders had indicated they wanted to talk, and the watching Nobles kept surrounding until Nina had come.

And Nina's fear of the unknown overwhelmed.

"Kill them," she had ordered, and these were not human slaves? But free soldiers who killed twenty ants for every one of their own slain.

"Must you kill everything you do not understand?" Governor Ziusudra demanded angrily at her side at the time.

"Yes, "her reply.

(Pink clouds)

"Do not kill them all, let us learn how to travel the stars from them," Governor Ziusudra and got away with his brashness by appealing to her logic. There was light in this Insect Noble.

And Queen Nina commanded the offworlders to surrender, or die, and they did talk amongst themselves and preferred to die with their secrets.

For they knew that if their ship was able to fly, they did annihilate these insects who had crawled out of the woodwork.

(Buzzing sounds)

Now there are species of insects, large and small. Now Governor Ziusudra summoned the small kind, mosquitoes, and flies to annoy the offworlders.

One week later they charged out from their burnt ship in a suicide attack and dozens killed and enslaved when their weapons fell silent.

And Queen Nina feared Governor Ziusudra for he was dangerous for he had a mind.

And from that day she plotted to kill him for she was indeed a black widow spider.

There had never been a king only a queen in any insect nest but World with its colored clouds were changing.

Now this off-worlder's ship provided the green-eyed woman sent with Lords Hupamuk and Enalusdra. She knew what she must do for the lives of her friends

depended upon her.

Already she had seen Queen Nina's mercy at work.

(White sky)

In Shurrupuk dungeon cells adjoining the circular goaler's room lit by burning bees wax seen her own father dissected, as had the first human survivors of Phoenix been fated to die before they were born.

(Dungeon stinks)

Vornalian technology was advanced, but the insects counted as the grains

of sand on a seashore and that counted

And she shamed and cried over her father's nakedness.

And she wished her father dead for he lay for hours as the teachers of the Insects cut, probed and took his organs to learn knowledge, for to them he was no more than an intelligent two finned green dolphin that swam in the yellow seas of World.

A laboratory specimen to chloroform.

Then they came for a woman, and she thought they would take her, but did not for they had plans for Nina desired to capture Luke for the girl was fair.

And she heard the woman scream as they did sad things to her to see if she differed from their own insect or human women. There were no laws prohibiting medical research and yet they were backward still in space travel.

(screams)

And the Insect Noble scientists clapped hands and backs for they had found this new star travelling race yielded a rich milk; so that females would become as the human cows, fixed to milking machines for Insect milk is not rich.

Insect evolution is void of breast feeding; why mammals have outstripped the insect.

Pink clouds

And the green-eyed auburn-haired girl knew she was in hell, where the tables had been turned. Instead of dissecting bugs the bugs were dissecting them. On the walls she saw stuffed creatures like herself, or bits of them in pickling jars.

And she did not know she was looking at humans, and she saw the Insect Nobles as demons and went crazy in the mind.

And they removed the dissected woman's eggs and took them away and allowed the green eyed woman to see her......her fate if she refused to help.

Saw the woman alive but stretched out over wooden tables, heart beating there and lungs breathing here.... over their bile produced, and dripping into a bowl......
and the legs jerking independently of the body by electrodes on other tables......she did not want the same fate.

And the Insect medical students came and watched the effects of new drugs on the exposed alien human body......and they took the green-eyed woman Ulana out for she had vomited, stinking the air.

And spared seeing the fetus taken from the dissected woman and placed in an artificial womb.... for later use......these people were wingless like the humans?

Insect Noble ethics were different from other planets.

So, that when this green-eyed girl, Ulana went topside with Lords Hupamuk and Enalusdra she went, anything to get away from this laboratory hell.

This poor girl had found two hells, mind, and physical habitat: the third, the Outer Darkness waited for her tormentors.

So, they took her to the chambers of Queen Nina.

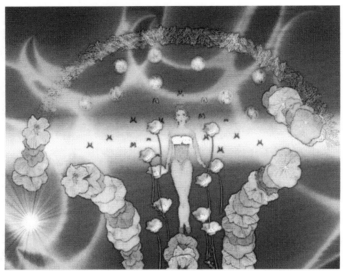

Solid green eyes and (WINGED RABBITS).

(Solid green eyes)

And she stood in her plastic silver and green transparent body armor trying to feel different and PROUD to be a Sun Traveler and not one of these BUGS.

And Queen Nina watched the lords take away her armor and kilt; but Ulana was not here for information extraction, they had gotten enough of that out of their captives.

Like the humans before them had come through a black hole and try as she might, Queen Nina never saw a black hole when she looked at the night sky.

"Perhaps they are witches and need burning like the humans," for Nina's imagination could not stretch down black holes.

But Lords Hupamuk and Enalusdra saw beyond the white sky seeing planets populated with humanoids and although they did not confide in each other, both had stopped believing in a god called Enil.

If heavenly Naja rested upon the clouds above and World was Enil's his foot stool, then there might as well be *winged rabbits flying about the three crimson moons.*

Lo, Nina, Enalusdra and Hupamuk were not good in human terms of thinking; but they were the masters and these newcomers' slaves.

Slaves were prey, food, and toys.

In this case the girl was a pretty toy.

And the girl had entered another type of hell, the world of the abused and abuser.

"Look what I lay at your feet," and Nobles looked and saw every creeping thing, *"Behold cast nets in the yellow sea and look,"* and Nobles cast and saw every fish that

lived, *"Lo fly the air and what you meet is yours,"* and Nobles flew the air and met every manner of winged beast, *"all that you see is yours to treat as you please for I god Enil have given all to you."*

*

Howal and I sat beside this green-eyed girl watching her eat knowing nothing about Vornals. The meal was not much, roasted lizard with tubers.

(Roast lizard delicious)

And very slowly she bit, slower chewed, and often threw hateful stares at us but ate with manners often wiping her mouth and fingers on a yellow leaf.

And the remains she threw into the darkness for others to enjoy.

"Some offering to her gods?" Howal gruffly for he would not offer gnawed bones to his.

And by her eyes I saw her negative reply and remembered what I used to do, leave what I did not eat for the regeneration of the wilderness and saw that Howal was right, it was an offering to the wilderness. Our slain enemies treated likewise; man, or beast was just ash and part of the cycle of regeneration.

And still did not see Howal left the Nobles as food for the wilderness out of nastiness and not logic.

In her eyes I saw recognition, for she saw my kind as the stuffed specimens on the walls......
and I forgot about Alana who I thought I loved but was lust. And where there is no love it is easy to forget.

This strange girl, her solid green eyes, they were magnetic.

It was her unusual eye coloring that captivated Luke.

I wanted the girl's friendship and offered her weapons back, but Howal went crazy,

"Too much venom there, I want to wake up tomorrow."

The last bit I agreed but not the rest. She had not asked us to invade her privacy; I wanted her to have freedom and like me in return.

And I did.

"What the blazes your stupid young fool," Howal went crazy when I handed her back her sword, point facing us.

I mean Howal he jumped up and drew his steel sword.

Me I just sat opposite her smiling, looking stupid in the dancing light of our yellow fire.

She questioned me with her eyes.

And saw a flicker of light, hope, questioning? **It was reward enough.**

(Cooking smells)

My heart fluttered; it was her solid green eyes as if a candle lit in them.

"Want do you want with me?" She remembered what the queen and lords wanted?

I went back to eating, or tried too until Howal picked me up and started belting me with his palms. "I give the orders here," he shouted and, "you and your stupid puppy dog eyes shining like stars. "I'll give you shiners," and raised his right fist.

That was a mistake; I had been a slave too long to want to return to it. It also shows how big Howal is? He is a cat man as I call them and I had grown to over six feet, was well-muscled for slaves work always.

But I valued my freedom and chinned him flat. I was not scared; it was the right thing to do at that moment.

And the girl just sits, and stares and I know from her eyes she is asking, "To the victor the spoils?" And that makes me angry for I knew there was truth in it no matter how my mind screamed "NO" I am just being fair.

Now Howal, he recovers on unsteady feet and finds his sword.

"I am a king and you a human slave."

"So what?" I say maddened and draw my Noble's sword, then there was this squeal as Utna pinned the lion creature, Howal's domestic pet.

(squeal)

That made Howal crazy again and I got my second swordsmanship lesson.

I think Howal would have killed me. Six times he disarmed me and still attacked and I only lived because the girl flashed a beam of orange light from a ring, she wore into his eyes, temporarily blinding him, where I read intent, kill.

And knew Howal was more beast than man.

Yet defended myself, each time avoiding his sword and picking up my own and I learned quickly.

I ran circles about Howal.

How did he do that? Get my sword out of my hand and each time he did I watched and saw him twist his wrist and then did it back to him.

The girl clapped and that defused the situation....... a bit of humor brought out the man, in Howal. And what were we fighting about, there could only be one leader, one lion king, one to impress the girl who to the victor the spoils.

Her questioning eyes had been right, "What do you want of me?" But I did not want to stop, that would mean losing my freedom of opinion, I would be just Howal's human slave.

So, fought and disarmed him again and gave him back his sword and sheathed me own.

And do you know what the son of a snake does?

Quick as a flash he has that sword at my throat.

Now the girl came towards Howal calling him all sorts of names, "Cheat, a king, yes a king of thunder boxes," those names and stronger ones.

But she need not have bothered because Utna he throws that red lion creature over his back and comes to the rescue so Howal throws down his sword begging mercy at my feet.

I stop Utna and the embarrassment is overwhelming.

I am not a king.

I am Luke Hoarder, no Luke the son of a cheese maker who smells of Stilton, Danish Blue and cheddar and ant dung. So, help Howal up and give him back his sword and hold out my hand, "Friends alright?"

Now Howal stands trying to figure me out. Never been around with humans before on social terms.

"You are a human slave," he quietly.

And he did not shake hands.

So, I shrug and lie down next to Utna and try to get sleep; but Utna that black ant goes to the girl and fingers her all over with his antennae clicking excitedly.

(Clicking sounds)

Seeing how I was reminded of my manners I joined my ant.

"Thank you for coming to my aid, from both of us," I say and hold out my hand offering friendship.

Well, she looks at my right hand and I see she is examining it next to her own.

We both have five fingers per hand.

"Do not mention it," she grins and sits down to smooth the red grass of twigs for a bed.

Now it is embarrassing standing, ignored by a fair woman and I hear Howal's sniggering remarks behind, so I retire with Utna for the night.

Not knowing the girl had last seen a human hand in a glass beaker under Shurrupuk Nest, why she was 'off' human hands for a while.

And later felt guilty over her mission to save her people.

(What she told Tarves Dallas her father? It was his shinning eyes that made me see Luke as good. How could I kill someone with shinning eyes?)

And things were never the same between me and Howal. He had more experience and being a king should have led, but I had to reach Phoenix. I also did not like his reference to me being a slave as if I were to be his slave.

But somehow felt I was the leader and he my elder protector, my companion who would teach me what he knew.

I must have been in a dream world; the man should hate me for his loss of face.

He was, but I did not know that.

And the girl smiles for she knows she has friends, *Utna had moved antennae over her,* Utna's thanks for helping Luke, Utna is friend.

Yes, she has guilt feelings.

Me, I am pretending sleep, but peeking with half shut eyes and she smiles.

Yes, I look more like her than Howal who is lion creature; so, feel bounded already.

The hate for a moment leaves her eyes and fondness is there. That makes me happy; I shut my eyes and smile.

(Smell of girl head hair)

Ten minutes later I felt her soft hair against my left shoulder.

I just lay there frozen sweating, hoping she thought I was asleep.

I did not believe in the victor takes the spoils.

Next day she was as hostile as ever.

And Howal, remote.

And thanks to a tapeworm the Lords Hupamuk and Enalusdra trailed and through spying insects saw and were pleased with the green-eyed girl and knew something she did not, scientists had pinned her father on tables waiting for the next natural science class.

And puzzled that I had not taken advantage of her that night.

She had had her orders.

She at school taught humans were promiscuous like monkeys.

This Luke did not fit into her perception about humans.

And above night jars swooped eating moths by the beak.

The joke was gorillas were our distant cousins, monkeys more distant.

And below warriors of Hupamuk, off duty used their slings but because it was night, missed the night jars.

CH5 Next Companion

I stood with my new friends looking up at the far embankment which we needed to climb to reach Red Mountain.

It lay on the route Howal must take to reach his kingdom and the way he looked at me sometimes he knew I wanted Phoenix. He never said anything though, he knew about the Time of Myth, it was part of World Mythology.

He also knew about the little creatures living there that ate Insect Nobles like mutated leprosy germs that reduced Nobles to white flakes in weeks.

Howal like everyone else knew humans were supposed to be resistant to these germs.

He only knew half the truth.

Queen Nina had tried sending human slaves before and none returned.

Whether Phoenix's bugs got them, or they attempted freedom in the uncharted wilderness of white World is something else?

Humans were not trustworthy to find Phoenix. Might keep Phoenix's secrets to themselves.

Just the thought of people like my friend Jack who escaped Shurrupuk Dust Bowl obtaining human weapons made Queen Nina paranoid.

Made them want to put iron balls on our human ankles.

Which they did.

I guess either Howal was coming along as a companion or to see what he might get for himself.

Yes, I was in a good mood feeling lucky. Not that I believed in gods, we humans had learned moral science was the answer to problems eons ago.

If we had any priests aboard Phoenix when she floundered, we realized the Insect Nobles would not permit any competition for Enil their god.

There was no religious toleration under Queen Nina.

Besides, it was hard to believe in a good god on World; so, stuck too our elders the so-called magicians who taught morals through fables.

Those humans needing saved became Ghost Dancers of Queen Nina, her Ghosters who ran about in insect masks waving fire hardened tipped wooden spears, they who bullied the rest of us to work faster for their Noble masters.

A right couple of crazies these Ant Ghosters were? Been eating Magic Mushrooms when the chef was not looking and then blamed the cooking.

Anyway: Howal was beside the green-eyed woman who still had not told us her name.

He was doing his utmost to chat her up getting nowhere, 'SPURNED' in capitals.

Why one time I heard him offer her a diamond embedded in his dagger for something.

"I owe you nothing," she wrote with a finger in the grey dust that was the soil here, I read, learned, and was joyous, **(Red Mountain).**

And knew she had written the truth. She owed him nothing, could match him I believe in physical confrontation with the sword and Howal guessed this too. He was not in his kingdom where he could send his armed men to kidnap her or take her possessions or endanger her young to force her to his needs.

"Why is there so much evil on World?" I asked the girl when Howal sulked out of hearing behind bushes.

She answered by looking deep into my eyes and saw that she was seeking if I mocked or was true grit.

She smiled; I guess I had passed something.

Me I figured if she wanted my attention, she would attract it so let her be and did not press on her like Howal who would soon give up, I hoped.

Should have awoken to the trouble he was making but figured if they wanted fun it was up to them. I was being naïve, but I was acting the good big brother, the nice brother, **(Cat scenting smell).**

Howal, his eyes just would not leave her alone, glued to her green pants. I guess he could have told me the times her lips opened to chew food. He was that obsessed.

It was male lust and made me shame.

Was glad I had no diamonds to tempt her, but **(Red Mountain)**

here we were looking up at Red Mountain and somehow, I knew she was staring at me, you just feel eyes on your back. Her solid green eyes were not quick enough to drop from me or she wanted me to catch her stare? It made me blush at first, then made me think more about her which I was doing forgetting my want for Alana.

I mean she was stunning in her silver armor, and her auburn hair, well I knew what people did; Nina had taught me and taught there is no real difference between races when a man and women is concerned in bed.

I am being honest, sons of cheese makers usually are, and we do not own diamonds, and we started climbing unexpectedly grey depression and it was a hike, the flowering shrubs became denser and then cleared to flowering trees and the normal sized bees more fearsome trying to bite always.

THEN.... *a faint call for help.*

Well, Howal and the girl stop, being more experienced warriors than me, so I and Utna go ahead. Utna as programmed would investigate a hole where a trap door

spider lurks and, Utna eaten. Me I went forward because I heard someone in distress and was human, also an apprentice cheese maker and so dumb.

(Red Mountain)

But the auburn-haired girl who is hovering on her shoes, did I mention her shoes?

They have motors in them that let her skip across the red grass, runs after me and Howal, he curses and flanks.

"Damn you Luke boy dam you," I hear him before he vanished.

Know he is always damning me for something?

And I ride Utna right into a clearing like I was Lord of all I could see.

And saw two blue winged beings that reminded me of Insect Nobles but without their chitinous skin and both were hanging from poles with rocks about them

ankles as weights, **(Buzzing).**

I did not take notice of the herd of flying bugs tethered on my right, but did see three Insect Nobles, three red ants and six centipedes standing waiting for

dinner.

If the girl had not come and stood by me, I might not have been so gun, Ho, "safety in numbers," Elder Peter had said and "impressing girls gets one into a mess."

I had also changed after leaving the nest and seen how easy it was to kill Nobles, thanks Jack.

As for the girl, she either thought I was stupid or heroic.

Let us hope heroic.

Girls oh why do they have to be so pretty and boys with puffed out chests, impressing only giggling whispers in the breezes.

*

As recorded on a red recorder smelling strongly of tangerines that Tarves Dallas was able to hear later.

"My name is Ulana, and I went forward with Luke for I had to protect him. It was what Lord

Hupamuk and Priest Enalusdra wanted, for him to give them the secrets of the human ship Phoenix, (Tangerines).

These Nobles Luke were encountering, accidental, but World is vast and communications slow, it was bound to happen.

I saw Luke as innocent and soon realized he was no danger to me. He had honor and might grow into a fine man. But the way Howal was chasing me brought a

bad taste to my mouth after what Nina and the Lords Hupamuk and Enalusdra had

done to me.

I was not something owned and passed about for use or sold as slave. These Insect Nobles had violated me and think they are primary now, but being of the Planet Vornal, know we all pay for what we do, what goes around comes around.

Even on Vornal there are good, behaved men till they get you alone and then ask for it; it is just the way, men and women, men want women, simple as that.

Luke might turn.

Howal I would kill if he forced me. My shield and spear would remain close always.

Luke if he forced me, I must allow, the lives of my hostage people depend on his life.

I am not a little girl, Vornal is a promiscuous planet. But the prospect of Luke both revolted and pleased me.

Pleased because he is a good man.

Revolted because I must win the secrets of Phoenix to save my people from the horrors of Shurrupuk.

Also saw how brave Luke is to just ride out just as the air filled with a sickening thud as a Noble knifed one of those blue insect men hanging from a pole. This was cowardly as the hanging man was defenseless and his tormentor was out to torment.

And it was the red and centipedes that rushed upon Luke.

Here was a black ant with a human rider. As insects they came hurrying to investigate and I was afraid.

They were so big and venomous; I was unused to them.

I am Ulana woman warrior of Planet Vornal and used to battle, but to see these giant bugs, their bristles the size of sunflower stalks, their gaping mouths salivating, it was revolting.

As the first centipede rose to crawl over Utna, Utna bit it in half.

At once the air with a sticky smelly ooze.

And Luke killed an investigating red with his sword thrust into the beast's eye.

Me, I threw my spear into the head of the other centipede.

That left two reds.

I look at Luke who returns my stare and I saw his eyes were like a child's, innocent yet full of knowledge it had killed life.

"It was a serpent and was about to strike my baby sister, so cut off its head with the garden shears," the child was saying.

Who was this chap, Luke? Then he uttered a human roar. A horrendous clicking noise,

(Clicking noise).

Then he faces our enemy, yes, **our** enemy for these creatures were of the Noble race that pickled humans and Vornals, and a cursed bond formed between us.

Cursed because for the survival of my people I was to betray him Shurrupuk City.

And we were successful because they never expected dissecting specimens to fight.

Now the Nobles calmly walked confident the reds would kill us now that surprise was no longer with us.

And pale Howal on the back of his red growling lion sailed through the air and landed on them, and they died under feline weapons.

Now I left Luke and Utna to fend for themselves for the reds battled with them and it was no place for a mortal like me on foot as they stamped the red soil of the lower reaches of Red Mountain.

See how my perception of Luke had changed. World was full of monstrous giant insects, only gods, titans, and seekers of the Golden Fleece roamed World.

Luke at this time still meant little to me which was a lie although I did not know it.

He was not my mate, he also had Utna black ant to defend him.

I only had my shoes.

My warrior training instructed me to fall back, survey, think, and then attack.

There was still one Noble left who was preparing to dispatch Howal who unable to draw his sword from the other Noble as it had stuck in something, was defenseless, running I drew my sword across the back of our enemy's neck, so his head rolled away.

Howal and I looked at Luke who was full of frenzy slicing at the red while Utna and the other red were engaged in a tug of war to see which would topple first.

I reach for my sword and find it has fallen from its scabbard and I am without spear.

I look at Howal my eyes saying, "You are armed, go help."

And he hesitates and clearly see his soul; he wants Luke dead so to the victor goes the spoils.

"The ants will kill us next," I spit at him, and this makes Howal mount his red lion and bounding forward he lands upon the red attacking Luke so that distracted turns to bite Howal in half.

And Luke thrust his sword into the narrow neck, so the head fell off.

And I having freed my spear cast it hard into the last red's soft body segment which allowed Utna to finish the beast off.

And I stood panting looking at Luke, never had I seen a man/boy like him. Only one untouched by civilization could behave as he, fearless and bold and I wished I were

not his enemy but his friend.

(*Now man/boy to Vornals is a late teenager struggling to become adult, the same goes with girl/woman.*)

With Luke rode love and right.

He had right inside him, and I asked, "Where do you come from?"

"From the nest Ur."

I did not speak again, that is not what I meant."

Howal and his lion charge out of forest.

*

The freed man could not speak our tongue but as he was a Noble enemy, he was welcome with Luke.

"Titus," he said repeating stabbing a finger in his chest. And the men introduced themselves likewise except for me as none knew my name.

Then Titus tended his injured companion, and it was obvious he was to die for the wound had smacked his left kidney and was bleeding freely.

Now Titus erected poles with Luke's help between the branches of a tree, and at last Howal let go his regal dignity and helped lift the dying man onto the tree bed

they had made.

And Howal was disgusted as the dying man released his bowels over him as he was lifted.

Now on the bed Titus put the man's weapons by his blood-soaked side with money.

Then Titus spread arms to the white sky and spoke to his gods. While he was doing this Howal examined the herd of flying bugs, it was obvious these navy blue

humanoids with gold hair and white eyes were traders in insect mounts.

"My people have traded with their like in the far north," Howal and shrugged to further questioning about them. He was as ignorant as us or lying?

Now Titus gave each of us a flying insect with saddle and Howal took his while Luke refused, pointing and hugging Utna.

The man took no offence; instead, he took from a leather pouch a honeycomb and gave it to Utna.

Again, I saw a different Luke from he who I was supposed to trap. "He is a robber of his own kind. At least I can defend my Insect Noble race in that we are not of his race and see humanoids as cattle. But he is of his own race and eats his own as cattle," ......

and Priest Enalusdra showed me papers......pleas from human nests to petition him to hunt Luke down.

He is everything base a man could be. No woman or boy is safe with him. He knows not the meaning of honor or loyalty. Then feel no guilt when you hand the secrets of Phoenix over to Nobles," what Enalusdra told Ulana the green-eyed girl.

And it confirmed what I knew about Luke with my own eyes, that Enalusdra was a lair.

Luke was loyal to his friends.

Titus the blue skin.

Now I Ulana took my offered mount, a blue dragonfly which meant I would not walk, for riding behind Howal was an experience in ridding his pawing fingers from my belly and thighs.

In the end I jumped off and restrained from killing him for, "Protect Luke, keep him alive," Lord Hupamuk and remembered the fight between Howal and Luke and

thought Howal the better sword.

Howal was a lucky man.

I never rode behind him again now I had a mount.

The crazy thing is Howal thought I enjoyed. There are men who think like this, Howal was extremely dangerous, but Luke saw otherwise, Howal was his companion as I.

Comrades, each protecting each other's interests.

Luke's naivetés made me want to cry. I was glad none noticed my anguish as I flew rear-guard.

Luke could be such a stupid boy.

At the same time, I hoped Luke would never grow up for adulthood, corrupts.

"When he has given you Phoenix's secrets you will kill Luke," Lord Hupamuk.

"Then your people will be freed," Enalusdra.

And I learned Luke was their enemy, a human, like those stuffed and pinned on the walls...... like the woman of Vornal who I saw dissected.

I saw humans that endured the whims of Insect Nobles were salves and anatomically close to the Vornalians.

Did we not all have five fingers per hand?

I could find allies amongst them against our common enemy the Insect Noble.

To ride behind Luke brought on strange feelings that a girl should have towards a healthy young man. But I had to fight them for Luke was enemy, he had to be, me

people's lives depended upon this.

"All men are the same," I reminded myself but knew Luke was different.

Yes, I was glad of my own mount for the freedom it gave me ridding me dependence on men.

It was two Insect men and one Insect woman who had degraded me not Luke.

Just remembering made me squirm as if I was still being their object and needed washed and fresh clothes. It made me see Luke as male, enemy and it would be easy to

kill him to protect myself from his wickedness.

Even he was good which confused me?

*

In my world we put light next to right, evil with cruelty and darkness.

Light springs from the infinite goodness that created life in the beginning.

The Ceugant Dana.

It struggles through science to rid suffering disease.

We seek light in unusual ways, through meditation, others in religious houses, but no religion has state control because all of us are taught science and morality at an early age upwards.

Science comes first and we remember that.

Most of us attend no religious worship but abide by "Love one another and treat one another as you would treat yourself."

And our elders the magicians knew light is good for it brushes aside ignorance.

Luke was like this; he was a light bulb attracting us moths to him and he did not know it.

The Ceugant Dana was manifesting in him as does darkness manifest in evil men who hurts others?

Instead of being his enemy I wanted to save him because darkness would want to extinguish that light.

Then his eyes would no longer shine.

And I rode a blue dragonfly.

Luke an ant.

Howal a lion.

Titus a fly.

And behind came an assortment of buzzing flying bugs.

And haunted that a man was dying on a raised platform behind, the way of Titus and his people.

We could not stay till Titus's friend gasped his last. Nobles might come seeking those we killed.

His friend was dead anyway, becoming one with the spirit flowing through all, the platform he was on, white sky, rushing pink clouds, the tiny flies landing on him.

The Ceugant Dana.

The dying man was leaving his body, it was the way his race died, and his spirit would enter the spirit world soon.

It was awful. (Taken from Ulana's perfumed memo bank diary.)""

*

"He will not talk anymore," Lord Hupamuk watching Enalusdra cut off the man's right ear, and then Enalusdra looked at the man's eyes, saw them glaze, die and what

Enalusdra did next was pure nastiness.

See, he was sure he saw the man's essence rise from his body and instead of pain on the man's face there was a beautiful peace; the man was going home to the other

side.

And Enalusdra cut the man's throat from ear to ear.

Hoping he had inflicted stinging pain to the last.

So died the friend of Titus in his tree bed.

"So, the boy Luke has four companions," Hupamuk mused.

"He is no longer a boy, "Enalusdra chided, and the two lords locked eyes, knowing that Luke was dangerous.

The tales from the Time of Myths were full of murders by humans who had survived capture. Now one Jack whose printed face on hand sheets nailed to blue

painted walls had rebelled, and he used only one sword.

"Wanted for the murder of Nobles."

Look well his face and report him."

A fearsome reminder of human brutality towards Insects.

Luke must die when he reached Phoenix. Humans must not get its secrets, the only safeguard was Ulana.

Now just before they left Priest Enalusdra got Noble warriors to completely destroy the raised platform and throw the friend of Titus on an ant hill.

Priest Enalusdra knew of the race of Titus and what they believed in was blasphemous, only Insect Nobles became part of Enil when they went to heavenly Naja.

All other life including humans did not have a soul!

Dozens of Enil priests argued they did but went to hell like mammals, not to heaven, reserved for Noble Insects. Humans could not feel higher emotions, so it was all right to slaughter them in butcher yards.

"What if Luke joins the robber, Jack? They were friends once," Enalusdra asked.

And Lord Hupamuk said nothing but stared down the trail that was leading to Luke.

*

A past event.

The wedding of Ziu and Lana.

And there was a great fanfare of drumming wings as red Ziusudra with red beard led his son red Ziu to the gold human crafted alter of Enil in Shurrupuk City atop Enil's Ziggurat. Queen Nina was not present, she had given consent to his son's marriage with Lana, **(Sounds of wedding celebration).**

Her absenteeism was saying enough is enough. I do not really approve and those that follow Governor Ziusudra cannot expect my support.

It is only an experiment.

"I also expose Ziusudra's supporters who will attend the wedding; am I not intelligent?" Queen Nina, "We wingless ones don't need to mingle with human blood.

Ziusudra must, he is winged, not like Enil our god."

And Ziu wedded Lana and after the feasting attended by winged Nobles, Ziu took Lana to bed.

She was beautiful and he a handsome insect humanoid.

His red chitinous skin velvety, his eyes bright with light and love.

And Lana was human; a lovely girl who knew life was in World now. Ziu was kind, wrote her poetry, gave flowers, and treated his slaves with respect.

The thought of his insect seed growing in her into a monster frightened her until she looked at Ziu and asked?

"Is he a monster?"

And knew he was not, but a kind caring soul.

She was salve, bedded anyway, and had already given birth to wingless Nobles.

She could remain slave traded from house to house or accept his marriage offer......and he did not even need to offer. He could have left things the way they were.

Would not need to ask, just take whatever her mood.

Ziu was good; he had an inner kindness as if a candle had been lit. Handsome which was lucky for Lana as Nobles who had forced their attention onto her had been repulsive bugs.

And Lana knew by marrying Red Ziu she was taking a giant step forward for humankind: others would follow, a path out of slavery illuminated, a path towards equality had been set.

And when the priest proclaimed Lana, as first wife of Ziu, the newlyweds exited a dining hall made of, the finest blue spider's silk hanging from the west wall of Governor Ziusudra's town house.

A fortress of rock built with human labor and designed by human magicians our elders.

Here guests would eat and drink and leave in their own time for none expected Ziu to emerge till sunrise.

And upon the feasting tables were no human sweetmeats or barbecued ribs or crackling; Ziusudra would not eat humans.

Now at that moment of intimacy the spider silk curtains opened and Ziu's father Governor Ziusudra stood there. His timing was out, he was a little drunk and only knew he must visit the newlyweds before they became too close.

"Father," Ziu astonished.

In response Ziusudra explained how his vast estates would go to his son.

"I know that father."

"And I know give you light or dark, day or night," and so saying Lana looked horrified as Ziusudra dug his left eye out.

Ziu tried to stop him, but his father halted him by holding out the eye. Apart from wetness it looked it was, clearing in the light, a glass eye with a map on the back.

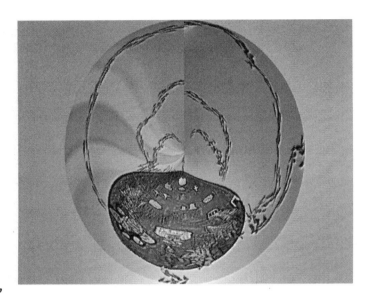

"What is it father?"

"The way to Phoenix."

Now Lana came and stood next to her husband Ziu staring at the eye.

And Ziusudra must have the actor in him for he took from his green robe a magnifying lens, and they saw the eye was a maze of rivers, trees, mountains, and a ship.

Phoenix.

"Why father?"

"You must decide but which way your soul goes I will support."

Then he left.

Like an insect Red Ziu liked the coolness of the forest floor, shaded

In Ziu's hands was "The freedom of slaves." Now this was a "Heavy Burden." His words spoken carelessly in front of Lana his human wife. His father had taught him

"To be kind to all things. Did not Enil make all things, so then all things have Enil in them," so Ziu spoke.

"The gods are hard and cruel, selfish. What you teach me is not of Enil," Ziu remembered telling his father and repeated now as he looked at the eye in his hand with his new wife sitting on their white wax bed.

"Enil, Enil, son, how many times have I made you pick up a human child or let a small beetle walks your palm. All is life, all have needs.

All belong to Enil; do not you feel him in your heart?"

And Lana understooo Governor Ziusudra was a great man, greater than Elder Peter who had been human?

"And it took me time to discard thoughts of yes; I feel strong and must protect the weak before I felt it, love.

And with it I became part of love which makes all things part of it.

That is love that manifests the unseen laws that allow us to exist, to breathe, to mate, to reproduce in diversity.

Love.

But I am still Noble Insect.

There is one thing marrying a slave but giving them freedom, equal rights to share my inheritance, my power by divine right of Enil," ....and Ziu realized his meaning

as his wife's human hand dropped from his arm.

A drawbridge had come between them.

The marriage was sham, another of Ziu's boyish pranks. And Lana knew Ziu was no different from Jack or the other boys that through intellectual boredom had sought mischief in the nest of Ur.

And insect rose in Ziu, anger burned so that he forced Lana back on the bed.

"I am Insect; you know what my father is asking me to do?"

And Lana was silent.

Only what Ziu had in his heart could help him. And Lana hoped the good there that had allowed her to love him as a person would win.

"There are many rights......I am right if I give the eye to Nina for my loyalty lies with Nobles......I am right if I get the eye to Luke for slavery is wrong," and Ziu

looked at Lana and saw humans in the future equal to Nobles.

No longer Ziu flying over his slave's heads in the tuber fields on a dragonfly.

And Ziu remembered his dragonfly's poohing on human heads and he laughing as a boy. Those where the days before his father had won his soul.

Dismounting and taking a human behind a bush because he felt like it. He still did that, it was his right to exhaust his lust with human female slaves.

Enil his god said it was.

And he caused bellies to swell; so many of the young running around his father's great ancestral brown wax hall were his children, and dozens had wings.

"A blessing, do you know humans dream of flight and we can? Never mind Nina and God Enil," father had said and spoken to him about his habit with the human

female slaves, then asked him to stop it, then ordered, then beat him for it. "You have forgotten all I have taught you that all life is same. You cannot force coupling

because you are the master.

Treat one another as you treat yourself, then treat the lower animals with respect for they are you, they share your spirit, respect all life, the spirit of God Enil is in all, what makes life; go look in a mirror if you do not believe me."

And Ziu had remembered his lessons and repented and stopped coupling the slaves for fun. It had been a passing teenage phrase expected of young Nobles.

And Lana did not know of this, why should he tell her, she was salve, still a slave......now wife, and Ziu allowed anger to consume him and tore Lana's white silk

clothes till she was naked, and then she knew she was slave and not wife and he treated her as slave that night.

And he was wrong, Lana knew his past, she was slave, and slaves talked.

Fortress ofZiusudra

*

It was early morning; Ziu had not slept, not allowed his salve beside him to sleep either. His anger he directed through his lions so that he woke Lana often.

And now he tired for his venom was embers.

Also shamed, he would not annul the marriage and give Nina the eye. He would give Lana, beautiful auburn Lana with gold eyebrows and blue eyelashes and eyes the

eye. If the salves were meant to be equals, then Enil meant it.

He would not like a dragonfly to pooh on his head as it flew past.

So, slept on the floor feeling unclean, that he had continually raped his new wife.

Six hours later she woke first and saw the eye when she sat.

"The eye to freedom," she and looked down at Ziu.

Now she was not sure if Ziu had given her the eye or what? But she did not want to go back to what had occurred last night.

So very stealthily she sneaked out the bedroom and then took hold of herself. She was a Noble's wife now, none would question as she found riding clothes, dragonfly and transport fly for the journey ahead.

And never saw a wanted poster nailed to the front of Governor Ziusudra's town house.

"Wanted for the murder of Nobles,

Jack."

Lana was slave,
had no rights.
She dreamed
of insect babies.

CH6 *Pretty but deadly.*

Lana

What Luke told Tarves Dallas the silver eyed recorder.

Lana my remaining sister had never been alone in the wildernesses which were lands outside a nest. Lands full of giant Venus fly traps that bit humans. Purple quick

sands were beetles lived waiting for runaway slaves to fall in. Giant wasps seeking humans to lay eggs in.

It could be a hell out there?

Lana had never seen the abundance of life of giant flowers that supported insect dominance on white World, or the blue, red, yellow, purple, and other colored grasslands all flowering. Which explains why she went to Alana her friend who had married the same time

Enbilulu for she had become a widow for the slave husband Mac had died?

Lo, Queen Nina on a whim had sent for Mac to examine, to become bored of, to be handed over to Priest Enalusdra minions to extract genes, and then sent to Dust Bowl a withered husk unable to run far from the giant desert scorpion loosened upon him.

And it caught, stung, and ate him.

And the watching Noble Insects were not envious of the lesser insect's dinner for Mac was no longer muscular.

There was no eating left after Enalusdra had what he wanted from you.

Just naked bones.

Such the work of the evil Lord Priest Enalusdra School of Science.

It was also Queen Nina's way of saying slaves shall not be our equals. Why all Nobles knew slaves were the descendants of illegitimate parents for the marriages their

magicians performed were illegal.

Could not be legal as slaves did not have souls. They were just white, black or yellow apes imitating their betters the Nobles.

And Enbilulu which means he of the pink hair, friend of Ziu red chitinous son of Governor Ziusudra had just finished breakfast in bed with his human bride and was

pleased with her. It was Ziu's idea he takes her. It seemed a wonderful thing to do for the human woman was fair and not multicolored like Insects Noble women.

(An insect trait.)

Why her hair was blond, long, not pink cut in a square stiff box upon his yellow and black striped face and what side hair remained was long and green. For Enbilulu had wasp genes inside him.

And his face tattooed with twirls and a diamond pin clasped the middle partition of his nose.

(He was a Noble dandy.)

And proud to have made a decent woman of a slave. Soon her belly would fill again, as it had over the years but this time the child would be his heir......and that made him think. A human plaything his heir?

(Cursed as was Ziu)

None had thought ahead their consequences of marriage.

A human woman was exactly that, plaything. Taking them out in public parading them as if they were queens had been a good joke, just to see the facial expressions on

Hupamuk and Enalusdra.

Having a beautiful slave sit on his lap while he exposed her bosom to the courtiers to shock them also was a clever idea.

The other Insect Nobles would never do such a thing in public, but he had, with Alana. "I am a beast," he admitted and remembered the execution of Mac and was

afraid of Queen Nina now.

The other Insect Nobles would never do such a thing in public, but he had, with Alana. "I am a beast," he admitted and remembered the execution of Mac and was afraid of Queen Nina now; but he need not have worried for the wasp genes would ensure the human child had antennae and a sting above his bottom that would kill unruly human slaves as his daddy had.

Even though the child would be flightless and human looking, it would be Insect Noble, his heir, he need not worry there.

And there was darkness in him as there was Light in Ziu.

And Queen Nina had overlooked the frolics of the young, until the marriages.

And Lana who fled Ziu landed outside Enbilulu's vined tree house whose walls were the red petals of a giant rose and called for Alana.

Now Enbilulu was annoyed at this sudden interruption of his love bed powdered iliac flowers, even though he had done so with his own thoughts.

"Tell her to go away," he said expecting his will obeyed blindly, but Alana now outside saw urgency in her friend's blue and gold eyes and came down the vines

whose white leaves where steps to see her.

(Sunflower horns)

"I have the map to Phoenix," the talk went.

"If he had not looked at me the way he did this morning," Alana explained, "As if you were slave and regretted marrying you?" Lana added.

"Yes, as if her had dung lying next to him."

And Enbilulu thought deep about his marriage as he lay on his bed. It had been a mistake; this was all the fault of Ziu and his crazy winged father Ziusudra.

And heard drifting voices.

"Can that eye take Luke to Phoenix?" Alana's bird like chirp, the tongue of Nobles....and Enbilulu listened with white elf like ears as small red mites scuttled from them with ear wax.

Ear cleaners.

All Insect Nobles knew of Luke, he was on a wanted picture. Them who provided blood sport for bored Insect Nobles.

A pack of them would fly dragonflies or ride red ants and centipedes tracking the hunted. The thrill of the chase, the sound of sunflower horns and finally trapping and allowing ants and centipedes at them.

All except the head which was bounty. And heads in varying degrees of decomposition decorated the cream pulp, green and red wax, and yellow brick walls of

Shurrupuk,

FOOD FOR LESSER INSECTS.

COUSINS OF ISNECT NOBLES.

But Enbilulu had stopped taking part in this sport to please his human slave girls; truthfully, it made him and Ziu different from other Nobles.

They were young and full of youthful pride and wanted noticed that was all.

"What have I done?" Enbilulu asked himself to regret his marriage. Fear gripped him; saw the future, isolation from court. "I hate you bitch," he screamed in panic.

And the girls heard and ran mounting Lana's green dragonfly and fled.

Humans were lap pets.

*

The sky was white, the clouds pink and Insect Nobles knew higher up it turned blue then black.

They did not call it space but Enil's heaven of Naja.

There was anti-gravity up there that contained billions of crystal atoms that were prisms deflecting all color but white from the sun's red rays back into space.

So, World people called white.

But the Nobles did not know this; to them it was the way god Enil made things.

And Alana and Lana flew past crystal rock hills not knowing that this rock spilt light into color giving the ground a hazy multicolored effect.

One moment the grass would be blue, next red.

But they did not know the crystal caused that......yet?

In fact, the real color of the grass was a very pale shade of green.

Luke if he reached the ship Phoenix would learn about gravity; but Queen Nina was taking no chances.

Lest he escape his drawn face was now

nailed next to another hunted.

Jack's.

And Ziu overcome by shameful; remorse for his beautiful wife mounted his fastest imperial blue Dragonfly and gave chase to Lana shouting, "Lana I am dung," and slaves heard and Nobles for it was Shurrupuk he flew over.

And Queen Nina heard of it.

And Ziu came to Enbilulu's tree house......where sat

Enbilulu thinking of new abominations.

"My friend where is your wife?" Ziu shouted through the open windows. And saw Enbilulu with a human who was not his wife Alana.

"Is there no privacy here?" Enbilulu demanded showing his nakedness to Ziu and was not ashamed.

So, Ziu looked away and asked forgiveness of God Enil for LIGHT was here.

And Enbilulu looked sick, his long green hair stuck out at funny angles as the lime he used to hold it in place, disturbed by the hands of human slaves.

It had been sixteen hours since Alana had fled with Lana; and as Enbilulu pranced his nakedness, his bed chamber emptied of slaves of sexes and ages, normal and

deformities for DARKNESS were here.

Even mammal pets scurried off afraid of his temper.

So, Ziu felt sick, Enbilulu his fiend was an abomination.

"Look at all life I have given you for your pleasure," God Enil commanded and Ziu knew Enil was wrong.

And Ziu took his bow and notched a silver tipped arrow and sent it through the open window and pierced the heart of a red wax image of God Enil above Enbilulu's

bed.

Ziu was disgusted with his old friend and feared Enbilulu had killed Lana.

And Enbilulu knew their friendship had ended. For it was Queen Nina's law……." If a Noble defile the image of our god Enil, then let him be put in Dust Bowl."

And Enbilulu drew copper sword from under his petal bed.

"What have you done?" Ziu shouted and Enbilulu, "Sent them away," and caught a human boy, swung him up by his red hair bun so that the child screamed.

Slapped his face.

Silenced him.

Kissed him with his humanoid insect humanoid lips.

Choking him with his long yellow proboscis that came out of his green tongue that spilt to reveal it.

INSECT.

"I am Insect, Noble, master of all I own," and saying dragged the terrified human child slave to his bed and attempted to be unnatural.

"Stop," Ziu begged but that made Enbilulu worse, and he cut the slave's throat with his copper sword for mercy was not related to darkness.

Then a human woman crawled out from under the lilac bed to escape the blood.

So Enbilulu threw the boy away and pounced upon her; insect he was.

"Here is human all human," by this he meant any human was his and from behind his sting stung the woman; he was insect.

And Ziu shamed and cried, "May the sun fall upon me, and tidal waves drown me."

"Look Ziu, like your wife," and Enbilulu forced the woman to show her bosom.

Ziu looked away to show the woman he was not guilty of this shaming; Light was here.

"Do you want her Ziu, ten a gold coin like her," and Enbilulu threw the slave forward and kicked her so she fell out the open rattan window and just managed to cling to the ledge half in half out.

"Slaves we have married.... you know what slave is? Something we buy or inherit like a nest of black ants," and Enbilulu took a mauve vase, held it, now I bore of it,"

and threw it out the window so it fragmented below, then stomped the woman till she slid all the way out the window.

In the end he hacked off her fingers with his copper sword.

"No stop Enbilulu," Ziu demanded and even as he tried to get his Imperial blue dragonfly closer to save the woman she fell screaming catching thorn creepers that

grew up the tree house so, impaled.

Her thighs in a post below the tree house.

She bounced in front of Ziu like a butterfly newly fixed in a human collection.

"What have you done?" Ziu stunned by the sudden destruction of life.

"Broken what is mine, the vessel belongs to the potter," Enbilulu.

Then Ziu watched Enbilulu's red ants eat up the woman below. Soon human spillage would be gone, and the lawn clean again.

And Ziu cast his steel javelin and the throw granted mercy to her.

And one unknown life went out, for they did not know her name.

But Enil knows when life goes from a butterfly, so why not a human slave?

It is rumored Enil named all the stars and gave her a new star?

"Murderer," Ziu jumping for the window.

Enbilulu drew back and as Ziu crawled over the window full of desire to destroy Enbilulu and privilege; Enbilulu hit a bronze gong.

Yet still Ziu pressed his attacked.

Only a man skilled in swordsmanship could use the gong while deflecting Ziu's sword.

And they came, Nobles, Enbilulu's house guard and Ziu, leapt for his dragonfly just as a javelin quietly passed him.

Fled with an arrow in his right shoulder.

Gave his mount a scarf of his wife to scent her pomegranate perfume in the wind.

Leaving behind a dead Noble guard.

He was now a **murderer.**

"Insect will not kill Insect," Queen Nina.

*

Shurrupuk City that same night:

Queen Nina listened to Enbilulu's story.

For he had come with his tale about Lana's eye map. Also, Noble had killed Noble and the murderer was Governor Ziusudra's red son.

"So, you have divorced your human slave?" This was a statement, which was good, showed the young mixed marriages did not work.

Nobles believed in Enil, humans in themselves.

One took humans discreetly, not to flaunt in front of Queen Nina. But it was not enough Enbilulu nailing his divorce proclamation in Shurrupuk's main market square, Nina's displeasure shown.

Enbilulu had forgotten it was time for the water festival where?

"An offering must be made to the beautiful water god of Wisdom, Enki to stop the flood returning. (A great flood in the Time of Myth had risen from the Great Dust Depression; the very one Luke had ridden across destroying Nobles.

Priests like Enalusdra said it was a cosmic sign heralding the arrival of humans and their plagues.

That God Enil had tried to drown humans but spared the fairest for breeding with Nobles to make Nobles wingless like Enil.) How better to offer Enbilulu instead of a human, Enbilulu who broke all God Enil's commands," Queen Nina, whose chitin is black, **(Sound running water).**

For it had been the practice to offer base insects like flies till humans replaced them. Pegging them on a platform in the middle of the flood plain about Shurrupuk City and when the floods came, the offering washed away and devoured by God Enki.

Lo the Nobles lived in terror of the floods. The floods had made them give up living underground.

And Enbilulu changed his color as is the custom with insects from pale green to dark blue, for he knew he was to die in two calendars time when the Shurrupuk River water rose again, an offering and execution.

"My queen," he stammered.

"Yes," she replied, craning head forward smirking, as if to say do not call me your queen, you do not obey my laws.

And she lifted her split crimson robe so golden stocking showed, and with both black feet shoved kneeling Enbilulu backwards. And his yellow eyes were wide with fright as he fell cracking skull, so that he was half conscious.

Then ordered Governor Ziusudra arrested and left court striding over Enbilulu's mauve lips.

Queen Nina whose hair is a blond-haired person did not belong to light but cruel darkness; she went to bath in milk, which was good for chitinous skin, to wash the contamination of Enbilulu away and thought of how to torture Ziusudra.

No one held her to ransom.

(Trumpets)

And her trumpeters blew hard on the copper encased reed stalks which were a pronouncement that audience was over.

The floods submerged the land, forcing Insects to travel by balloon and the water full of angry snakes seeking dry land and pregnant bull sharks, which swim up freshwater rivers.

*

Later in the wilderness: for time does not stop.

Ziu flew his beast till its thin wings fell off and now stood with his sword dripping yellow insect mess.

He had cut off its head for without wings the beast was dead. For two weeks he had flown nonstop, sleeping tied to saddle and knew he must be near Lana and Luke, but where?

"To the Red Mountains," he said looking at them from the edge of the great depression Luke had entered. For two weeks he had examined his life and had not been

happy with what he found.

"Life is hard under a great man," he referring to his father Red Ziusudra. "A man of principle does not like me. He's fearless and doesn't kiss Nina's bottom, not like me," and hated himself for the harm he had done Lana his wife.

"Each marries his own kind. She is happy with them," but "would I listen," thinking no one could be happy as a slave.

"She would jump at the chance to belong to a Noble," and that word, "belong, Belong, belong, it was discriminating."

"Did I ever ask her if she wanted to be part of our society?" And he knew the negative answer, "Just presumed because she was in Shurrupuk she would accept her

fate as my wife.

To lie with me the first time must have been a terrifying experience for I am an insect. How brutal of me, of what terror she must have gone through but because she is slave remained silent.

Ziu had a soul.

Was she invited to the city? No, taken by force. Accepting fate as an Insect's wife," and Ziu each time he stopped for rest sought his reflection in a pond, and saw his face, it had black bristles growing, not soft hairs like a slave's beard, but hard black bristles like a fly.

And he would shave with his copper knife and cut his face often, in disgust at assuming he was handsome to his own kind did not mean he was beautiful to a slave

without opinions.

And he would take off his clothes seeking bristles and was wrong in one respect, his body bristles were soft as sable not hard as a fly's.

He had human slave genes in him.

And he had a conscious.

He had a spirit.

He had light in him.

His father Governor Ziusudra knew during the Time of Myth an ancestor had taken a human as mate. Human genes that prolonged life, also insect genes that regenerate tissue.

And Ziu cried for his sins.

He was becoming mentally unstable.

He was good but his guilt opened the door to darkness for he should not have thoughts of self-harm, for he was guiltless for he was a Noble Insect, and

was on the right path that he and Lana were of the same flesh for they were of the same spirit.

Ziu had rejected Enil his god.

"The gods are false."

And Ziu did sad things to himself to atone for his guilt. Did not Priest Enalusdra allow the priestesses of the goddess Adrastea to parade her mummified remains down Shurrupuk streets, and the priests herded drugged drunken Nobles behind were they mutilated themselves and threw the organs to girls as fertility charms.

Like Celtic humans but Insect Nobles.

He had become his own judge and jury.

"The gods are humans, space walkers. It is we Insect Nobles who should be the salves and humans' masters.

May the gods forgive me," Ziu moaned surrounded by giant pea flowers.

But no gods heard him for he no longer believed in gods......he believed in humans.

*

And Lords Hupamuk and Enalusdra were only a day behind Luke when Lana and Alana met them......at a night camp which was upon a black tree lily which they had cut drainage holes in.

Sixty feet above ground safe from evolving ground mammals who would devour a sleeping Noble given a chance.

Evolution was working.

Offworlders needed to tip the balance.

There had been subtle climatic changes over the millenniums, and it did not favor insects or dinosaurs.

Now the campfire had attracted the girl's flying mounts as they slept exhausted upon them.

"Wake up little girl," the hard voice drifted into Lana's dreams of......Ziu banning slave whipping in his estates.

And Lana awoke and found hands and feet held as she lay on the unstable black leaf.

(3 crimson moons)

A six-inch brown leaf worm rolled trapped under Lana's back.

And the Lords Hupamuk and Enalusdra could see why Ziu fancied her, for she was only in riding shorts and yellow cape to protect against passing branches.

"She is welcoming me," all the Nobles about her thought for they did not have light but hate for slaves and not respect. Even the cicadas stopped, and the night fell silent as insects were ashamed to be related to these two-legged cousins that called themselves Insects.

Now the Lords knew naught of the eye and guessed the two wives had left husbands to seek Luke whom they were following as Queen Nina had planned.

"There is no other explanation," Enalusdra the priest as he pinched Lana till, she swooned.

"When a slave runs, ITS punishment is at the discretion of Nobles," Hupamuk's reply and with right foot stood hard upon Alana's belly so, that her chest arched upwards seeking breath,

(3 crimson moons)

And she breathed hard under the light of World's three crimson moons. Then Enalusdra cut open Alana's soft yellow riding boots with his sword, so, a red line appeared on each leg.

But Lana did not fight for she knew the Nobles loved a frightened slave; and accepted her fate, they would not be returning home as would be, eaten. "I must escape; I have the eye, but how?" Lana thought when carried into Hupamuk's skin tent. Skin from humans mixed with bee's wax and stitched by leaf cutters ants.

She did not respond to Alana's screams.

"Look at me," and she obeyed out of years of servitude and saw Lord Hupamuk was removing his shirt.

"Do you find me handsome?" He asked.

"Very my Lord," she lied as years of slave hood showed itself.

And the insect used his hands not the sword.

"We are the masters you the salve.

There is one God Enil.

All unbelievers are ours to do what we wish with.

To kill humans is a surety to gain entrance to Naja, Heaven.

Enil made this law, "a Noble Insect saying.

"I know where there is a map," Lana whispered into Hupamuk's ear as his green antennae bobbed comically over her small head.

The words went in but did not register for like an insect Hupamuk was completely immersed in his food, Lana's body, for his green tongue had parted and a blue

proboscis had slid out down her esophagus into stomach, taking strength from her digested food: fly genes were present. Also, devil's Coachman genes in his ancestry

that demanded he have human juices.

For the Devil's Coachman feeds in slave cemeteries? And Hupamuk finished his business and stood and shouted for a guard who dragged Lana out of the tent, not caring what cuts she suffered on the black lily leaf hairs.

Now, Hupamuk's tent Alana in smeared in her own blood. Outside half a brown leaf worm now wriggled free of a human's weight.

The other half was on Lana's back.

And Hupamuk smelt Alana's blood making him ravenous like a praying mantis excited over the moth's body juices swimming about in its mouth.

And drew a dagger from his pile of clothes, and he cut Alana up, eating her slowly in the fashion of insects.

For indeed he had the genes of a praying mantis in him, and they dominated his human genes at this moment.

And shouted for his guards to threw her out onto a leaf and ate her.

And Alana would not stop screaming so encouraged her Noble captors into further degeneration.

"*My people are not really evil, cannot you understand we are Insects,*" Governor Ziusudra defended inside his dungeon when he heard of this outrage.

And one guard thrust his dagger into her and was innocent for his founding father had been a water beetle, vicious hunters of the pond.

"Bring me the woman," Hupamuk bellowed and the one with Alana held up her head by her blonde hair and Lord Hupamuk peered his eyes and focused identifying what hung from the insect's man's mouth?

Saw it was a hand.

Saw the man swallow.

Saw the bulge flow down the man's arched throat; never mind he was eating cattle.

Saw Lana look at him as if he was carrion.

Saw slaves did not behave in this manner, only insects.

Saw Alana die and his spirit sickened.

Sick with knowledge that salves were better than Insects.

He had human genes in him.

(*The evil Insect Lord pounced upon the human slave as if prey and she was, her friend Alana just eaten in the fashion of the Black Widow spider but in reverse. Get up girl, run for your live, but where could she go? She must bide her time and wait for Madam Vengeance.*)

And he attacked his own degenerate kind, for as Elder Peter had said, **"Their mixed genes have given them many voices in their head."**

And Lana crawled into the darkness, found her mount, and heard sounds of sword against sword escaping. "Dung heaps," she called to them; and never saw Alana die.

All under the light of three crimson moons, (3 crimson moons). Insects and insects knew eggs, larvae and pupae were full of protein and vitamins.

Lo, the Noble Insects kept baby insects' farms apart from their human nests, baby insects were cheaper to rear and very nourishing.

Humans were expensive and troublesome but nice to eat, tasted like pork.

(3 crimson moons)

CH7 Alana

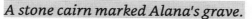

A stone cairn marked Alana's grave.

And they did not even bother to dig a shallow hole for Alana for she was human, dung, slave, and theirs to do with as they pleased.

She did not believe in God Enil.

Therefore, belonged to the Lord of Darkness Apsu so had divine right to kill her as a blessed Insect Noble.

Also threw her body off the black lily leaf to crash vines and ten feet from the ground hit a Venus fly trap which held her prone.

It pleased them to leave her sprawled the way she had died. Unladylike, half eaten and exposed where an Insect Noble in a frenzy to suck her body fluids dry in the fashion of insects before she slept. It was the way of wasp, water beetle and other insects; to suck the victim dry while it lived under the mandible.

Insect way, *hopefully not human; fortunately, insects had not thought of slaughterhouses?*

Now Alana soon covered in ants, flies and clothes moth eggs that would hatch and feed.

So, when Ziu found her and stood there full of blame with the same feelings as a human seeing roses destroyed and sickened. And rent his clothes and threw dust on his red hair.

And nor possessing a shovel covered her with stones knowing this was a waste of time, for he saw predators. Mammal and insect in the trees waiting for his departure.

"Enbilulu, you fool, here is your wife," is all Ziu said, he had no idea who had done this only guessing Nobles, then saw the diamond ring.

Hupamuk's ring.

And Ziu with blue eyes looked ahead through the trees and swirling midges over waterfalls.

"They seek her?" And was afraid Lana being captive with them, "I will kill you Hupamuk," he swore fearing harm done to Lana. "Someone must avenge Alana; I must regenerate what parts I have cut off. This I can do for I have insect in me.

My children will be human and not insect," also "I will build a new nest and there will be no queen but elected elders like humans have."

And followed the trail.

Ziu had reached a plain of thought where he saw no difference between killing a slave and one of his own, Insect, it was murder, a killing.

*

Noon next day:

Jet shoes cool.

"Well Luke, I will tell you this, we are being followed," Howal peering back.

And Luke saw three parties watching them from the edge of the grey depression, half a mile below.

And Luke's face became like a cornered dog's and Ulana was afraid of him for she saw he was primitive and was becoming his own master.

A man out of a boy.

"Luke, we must go on." Ulana advised resting her soft hand on his arm; at once electricity flowed through him, and he blushed.

Howal noticed grunting annoyed jealously......

Ulana had strange thoughts......she could easily manipulate this Luke and win her people's freedom......and seeing Howal's reaction she too blushed for Luke's innocence was attractive: so was his body for he was not ugly.

And Luke did not just see Ulana as gratifying flesh, and she was not afraid to squat examining the trail allowing Luke to see her green pants; or she did it on purpose for she was dealing with stupid adulthood.

Any lust produced in him was his, how he controlled his responsibility not hers.

She could wear what she wanted, how he reacted was his learning lesson.

It was the way of the nests.

Howal was different, he blamed her for his lust.

(a red sun)

And Luke the same age as Ulana mentally was younger. For world's red sun produced a healing effect on body tissue. Luke did not need the science of Earth and Vornal to have long life, a day on World was not twenty-four hours.

Ulana's world was what Luke's ancestors had left, a world of science where people lived hundreds of years, had so many things done to them that they could think like a commuter.

 In her early teens Ulana's speed of thought was comparable to a small PCW but by the time she was a hundred her brain could think as a P.C. for microchip implants
made it thus.

Her conscious was a computer.

And Luke was her primitive Tarzan and she, Jane. He was foolishly brave, seemed honorable and rode a black ant.

Her world as on Earth people rode machines not ants.

All these conflicting thoughts came to her at once.

Now she had good mind stability, or she would go crazy with such speed of analysis. Also, logic and knew she could not allow Luke's attractiveness to divert her from her mission.

"Luke would hate me if he knew," she thought.

"So, what, there are many pretty boys," conscious.

"The Insects will not free my people anyway," she.

"That risk is no for you to take," conscious.

"I will take that risk, I want Luke," she.

 "Then you will lose both," such the voices in her mind, one computer, one her own.

Anyway......the watchers were moving towards them.

"You go on Luke, I will circle and scout," Howal with gritted teeth.

"If you go on so, do I," Luke replied with one hand on his sword hilt and the other on Howal's tanned chest.

Howal stared into Luke's clear blue eyes. Never had he seen anyone so open or stupid. Now pale Howal knew one of them should scout if they had a chance of escaping pursuers, a chance of getting home.

The best one here at that was himself.

He wanted home with Ulana.

He also would like to better Luke for the humiliation he had suffered.

He would show Ulana who was dominant and the position of women in a man's world.

He saw and felt Luke's comradeship flow to him and shamed.

He had never met anyone like Luke, never talked with a human.

He had taken human women stolen like cattle from Noble Insects.

He even kept humans at home as domestic pets.

He saw Luke as slave and not free man.

He knew if Luke came to his home, he did have him chained and beaten till his spirit broke and became slave again.

There were no such thing as free humans.

Now he did not say this but, "May the best win for the prize is great," and the prize was Ulana.

For Howal was still who he was, a warrior king. Now his warrior self-criticized his own dishonor so he politely refused Luke's help, and when Luke insisted, he accepted

and held out his hand high, so their arms entwined like a snake's.

Comrades in arms,

for as long as Howal felt it so.

A minute?

Howal was a shallow selfish lion man.

And Luke spoke to Ulana with his hands.

"What did you say?" Howal asked as Ulana watched.

"That Titus may protect her till we come back."

Ulana was annoyed, no one had asked her opinion, and could protect herself.

"Just tell the ant what to do," Howal.

"He is my friend."

And Ulana lost her temper feeling insane that anyone could have an ant as a friend.

She wished she were Luke's friend so she could have a choice too.

So Howal scratched the blond stubble on his chin.

"Alright," he replied, mounted his red lion beast, and rode.

"I follow," Ulana said and again used body language, a simple hand touch on Luke's chest.

Luke liked the feel of her hand.

Made him excited, so strange feelings stronger than lust filled him. This he could not understand.

"Your choice," Luke grunted with effort.

And Ulana was happy to have choice; but as she tried to move off, she found her Vornal sole pads defunct for they needed recharging. So, looked at Luke and Titus, this is how she had been able to run with them; her shoes had projected stabilizing fins and a microchip jet pack that allowed her to skim soil as a skateboard.

To Luke she was WONDER GIRL COME ALIVE.

Luke also liked holding her slim waist, seeing her hips curve as he helped her onto Utna, which he did.

And she did not protest, she insisted, she go with him. Luring him; her people's lives were at stake.

And felt his hands desperately trying not to touch parts of her he should not and Luke's mind flashed memories of Nina and he remained excited and with difficulty

and embarrassment mounted himself.

The boy was now a man.

And all Ulana wanted his hands to slip and touch her hips where he was desperately trying not to touch.

"Foolish girl," *her computer brain rebuked.*

"Hold on," Luke's voice was a squeak.

Ulana smiled; it was not the fish that had taken the bait but the angler.

She was wickedly female.

Her hands slid about his belly and Luke was ready to die if she dropped them by accident of course below his loin cloth.

He was all foolishly male.

And she did, her people were at stake; Luke died.

His blushed face went deadly white. And was too afraid to speak for he did not trust his own voice, so decided to concentrate his thoughts and vision on Howal.

Just as well Titus remained behind with the herd of flying bugs and had seen all and watched amused. The fool Luke, all he had to do was ask and the girl was his.

None knew of Luke's experience with Queen Nina, but that was the past.

King Howal fueled his lust with alcohol.

*

And Luke somehow could not concentrate on matters, was aware of Ulana's warmth, her soft auburn hair breezing his cheeks.

Luke was not happy, a part of him wanted Ulana the 'cave dweller style.'

And hidden onlookers who had been watching Luke from behind vegetation, advanced out seeing seen by Luke's friends.

Luke clumsily drew his sword, "I will protect you," he wanted to say but garbled a grunt.

Ulana smiled and dropped off Utna knowing it was Luke who needed protection.

She was a warrior woman of Planet Vornal.

And Howal gave chase behind an advancing unknown figure and Luke saw it was his sister Lana running to him.

That was one party emerging from the vegetation.

Ziu saw also, Lords Hupamuk and Enalusdra ordering Nobles forward and Ziu remembered Alana in her stone grave, "Murderers," he spat and drew sword.

Ziu was the second secret watcher to emerge.

The Lords the third party emerging.

"A fight," Ulana and Luke stopped kissing his sister's head and hugging and looked to the sounds of war.

(Sounds of fight)

A lone Noble sunflower reed blower was playing a lament to encourage his kind to fight bravely, the sound was like a lyre.

Now Titus seeing the Nobles riding down the hill blew his carnyx horn and came forth.

And the sound was strong and metallic.

(Carnyx horn)

And the wilderness quietened and the scavenging eyes of carnivorous mammals watched what was for dinner.

"There cannot be more of them?" Hupamuk fearing death as they saw Titus's herd in close formation approaching thinking them flying warriors.

For the red sun was in front and blinded them.

Their own fault, every kid on the block knows not to fight with the sun in your eyes.

And Priest Enalusdra did not answer; Ziu was hacking dents in his copper sword with frenzied madness.

So Hupamuk the brave fled.

Then Enalusdra.

Then the soldiers.

All wanted life and a chance to bully again.

And their lie to Queen Nina was immortalized for slave stone masons etched a great battle in hieroglyphics in Shurrupuk Market Square showing the Lords fighting a great host belonging to the people of Titus.

And Ziu chased catching a Noble straggler, hacking till the Noble fell and Ziu cut sliced till an insect man lay at his feet, yet still Alana would not rise from the dust alive.

So, calm overcame him since he had no one to kill. His anger spent he looked at the distant depression where he knew the Lords had fled and with-it knowledge, he had helped slaves......" I am a murderer twice condemned," meaning he had killed his own twice.

No Insects would forgive him; he could no longer live amongst Nobles.

But Lana was running to him?

"Husband," she called.

And he turned and she saw his thought in his eyes.

So, cradled him comforting and he was glad he was not lonely. Being Outcast with her would be good, World was big, he knew places they might be able to set up

nest.

Being an insect, he was already regenerating parts; **gene fifty-one.**

And Lana looked to the future when fine healthy young red Ziu's would run at her feet: she did not see his beauty in his face but in his soul, and he was Insect Noble of the religion that said only Nobles went to Naja, Heaven and no others, yet she had a soul that saw his.

Anyway, who would want her, a Noble's plaything, no humans anyway?

Meanwhile: Shurrupuk City, dungeons.

The great fortress that was Governor Ziusudra's town house, human slave workers boarded up with planks of wood.

Lo, in the bottom of the moat lay the governor's loyal House Carl's, chain mailed Nobles who fought with long two-handed axes.

And they had slain dozens of Queen Nina's warriors.

Behold now Ziusudra sat in a wooden chair with clamps screwed to it, and the clamps were iron vices that tightened till wrists and ankles crumpled.

Queen Nina had done all the speaking necessary.

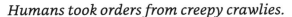

Humans took orders from creepy crawlies.

*

Ziusudra's voice would soon be silent forever; no more would she hear his call for cooperation with slaves.

His one remaining white eye puffed from beatings.

His clothes taken for humiliation's sake. No Insect likes to be naked inn public, degrading.

"All these years your eye held the secret, why?" She had asked a hundred times already.

"Because you are unworthy of Phoenix's secret," his reply.

And beaten him herself with a rose bush. No one spoke to her like that.

And when the bush was useless had picked up his own discarded thick blue dyed leather belt, bent it so that the buckle showed......and used as if she was beating a disobedient slave.

There just were not any more questions to ask, Ziusudra had talked feely. What was happening now was punishment, slow execution.

"I never did like the sound of your voice Ziusudra," Nina said looking at the Noble goalers.

Then Nina walked to the top of the dungeon steps and conducted her command again.

It was one goaler yanked Ziusudra's mouth open by his red beard while the other pulled his tongue out with tongs.

Poor Ziusudra.

Then his tongue was gone.

Nina smiled, "No one speaks to me like that," she repeated leaving.

How the dungeons stunk, she would bath in flowered petal bath and lead her courtesans after the human woman Lana who would trail blaze to Luke and Phoenix.

How could Enbilulu and Ziu think slaves could be legal wives?

And as Nina slid into her hot bath a human harem slave waited to soap while another prepared scented oils to massage her chitinous Black skin.

And fifty feet directly below Ziusudra managed a gurgled silence as a goaler played a game of Chinese checkers on his chest with a dagger.

The man enjoyed his work; he did not love anything but himself.

Then he prized off Ziusudra's right thumb nail; the prisoner passed out.

So peeved the goaler fearing Ziusudra would die and not entertain him cauterized the mouth wound, then sat down, emptied a wine jug, and fell asleep.

There was no hurry, Ziusudra was not leaving.

And Ziusudra was not alone; no new wanted posters for a man called Jack would be going up in market squares.

He hung from a wall next to Ziusudra, his race was dead.

And those enlightened once like Ziu now quickly copied Enbilulu and rid themselves of human wives or husbands or fled with them and their estate workers and warriors into the wilderness.

And those who delayed chained taken to Shurrupuk. Lo six hundred chained smeared in honey for World's small insects to feed. A public reminder to Nobles who ruled, and the old ways stayed.

The stone mason carvers showed Queen Nina the great general whose victory over her blue skinned enemies was complete; and what happened to the vanquished, scores slain, hundreds now slaves and if you note, dozens kept fighting and it went unnoticed in the carving! The stone masons not only had the Tequila but the grub at the bottom of the bottle.

*

And twenty thrown in dungeons and tortured.

And hundreds joined mixed human other evolved life unpaid work chain gangs, that worked the mills, water wheels and pumps that cleared sewage channels and provided cold and hot water in Shurrupuk City and the hieroglyphics recorded and called it the Cleansing.

*

The new arrivals from space, Ulana's folk where solemn as they swept Shurrupuk's nest tunnels helped by black ants guarded by reds and centipedes.

It had come to the attention of Nobles that black ants, were not trustworthy.

Queen Nina's cruelty had opened evolutions of war between red and black.

"Fine, if blacks see their humans as brothers, then we shall treat them as such," Queen Nina.

The black ants humans knew the price of disobedience, had seen those that did not work or escaped as chewed bits by their insect watchers.

Humans and Black Ants were on the menu.

Even now a centipede was eating the latest to escape. Chewing the legs as the food struggled to escape, and fed up with its food flipped the Vornal aside and injected venom; now dinner would be patient as devoured,

the

insect

way.

And Ulana's father silver eyed Tarves Dallas crippled and pushed in a burrow, made Elder, by Nina to bring order amongst her newest slaves.

For Nina did not want them exterminated, just controlled.

She also waited expectantly to see what the new Vornal magicians would show her.

Would their architecture be different from the humans?

Life was good Queen Nina knew, it was bountiful, and God Enil had blessed. It was the Noble birth right to be such.

Already Nobles took away Vornals and dozens did not return.

Those that returned spoke of nightmares, of having to provide genes for Nobles.

And Vornal women their bellies round with pupae spoke of Noble scientists injecting them full of Noble genes. Insect genes to speed up growth.

Insects used up slaves at an alarming rate.

And Tarves Dallas knew the meaning of hell, he had seen the nursery, forced to draw up a birthing schedule for Nina wanted Vornals bred, not only amongst

themselves but with Nobles.

And this is how Tarves Dallas was crippled:

"There are Enalusdra's dungeons, here he works," he remembered Queen Nina, and saw his people dissected on tables as Noble students extended the boundaries of Noble science.

And guessed Nobles needed fresh genes for they were becoming sterile and extinct.

And he was happy with that knowledge.

"Is this your god?" He had asked of a red wax image and Nina in good mood since things were under control again, "Yes."

And saw Enil was wingless and examined the hieroglyphics and his computer brain deciphered the story of the Nobles without Queen Nina understanding what was happening.

That space travelers as themselves, humans as the other slaves had come through that black hole and the primitive ancestors of the Nobles captured them, saw they were gods who had come to walk amongst them.

And God Enil was one of these first astronauts.

Wingless, not Insect.

This Vornal lost his head to a jar.

And the Nobles raped the gods to be like the gods to rid themselves of insect traits thinking they could then reach Naja their heaven and the stars.

It had worked, cross breeding for the priests knew their work but there had been a disastrous side effect......sterility. For the new traits were stronger than the insect inheritance which began to die out.

"And demons came upon us and had our women, and they gave birth to dead ones, children with no eyes, mad ones, and people were too sore to touch one another and the bed chambers stank of pus," he read and guessed some new arrivals had passed on an aggressive venereal disease.

And Insect Nobles needed humans to kill off that gene.

So far it had worked, new human seed was healthy. But seeing how Nina behaved he wondered if the disease was now hereditary for Nina was cruelly insane.

His thoughts interrupted; a priest had entered talking about one Vornal being useless, that all his genes were dead.

And Tarves Dallas looked at the young man in question and remembered he had chosen to become sterile from chose for were too many in existence.

And saw Nina nod and the priest picked up a dagger; she wanted a new Vornalian shirt.

When done, parts examined for disease and the dead slave kept for taxidermy, where stuffed, and his body stuck on a wall.

"Vornal," with glass bead eyes.

And Nina let Tarves watch for Nina has a reason for everything she does.

Tarves Dallas looked away and focused on a hieroglyphic picture……." And the demon seed was bad, so Queen Hostala led her Nobles against the new space comers and slew giving their carcasses to her friends the red ants and centipedes.

To cement the new friendship with lesser insects ordered all Nobles to take the genes of red ants and centipedes to strengthen their stock, for we are insects," he read.

"Let us go," Queen Nina commanded and Tarves Dallas allowed his silver eyes to see all the walls, his brain would decipher later over bedtime hot drink.

And outside Queen Nina had his legs broken so they would not set properly. A last instructive warning to Tarves Dallas and his people. Such Nina's darkness of spirit.

So, this is how Tarves Dallas became cripple and ended up pushed about in a barrow.

"And Nobles selected their queens from those with proven traits able to lay a hundred eggs a time from Noble families.

And the hieroglyphic list gave their names till Queen Tukania seized the throne for herself a thousand years ago……and gave birth to Princess Nina our Queen…….and the custom of selecting queens was stopped," Tarves mind memorized the hieroglyphics when wheeled away in a in a barrow.

Lo he saw **new** pictures of a human in a lion cloth riding a black ant and beside him walked a green-eyed girl and knew he saw his daughter Ulana; but as for the man on the ant he could wonder but was pleased for under the black were slain Nobles. And he smiled that his daughter was not helping Queen Nina. Yet she had to save her people, how?

And read no more as the chiselers needed updates to keep working and they had not arrived.

Treves's mind felt no pain from his crushed legs as his computer brain read 'MALFUNCTION……ceased to operate and shut down the nervous system to that

area.'

And Queen Nina who survives on pain, terror, dominance, and darkness had no idea: cheated by a computer.

House carls trained to ignore all while guarding a Noble's home.

CH8 Sister

*Alana and Peter were dead, now spirit folk, you soon realised clothes,
food, those basic physical yummies were not needed.
They say space is freezing, so gather spirits having no nervous system do not feel the cold, better not?*

One week after the fight with Hupamuk and Enalusdra.

Luke's party had travelled a yellow river full of leaping pink salmon towards Red Mountain and Phoenix.

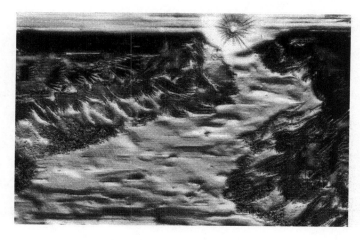

Luke's time of sadness for Alana was past. She was now sacred private memory.

Titus was struggling as fast as he could to learn the tongue of World which Ulana had mastered through science; she had a computer as a conscious.

Ignorance is darkness so Titus remained in his misunderstood world; deaf mute yet was neither.

And Ulana's computer deciphered his tongue, and she did not reveal its success for she feared Howal's reaction to accompanying a woman superior in intellect.

Would be like waving a **red flag** at a bull.

Lo Titus came from an Island in North World from mammal stock that had evolved separately from Insect Nobles.

A well-kept secret from human slaves.

Another reason Queen Nina wanted Phoenix and its weapons.

World animals had learned to walk and free their fingers to make tools. Now Ulana's distant Vornal had given her a computer brain with dictionary, one book provided by Governor Ziusudra to her imprisoned people and

(Bird like chirping tongue)

passed from hand to hand, deciphered and enabled the stranded Vornalians to speak the Noble bird like chirping tongue.

If Luke had been on Earth the same technology would have been available to him.

He was not on Earth, was he?

He just thought she was one very smart pretty girl and knew every patch of her skin on her arms.

The flow of her auburn hair.

Each root follicle.

The depth of her belly button.

The smell of every flower she rubbed on her skin as natural perfume.

"Your sister is different?" Ulana sitting down beside Luke at campfire.

Howal stopped eating, the human slave Luke was foolish, the girl wanted him. **Dark** thoughts from friend Howal or a misunderstanding from a clash of cultures?

"Lana is now Noble," Luke falling silent more interested in this green-eyed girl than his sister.

One look and conversations conjured fleeting pictures of Lana's life in Shurrupuk and the acceptance of pain that went with human slaves.

Besides Lana was more interested in Ziu than pouring out her hurts to Luke.

But Ulana was different, not two doubts about it. Strange, intriguing, and pulling Luke into maturity, all to *save her people.*

"Pop," as Titus uncorked a bottle, drank coughed and handed too Howal, and still Ulana questioned Luke on Lana.

"They killed Alana," the voice his sister who hugged her brother now deserting Ziu who belonged to the race that committed the murder. Luke felt bad at this; Alana had once been his intended woman, now killed by

Nobles.

He looked up towards Ziu.

"I am ashamed, also sorry to be Insect," he was real torn up.

Howal and Titus stopped drinking.

Silence, only fireflies moved about their heads.

Ulana watched Luke's hand drop to his sword. Ziu to Luke was just a Noble Insect, someone who came to the nests to take away pretty girls and handsome boys. As Queen Nina corrupted him and......that did not mean he did not end up enjoying; one adapts, one lives, one has a physical as well as spiritual body.... besides, he did not have a choice in the matter, Nina needed his DNA.

It was not Luke; it was a bit of his past he would like to forget. Just as Alana was past, now ashes, and a painful memory; but her spirit lived on like Elder Peter's always willing to come and help him.

So, Luke's iron sword slithered out shining in the fire.

"I deserve death," Ziu said and held up his arms, so his chest armor lifted revealing a two-inch gap of belly flesh.

(Owl hoots)

"I love him Luke, he is a good man, my husband," Lana defended.

Silence as Luke wishing enlightenment.

An owl hooted from a tree branch with a moth in its mouth.

"Is not your fault, Insects and humans being different. What you have done by marrying Lana is good," and Luke dropped his sword and picked up a burning twig......" Not all men have light in them," and gave Ziu the stick also, "same spirit, one spirit, same body building blocks, all brothers and sister, all go home to one source."

Ziu was astonished, he was all Insect pride waiting death which was suicide.

Ziu, allowing slave to end his life, had done this human a great honor. The slave refused insulting Ziu allowing him to live.

Ziu was Insect.

Now Ulana, Howal and Titus wondered what would have been Ziu's expression if Luke had gutted him.

They would have, Ziu was just one big bug.

Insect......enemy, someone who bedded a girl called Lana who thought she was not His equal. The three knew nothing about Ziu......in fact neither did Luke except his sister had vouched for his goodness.

Ziu was one lucky Noble Luke thought. If his sister wanted Ziu he was not interfering, he knew once a girl made up her mind there was no way changing it.

Ziu was a mirror of his father Governor, imperialism at its most foolishness. Brought up to commit suicide over dishonor when good men where needed. So, Ulana warmed to Luke's inner goodness; but Howal thought Luke a fool, an Insect wanted killing.

And Titus had never seen the likes of Luke. After all World was a violent place that never gave quarter, just death in the form of the victor's whims.

(Sweet
tangerines)

And that's why drunken Howal suddenly slashed with sword and cut off Ziu's left antennae, so that the twinkle of life vanished now from his left clouding eye.

At once Luke stood beside Howal, his chest bare heaving, snarled lips showing teeth, spittle running free, veins bulging from expanded muscle.

Fight in the playground.

He did not need a sword for righteous strength flowed in him. His eyes his eyes those shinning eyes were the pits of hell to Howal. And his left hand was a vice over Howal's left kidney and his right choked life from throat.

As Howal began to sink to knees into oblivion he saw a giant black ant in each of Luke's eyes and something told him *Luke was not human.*

And Ulana slipped between them for none could pull Luke away. Her sweet tangerine scent filtered through Luke's mind, and he released Howal.

And sat next to his ant Utna.

Ulana sat next to him.

And Ziu allowed Lana and Titus to tend to his wound.

While Howal slept off his drink.

And all knew Luke was different.

*

Two weeks past, (Insect chorus).

Ziu and Lana lay near their own fire a distance from the camp for they were married. Ziu had regenerated all except his left blinded eye.

Now Howal decided to take Ulana by force; if he had been sober, he might have acted like a man and not a despotic king. But the night was for lovers and an

insect chorus was working on his ears.

He might also have remembered Luke was different.

He did not, more the fool him.

So, thinking the others asleep he sneaked into Ulana's tent of leaves and was annoyed for she slept with silver armor on which would not make his task easier.

Knew drink was making time run out, soon he would collapse so full of alcohol that he was. But first he must unclip her armor latches.

Not that he intended rape, but he was Howal and never refused because all knew them place in his lands.

So, did not know what 'no' meant.

He also knew by experience when a woman said no, she meant yes.

What he wanted he took and in his warrior kingdom it was a woman's duty not to refuse a man, especially an important man like a king.

But Ulana was not one of his subjects. She woke and sat up, the latches open and her silver chest plate fell forward and Howal was pleased; Howal was not a good man.

So, at once she slapped him and spat on him.

To Howal this was fun, women he knew had to keep an air of decency about all this when in fact they were pleading for him to love.

That was the way he and men saw it, unfortunately his kingdom was full of them.

So, he pounced lion fashion.

And Ulana did not scream, that would be a waste of breath needed to think and so, fought him silently with intent to kill, drag his body into the bush and leave it for wild night insects and mammals.

For she thought he was still a companion of Luke's whom she wanted no trouble. "Howal went for a leak, drinking too much," she imagined Titus and Luke would think, Howal had been too drunk to stand so, fell asleep and eaten by a carnivorous insect.

Titus would agree Howal deserved what he got.

In fact, Howal was becoming annoyed with Ulana's persistence in struggling.

There was a limit to saying 'no.'

Lo Luke was not asleep as he lay across Utna thinking how his band was growing, for that is how he saw them, his responsibility, and wished Howal would not drink the sap of the Mandarin plant for it was alcoholic.

And heard the grunts and rustle of limbs, heard fist smack flesh.

Luke rose.

And saw the empty jug and remembered his time with Queen Nina and was wrath.

The sound of Queen Nina was coming from Ulana's tent. He did not shout, just strode purposefully, and stood outside Ulana's tent allowing his senses to tell him if a struggle was occurring within.

Luke had sour grapes as he liked Ulana a great deal, and part of him was telling him Ulana preferred Howal. *She was not screaming.*

For he remembered how he had struggled against Lord Hupamuk, but not against Queen Nina.

This then made him throw open the tent flaps and, in the moonlight, Ulana.

(Strange clicking sound)

Her face under a cape, with Howal sitting on her, his weight pinning.

A click alerted Howal that all was not well. Luke was more ant than human, brought up on ant milk, chitinous food, absorbing their DNA.

So, with one blow across Howal's he winded him, and then threw him sideways so the leaf tent went with him. And Luke looked down upon Ulana and shifted his eyes from her for he was decent, "I am sorry," it was barely audible, sounding more like an ant clicking than a man speaking.

He was ashamed.

So, Ulana hugged herself, she did not want Luke to see her thus although her computer brain demanded she hesitate for the good of her people......let Luke look,

make him want, entrap him.

But she still had her sense of right and wrong that pushed aside computer logic and said "No." Luke is good; I do not want to cheapen myself in front of him. Another part of her told her she had him anyway eating out of her hand.

Then Ulana froze, the red lion creature belonging to Howal was growling and advancing upon Luke. At once Utna black ant ran to help Luke, but not before Luke had landed on the back of the lion, slid off and was holding the beast by its tail.

Ulana had never seen such strength without implants.

And Luke had never been aware of his strength and unknown to his people evolution was happening.

Had taken place, eons brought up on black ant milk......were indeed superhuman and needed anger to trigger this strength off.... also, it was time the new trait was showing.

It was a trait the Insect Nobles had but suppressed thinking it made them too insect.

None knew that insect food on World is full of steroids that build up in your body, waiting to release strength.

Then Utna pinned the lion down, waiting for Luke to decide what to do?

Utna without Luke, a lost sheep.

Luke was soldier, queen, and goat.

Utna bred to take orders.

And Luke sat on his hunches and stroked the lion till it became quiet, then allowed Utna to release it and it stayed pressing the dirt.

And Luke roared a strange clicking sound through the night so that even the fire flies fled, the cicadas stopped singing and the mammal wolves stopped howling.

Then all at once joined Luke howling to the moon and making noise.

"Who is he?" Titus asked.

"Light," Ulana still holding her armor in one hand, dagger in other and only her short kilt covered her.

Now Luke approached, took her armor, found her other clothes, and walked away.

Utna followed.

Ulana felt she was the prize.

Just somehow seemed right for Luke the victor. She was not naïve, her society was prolific as on Vornal the young cannot wait to grow up and do what adults do.

"Good, good, good," her computer flashed in her mind.

"Shut up," she said aloud.

Now if she thought Luke was to take his spoils, she was wrong, instead he fastened her armor to her when she came over and handed her the rest of her clothing. She knew each time he touched her flesh he felt uncomfortable; sensed his fingers lingering and smiled.

She was all women.

And he was silent for he trusted not his voice.

It might squeak.

He was all growing up boy.

And Ulana seeing him going red in the face moved, sparing him further misery and her computer brain was wrath; as well as confused.

Women are a mystery to themselves.

He was more confused as part of him was saying "See she don't like you for she has moved away," so she hadn't done him any favors.

"Thank you," she said dressed.

A mumble escaped his throat.

And he stood lost, unable to understand what was happening and Ulana faced him waiting for him to kiss her.

She had a long wait for he never did, just stood there.

In the end Utna came over and pushed the idiot away.

Utna was jealous.

And Ulana broke the ants stare by holding out her right hand which Utna smelled. Then Ulana slowly hugged Utna whose programming prevented it killing a human brother/sister worker......and Utna liked Ulana, she smelled nice and so was confused.

See, she had this endless supply of dried honeycombs.

A woman's charm.

Howal pounced on Ulana.

Shamed

Ch 9 Betrayal

The Vornalians came from Planet Vornal where gaseous clouds swirled in the atmosphere and herds of deer ran across farmers' fields, fruit trees bloomed, butterflies played on the spongy grass and hawks hovered waiting for field mice.

None helped Howal disentangle himself from the knots he found his limbs in next day, none laughed as he rolled down an embankment under the leaf tent and winded himself against a fallen tree.

A tree a thousand years old but now a victim of lighting.

And a red snake slithered out away.

Then Howal sat thinking how he was here......and remembered and roared "Luke."

At first his head did not affect him but before he reached the top, he was staggering holding its thumping sides.

No words passed between him and Luke as they looked each other out. Then Howal snarled spitting as the cat he was for his race had evolved from cat like creatures.

Luke grunted.

None told Howal to depart, he did that himself. Luke would have given him another chance to redeem but Howal's self-ridicule made him go.

Also hated Luke to be anywhere near him.

And a lion roar made every fruit bat fly back to roost

And Luke answered with a clicking roar as if the rocks had split open and all life fell quiet, **(Lion roars).**

*

A day later.

A lone green bush baby, the only witness to what?

Howal gritting his teeth and not aware of his surroundings because he roared his anger frequently, so never saw the green barbed net land on him. And as he and his lion creature hung upside down Priest Enalusdra poked with sword piercing his flesh further.

Just enough for the muscle underneath to bubble through cut.

"Spare me and I will help you," Howal shouted.

At once Enalusdra dug deeper.

"We do not need you friend of Luke," Hupamuk answered drawing his sword, pushing the priest side. Now Hupamuk respected no one, had no friends but foes: *but Priest Enalusdra thought he was Hupamuk's friend.*

And Howal felt the cold metal slide along his spine. *Fear gripped him,* "I want to kill Luke as much as you," Howal and quickly explained his hatred two words a second for he was a lion man in a hurry.

Now Priest Enalusdra took Hupamuk aside and suggested giving Howal a vile he carried amongst his belongings, containing a parasitic worm that would eat Howal's heart unless a poison administered to kill the worm.

Lord Hupamuk laughed at the wickedness.

"Drink," Hupamuk commanded and Howal eyed suspiciously, looked at Hupamuk's sword and knew he must too live. And he drank the parasitic worm as the barbed net plucked holes in his hands and arms all the while he hated Luke for his predicament.

And Howal now stood in front of his enemies while Lord Hupamuk watched Enalusdra give Howal back his weapons. Hupamuk knew Enalusdra was a pawn, not

friend: he was his own friend in this present life.

"What have you given me?" Howal asked fearing the answer.

Hupamuk gave him a warm smile back.

*

Luke and Utna his ant

A week later, (Army sounds).

Queen Nina's great Insect host covered the land quickly for all flew the fastest dragonflies, blue imperials.

And the noise was like all beehives on white World had emptied.

And a mile ahead where Lords Hupamuk and Enalusdra following Luke's tapeworm signs unaware Nina was behind.

And Luke saw their dense green cloud and hurried on for he had the eye. But the nearer he got to Phoenix it became apparent that Queen Nina would catch them first.

There was no escape.

And Hupamuk and Enalusdra halted to allow Queen Nina to join them.

Good company for each other.

And Luke looked down upon a mighty Insect host barely half a mile behind, so that

his heartbeat fast, become tense, knew what he must do.

"It is me they want," he and they read him, and Ulana's computer mind suggested he give her the eye at the same time her spirit was mightily impressed at Luke's offer of self-sacrifice for them, *she was doing the same for her people.*

And a part of her did not want him to die.

"I will give her the eye and all of you must race to Phoenix. I alone will buy time," and he looked at Utna for he always spoke with his hands as well when the

black ant was present.

Utna moved beside him.

(Flower perfumes)

What Ulana did next her computer brain did not approve, her soul yes, for she took Luke's mouth and kissed. And Ulana's computer brain at once analyzed his saliva for gene compatibility and was worried.

The match for love had sneaked into the equation; Ulana was no longer listening to her computer brains.

At first Luke blushed and stood trembling but she knew how he felt about her. He had enjoyed every minute of her touch.

"I am a man now," and kissed her back and she did not refuse; nature had intended the process of baby making to be nice or there would not be any people!

So, she drew him close to her, so he smelt her flower perfumes and was overwhelmed.

"But not your mate," she whispered so only he could hear. At once his old self prevailed and he looked sheepish.

And Ulana felt sorry for him and wished she had left him alone, innocent, and wild.

"Give me the eye Luke," she said, her computer brain ordering.

And he did and her hands tightened about the eye.

She could save her people.

He could not save his people now.

Was this another case of Delilah?

Luke a Samson with a haircut?

Together forever cursed.

"There are many like Luke," the computer spoke to her, "be sensible, it is only his smell that attracts you."

And Luke mounted Utna and waved to his sister who knew he would not come back.

He locked eyes with Ziu and knew Ziu would protect Lana.

Then rode away to meet Queen Nina with his clicking roar deafening attentive Insect Nobles.

"I can save them all," Ulana aloud and Titus drew near saying, "Are you to trade for your people?"

And she flushed.

"Have you no idea what Nina is? She is a lie, even with the eye your people will be slaves give me the eye," Titus.

And Ulana would not but dropped one hand on her sword.

"My father is prisoner," Ulana.

"And they killed ours," Lana.

And Titus dropped his hand to his sword.

Now Ziu spoke, "Do not draw swords, Luke did not mean us to die but live. The eye has shown us the way to Phoenix and new nests. We don't need it now," and he

pointed to the Red Mountain behind, "but the question is your heart good or bad Ulana of the Stars?"

And Ulana felt her heart wretch and pull apart as she knew the answer. *"Fool, do not listen to him. The eye must be returned to Nina,"* her computer.

And saw Luke riding hard with a host of Insects flying after him.

"Good," she and mounted.

Titus smiled, "Ziu takes care of my herd, see you at Phoenix," and followed because he saw in Luke hope for all against Insect Noble exploitation.

"I will not risk you my love," Ziu to Lana, "it is up to us to reach Phoenix," and he tilted his wife's head towards Red Mountain.

"My brother Luke?"

"Gives us life," and led her away.

And Ulana drove the herd towards Luke and Titus laughing helped her for he knew what she planned.

And flying wasps, red ants and centipedes saw seeing an army approaching and became insects ignoring the commands of the Insect Nobles. As there was confusion

amongst the Nobles who strove to get their mounts to obey and chase Luke.

And did and these Luke fought on the run, slaying ten before Titus came to his side.

And Queen Nina did not see Ziu and Lana escape for Ulana was calling to her.

"Your promise Nina, my people and friends lives for the eye," and knew the eye meant little now for Ziu had seen it and would *"Learn its secrets, build new nests, breed his descendants and liberate slaves, how quaint,"* Ulana's computer brain could be sarcastic, even though it had won its argument by forcing Ulana to go to Queen Nina and bargain for her people.

And Ulana ignored her computer.

Queen Nina was listening.

"Bring me Luke back alive," Nina ordered Hupamuk and Enalusdra who knew this might be impossible.

Somewhere deep in her mind insect had taken over. It told her Luke was the strongest male for genning her young and then he was supper, for Nina originated from a Black Widow spider.

A thousand years past, **(Smell blueberry).**

And Luke roared a strange clicking sound, the sound of a black ant fighting the enemies of its nest.

And brought his iron sword down upon red chitinous ants and cut off the heads of ants and centipede.

And Lords Hupamuk and Enalusdra were afraid and ordered Howal to stand in Luke's way with his lion.

"Do not kill me Luke," Howal shouted, and Luke remembered they had entwined arms and were companions and hesitated and Hupamuk and Enalusdra escaped

amongst a mass of Nobles.

Then Howal cast a dart at Luke, and it stuck in his right hand. And Ulana seeing Nina as lies threw the eye into green bubbling marsh and it sank amongst the blueberry flower which is venomous to all insect life.

And the mighty Nina glared at the bubbling mud then suddenly jumped at Ulana, who mounted with sheathed weapons, fought with her hands?

And Ulana was smaller than the Insect Queen so was succumbed.

And Luke saw and roared his rage.

And upon charging with Utna came upon the queen's bodyguard, and slew half of them with his great strength and iron sword.

Thus, Howal managed to escape.

"Look human," and Luke saw that Nina held a jeweled dagger at Ulana's throat which it pricked, dribbling red blood.

And Luke felt his innards melt with terror.

And Titus cast a copper spear which would have struck Nina in her left eye if a Noble had not thrown an

Ant Ghoster in the missile's path.

And fell happily skewered at his queen's feet.

And she ignored his dying wish which was her blessing to obtain maidens in heaven, Naja.

"Surrender Luke or she dies," Nina meaning Ulana.

And Luke threw down his weapons looking at Ulana.

"Forgive me Luke, I did it for my people's freedom," Ulana grunted squirming in Nina's grasp to force the dagger into her own throat so Luke could fight for his freedom.

But Nina having insect intuition guessed Ulana's plan and held her head back by her auburn hair so Luke could see the smooth fair throat which she would cut deep.

And Nobles beat then chained Luke.

And Titus threw his weapons aside and was prisoner.

"Luke," Ulana moaned chained for, she wished she were dead for never had she encountered his likes or Titus. Luke had surrendered his life so she may live and Titus also for he was a true companion.

"Liar," she spat at Nina who replied by pushing her right foot in Ulana's mouth so she fell back gums bleeding.

Truly a sign of who was 'boss' and who salve.

And Ulana thought she was unworthy of Luke and Titus' friendship and wished for the same misery as her people as punishment.

And the red sun began to set, and day closed.

And small insects covered the red grass of the lower slopes of Red Mountain to feast upon slain Noble cousins.

A feast was a feast; all their birthdays had come in one day.

Ch 10 Sentence

The lakes were frozen.sensible insects crawled into cracks

in walls to huddle, chatter while mammals skated.

(Luke roared his rage.)

Noon when the red sun makes the white sky of World pink.

Luke and Titus stood chained to great iron balls before Queen Nina; Luke had failed to free his people for love.

Love is the greatest force in the universe.

And Luke was confused for Titus had told him about Ulana. How he wanted to blame her, if it had not been for her, he would be free, but he knew that was rubbish,

Queen Nina had come anyway for Phoenix and there was just too many Insects.

"I overheard Nobles thank the tapeworm inside you, for leaving a trail for them to follow," Titus in Ulana's defense for he knew about love and her predicament that her people must come first.

Luke was human, it would take longer for him to understand. Also said, "She tried to trade the eye for all our life's and believed in Nina's lies."

Now Nobles roped them with raspberry creepers to a seed cage that lifted with attached light blue transport flies.

"The way she went to your aid, she loves you fool," Titus laughed.

"It must have been horrible for her," Luke replied remembering the dagger at her throat. Always a white scar there now to remind Ulana of her treachery to humans but not her people.

Luke, you see was in love and hurting.

Now Titus understood, so did their guard Howal, who spat at them from above the seed cage float, "Not as horrible as I will make her life. Little vixen, ah ha," and hated himself for what he said for these were supposed to be companions below on the dirty unwashed filthy ridden seed floor.

"You do not understand love, that poor girl had a responsibility to her people not Luke and heart," Titus and spat at Howal but the wind blew his spittle back into his

face.

And Luke knew Titus was right, one does not allow the heart to rule on World and he realized how selfish he was.

He had betrayed his own people for his emotions whereas Ulana had not. Howal had lost the right to walk in Ulana's shadow.

And Howal was angry with himself so prodded Titus with a pole.

And Howal looked towards the nest of approaching Shurrupuk and threw the pole away hearing Luke speak thus.

"I do not blame her Howal, hear me; it's you I blame," and Howal felt uneasy though Luke was in a cage. That boy had strength and he called Luke boy as insult and as an imaginary safety barrier; buys he could batter, men was something else, and an ant man needed caution to be near.

"Do you want to know where Ulana is? Bet you do?" Howal shouted down and saw their expectant faces, "Riding with Queen Nina not sitting in pig swill. She betrayed you Luke," and Howal seeing Luke anger saw Ulana was triggered to his own life. If Luke stopped caring for her, he did fight to kill him; she, her safety was the restraint.

And Howal knew where she was, in a cage behind with swine. And there are times when men cannot stop being nasty and this was one. And Howal hated his lies that tumbled from his mouth.

And Howal through fear wanted to empty his bladder and bowels and could not for the Noble column was not stopping, and he did so over those below and hated Luke for it.

"Pig swill scum," he called to them in defense.

"She helped kill Utna your ant, didn't know that did you?" And Howal heard an animal growling below and fear gripped him so told the truth, "No, I lie son. Utna

fought till she fell with spear. And Ulana caged like you and do not forget her life depends upon your good behavior, **do not forget?**" For he was afraid of the ant man thing.

And Titus told Luke for once Howal spoke the truth for he had seen Howal cast spear aimed at Luke, a bad throw and it would have killed Ulana if the ant had not

stopped it.

And Luke wiped his face and thought of his friend Utna. "Go with the warm wind friend and be free," Luke knowing Utna's spirit was indestructible and lived on; gone back to same source for all life came from there.

Shurrupuk Dungeon.

And Luke and Titus lay chained to grey granite slabs, Queen Nina had just left.

Only Hupamuk and Enalusdra remained with two human slaves closing a freezer made of natural ice for the dungeons lie above a frozen lake.

Titus could not speak; lips stitched together out of cruelty and too silence him for he had witnessed Queen Nina couple with Luke to ensure her hundred eggs would use his genes; it was gene robbery in a big way.

Enalusdra was a natural scientist, explorer, archaeologist, and social scientist; he gives alms to the Insect Noble poor and orphans?

And he had inserted a Vornal device into Titus's veins, a robotic machine that cleared away fat blockages to prevent heart attacks; *what did you expect an Insect*

Noble to volunteer as a guinea pig?

And Enalusdra was pleased, Titus still lived, and another robot cruised the man's veins, his own invention he had stolen from human elders while they were being

explored on dissecting tables, well Enalusdra did sleep well at nights as humans and Titus were only laboratory creatures.

And the second robot was a bomb that had given Titus a headache as Enalusdra had exploded it, wiping out a section of cerebellum in the laboratory animal called Titus. Titus lived; anytime detonated, any time.

At once Enalusdra saw the assassination possibilities of such a bomb that could advance his claim to the throne.

With such a device there would be no opposition to the coronation of a male as king, he could dream.

And Enalusdra investigated the freezer and saw jars containing bits of Titus's pancreas, liver and for the wild beast's genes were worthy of further experimentation,

upon slaves and criminal Nobles.

Was Enalusdra not the man to take the insect species forward out of their dark age into the modern world?

And he looked at Titus, saw the large stitches, and thought Titus should thank him, he had inserted insect genes into this slave's arms and back, to give him strength to row the oars.

Enalusdra had granted him extra life; it would take years for Titus to die propelling galleys now.

And Enalusdra grinned seeing Titus fed gruel full of mold.

(MOULD)

There could only be one master race on white World, the followers of God Enil who promised his followers Naja, heaven.

And the Nobles knew how to achieve it, cross breed between the species. Gene robbers in a big way, even bigger than Burke and Hair but human cemeteries on White World, were open at night so grave robbers was not the profession to join, insects just robbed the graves of everything that was in them, a slave was still a slave in death.

And there would be no Naja heaven would there if everyone got in?

And in his species Titus was big and strong. His skin was a navy blue, his gold hair long and curly and his eyes white pearls. Enalusdra would multiply his genes and as

for Titus since he had no race left in him, so, to the oars he would go to die silently with his mouth stitched shut.

And treated Luke differently for Queen Nina thought it humorous for Luke to want Ulana always. Ulana now given to Howal as reward.

See Queen Nina understood the heart was a dagger.

*

The Insects did not believe in commercial fishing but sent individual

decorated fishing boats with Ant Ghosters as guards out to fish. It was

like a painter's competition as each design of fishing boat competed to outdo the

other. It would have provided dignified work for Nobles also, but they had slaves.

So, thousands of colorful boats went to sea instead of one giant fishing

boat that could put Insect Nobles out of work. What work, the humans faced sea monsters! And they sang songs to become brave.

Later above in Queen Nina's audience chamber, a chamber lined with gold and red wax. And there were niches with statues of God Enil.

And a new trophy on the wall, a human head to remind slaves who was master and it did not matter if it came from the dungeons, it was still a symbol.

And Nina had just pronounced sentence on Luke and Titus which tightened the guilt about Howal, for they were to be rowers in war galleys. Luke had never known of the existence of the Yellow Sea, didn't even know what a war galley was? Well, he was about to find out the hard way!

And Queen Nina seeing Luke's lack of dread, ordered him taken to a veranda which was a ventilation shaft of her nest, and have him shown the Yellow Sea and the

war galleys in the bay.

(Gold and red wax)

And he smelt fish, not salt which is the smell of the sea.

"How beautiful," he thought, and they read it in his face for the sea was dull yellow from algae living in it. And sea birds filled the white sky eating insects and the galleys painted in reds, oranges, shades of green and blue and surrounded by pink flamingos as the tide was out and the estuary stunk of mud and little crabs ran amuck, mud fish gulped air and walked on primitive legs.

And in sixty million years their descendants would threaten the Nobles too.

And life abounded for small insect life was plentiful and eaten.

Behold Luke saw the wonder of creation and became part of it, so his eyes shone for he was conscious of the universe and its force.

But Queen Nina became a wrinkled mass as she peered into Luke's face wondering if she was speaking to a simpleton, even as far as press his cheeks together so his eyes watered.

But Howal knew Luke was not simple and wondered which realm the boy lived on,

World or with the gods?

Now Luke or Titus did not know Ulana of the Stars was present, chained, for guards surrounded her for she was squatting as good dogs should.

"Meow," Ulana to annoy.

"Luke, don't let them break you," she suddenly screamed, and Queen Nina turned, comprehended quicker than Luke and smiled. Maybe rowing the Yellow Sea might not wilt the boy, but Ulana would.

"Bring her here," Nina commanded.

Why Ulana dumped at Luke's feet, her silver armor digging trenches in the opaque wax floor. "Meow," she loudly.

"Look at her Luke," which he was for her green leather kilt messed up, and her legs were long and smooth. Yes, just like a boy at a time like this?

And inside he lusted and cried for her humiliation.

For the kilt had a dog's tail stitched on its rear.

And on each of Ulana's feet and hands paws.

And about her neck a spiked red collar and the spikes drew blood from Ulana when she fell.

But she did not scream for she was a woman with dignity. She was also a star traveler, a Vornalian.

And Queen Nina saw Luke's eyes and knew he did not know himself that he loved Ulana.

"You may hold Luke," she told Lana and she did, and Luke felt himself go weak and Nina laughed.

And Ulana kissed Luke with these words, "Never forget me for I will never forget you."

"Howal come for your prize," a cruel queen.

Now Luke felt his heart break and spirit dip.

Now Howal the real dog, for he salivated over his Vornalian bone.

"Help me Luke," Ulana begged for once allowing her soul to speak and not her computer brain. She wanted Luke which made Howal realize that witch Nina knew

what made him tick; lust and did not like it made public.

And did not realize as Luke did that there was no such thing as real privacy as it is said, "What animates us knows when a sparrow dies."

So Howal was animate dung.

"Take her," and Howal heard the venom in Nina's voice and obeyed wondering when he would be her victim, so took Ulana screaming from Luke.

This, Howal enjoyed for part of him had diverted from the path to light to darkness.

Now he joined in the slippery road to ruin and lessons relearned.

Why Luke found rage swell in his bosom and the anger of ants' milk flowed so he forgot his good behavior kept Ulana alive.

And broke his chains by spreading arms roaring the sound of a Black soldier ant.

Lo his enemies drew back terrified.

And Queen Nina marveled seeing Luke's children from her as Noble Insects

possessed with his **strength.**

And shining eyes.

So Howal tried desperately to withdraw with his booty but tripped over Ulana's Dog tail and fell.

And there coming to him was Luke, who opened his mouth ripped the stitches apart there as Titus had, so he could do what ants do, fight with tremendous strength.

And he sat upon Howal, no longer seeing him as friend but foe.

And black ants are not killers like reds and Luke hesitated, so, from behind felled, by a wooden club, **(That hurt something).**

(Out of this world)

*

(Smell of alcohol)

That night Howal came for Ulana full of courage from a bottle, drunk. He wanted his prize and rid of his guilt. Drink always made reasoning easier; specially to bring things to the way he reasoned.

And Ulana chained to his bed post saw the cell door open and dim corridor light and smelt Howal.

Cat pee and drink............**for he was a lion man king and shamed his specie.**

And Howal staggered in wearing a purple robe and crown which Queen Nina had given him her royal prisoner. This made Howal feel important, he was a king and could do as he pleased, even with Ulana.

He had the divine right of kings on his side.

He had the divine right of his priests.

He had the divine right of God Enil for Ulana was not a believer and so deserved her fate; **HIM.**

So, lighting a candle he saw that Ulana had no clothes, bathed, and smelling of primrose but remained in her dog outfit. Now this inducement gave him strength for the drink was ebbing him of it.

"Ulana, you mean nothing to me," he explained discarding his purple robe. Yes, that was true; it was Luke that made him feel guilty.

As for Titus, he reminded Howal what friendship was and hated the man for that............AND ALL HE HAD TO DO WAS ASK FORGIVENESS.

But Poor Ulana meant nothing, she was a woman, and, in his kingdom, they came to him when he demanded. They had little rights; they filled the taverns dancing on spinning tables flashing their bottoms.

They pranced the stages of inns stripping.

They loitered street corners for the gratification of men.

They had your babies, cooked, and bathed you.

They filled slave markets.

They slaves needed; the slave economy based upon slavery would collapse without flesh too sells.

So, to, would the fashion and jewelry industry; need gems to add sparkle; and women were exactly sparkle, show pieces of ego. Men killed each other to possess the most beautiful and to parade them to show off their virility. All powered by slaves at sewing wheels.

"Roar, I am sixty-eight and have an eighteen-year-old girl, roar," a lion man.

Women had no rights, especially Luke's woman right now. Didn't God Enil curse them with monthly problems and child labor? And if God Enil could curse women *so could Howal.*

"What are you looking at?" He demanded realizing she was crucifying his body with her **solid green eyes.**

Somehow, he got the impression she was comparing him to Luke and saw himself as extremely distasteful, it must be his tail.

He looked down at an extended belly from years of beer drinking, saw his chest and belly hair patted wet with beer saliva and smelt drinkers' vomit.

Saw his limpness as he had drunk too much boasting his prowess to his Noble drinking comrades.

And knew he looked stupid; swished his tail in anger and drank more to get strength belched and vomited against a wall, then fell heavily beside Ulana.

And that last bit hurt more than emptying his stomach lining.

Tomorrow his ulcers would bleed, and he doubled up in pain.

Well, he did like his drink, didn't he?

"I hate you Luke," he mumbled and reached out limp cold wet sweaty hands for Ulana's body as his mind span and it took real, effort to raise his head, even now to open his mouth and eyes that could no longer focus on three spinning Ulana's.

He needed to admit he was alcoholic as a step to healing. But he was king Howal.

Year 2003, Calendar 1. DAY 354.

Luke had given up counting the days he rowed oars across the Yellow Sea that stank of mold. That Titus lived he was sure for he had not seen his remains thrown over the side.

And drummers pounded.

And Luke arched with the oar and the war galley sped on.

"Cause trouble and Ulana dies," Lord Hupamuk's words to him and he remembered always.

Luke the only rower chained more than the others, the only one with a Noble sitting behind pricking his back with a spear, hoping Luke would be bothersome so he could kili him.

But Luke was strong for the rowing was exercise, and something else gave him strength that which made his eyes shine, light.

"And when the wind blows," the slaves chanted, bent, pulled, leaned back, reached forth, and the wind hit the red sails lifting the ship and throwing it down amongst the yellow algae.

And the spear man was seasick, bored, and often left Luke.

And Luke having knowledge of Ulana's fate was worse than not having. Howal, always Howal, how evilly selfish to hate like Insects, but Luke found hating got you nowhere, just bitterness which made your day a misery.

And there was enough misery on ship.

So, he dreamed of better days to come and knew they must. With each action against whatever enemy they fought ships splintered and sank, and from his row hole he saw slaves foundering in the sea and others huddled on timbers.

That was his simple hope that their ship would suffer a like fate so he could escape on driftwood and his enemies think him dead while he would be free to rescue Ulana and his people.

And one day they sat Titus beside him, so Luke could see his friend but never hear his voice. The Insect Nobles thought this jolly wholesome fun. Poor Titus to be alone till the day he died never speaking, so never spoken too; but he was not alone, the grey gulls and white albatrosses sang to him uplifting his spirit.

And the yellow froth slapping the hull told him about whales under the ship.

And Luke saw his guards hoped he would get troublesome, so they could kill him, sitting down here amongst the slave stink was something else so wanted fresh air!

Besides Queen Nina was hundreds of miles away in Shurrupuk City, was not she?

Anyway:

And Titus was glad he was beside Luke for the boy's inner light gave him hope in their present dark state. Luke had changed, more silent, but the soul had withdrawn places were love existed.

"We will escape," Luke whispered to Titus hoping to cheer his friend.

"How?" Titus with his eyes in the dimness as they rested and by writing a '?' on Luke's arm.

"Out there," Luke answered and looked at the Yellow Sea, and Titus shivered. At first he thought the boy mad, but Luke was a man now. He rowed as hard as any of them, shared the whip, saw the hearts of others burst and their mouths gurgle with blood drowning.

And in the hieroglyphic reports sent to the admiralty scribes chiseled the expedition against the pirates, and one rower was larger than the others.

For over them Luke showed he was special. He was kind, offering to row for others who if he had not taken their place would die from exhaustion, and now others followed Luke's example and his guards thought it a joke, he was trying to row himself to death faster than planned for him?

And all the slaves shared a common burden, that of rowing the ship.

And the whip ceased for the Slave Master at first thinking Luke crazy whipped him, spat and peed on him, till he saw it had no effect, then afraid left Luke and was happy the rowing done more efficiently, so Luke praised instead.

And Luke's fame spread for it was the second time Insects learned to fear him.

The first when Luke became strong with anger and fear brought respect and Nobles as Ziusudra before tried You r\ammed, they sank.to understand humans without resorting to dissection.

You rammed, they sank.

*

Shurrupuk City.

Ulana waited on her haunches while her master Howal held the gold chains to her neck for she was a pet, at least a station above the slaves.

Every time he brought her anywhere, she listened and learned, but this time with greater interest.

Queen Nina was having a scribe read a report about Luke and Ulana glowed, Luke had not let them break him, if anything he was breaking the hate Nobles had for

slaves.

"Howal, you know this man Luke better than us," Queen Nina had said, "you will command his ship, destroy our common enemy the pirates, do this for me, do this for our kingdoms," Queen Nina told Howal, and Ulana could not miss the softness in the queen's voice. It would not be the first time Ulana had witnessed their games after dark.

First chained outside the queen's rooms, then brought in, forced to take participate for Queen Nina was insect who took a hundred mates to ensure her eggs were alive.

Enil their god was male, so Nina strove to be like God Enil and so was perverse with Ulana.

And the only good that came out of Howal's affair with Nina is that he left Ulana alone. And if the queen were in a temper, he would come to Ulana's cell, drink more and sleep snoring across Ulana and she would roll him off her bed, so he crashed on the wax floor and woke the next day with a sore forehead covered in his vomit.

Shame.

(Red
mushrooms)

But Ulana never told Howal she did this too him.

"I will destroy our greatest enemy," and Ulana knew Howal spoke of Luke, and the joy she had experienced expecting getting near Luke turned to apprehension.

And Howal knew if he ordered Nina about, would end up in a shallow grave, so, accepted with an air of bravado, her.

*

And Ulana's life as a pet gave her freedom for her handlers took her places they should not.

Like to the witches.

Now the witches,

Were composed of young girls to elderly women.

Did live in a holy red mushroom grove sacred to God Enil.

Orange mist shrouded the place.

Laughter and screams.

Insect and otherwise.

All feared them.

And Ulana saw her handlers sought love potions from the witches and paid dearly and tested potions on the young witch apprentices.

To Ulana the place represented all that was bad in Noble society, but superstition said it was here that the gateway to God Enil was and the witches guarded it. None knew if truth lay buried underneath the purple soil of that holy grove.

(Purple soil)

Luke would find out.

And it was on Ulana's visits here she saw her people sometimes as slaves and knew,

Titus had spoken the truth not to trust Queen Nina. That Nina would never free her people for the eye and map to Phoenix.

And here Ulana shown the truth by a green witch. Half insect and half bird creature. Taken to the grove as a child and Noble genes inserted into her back so fly wings grew.

For she was not of World nor come through the black hole, World's universe had habitable planets.

A lone survivor of a star ship crash; a girl who had suffered the same fate as all non Insect Noble women.

"Pretty, are you not?" The green witch.

As for Ulana she sat on her haunches, dog tail out, waiting to see which way the old woman's whim would swing.

Instead of giving doggy Ulana bone to chew *she offered drink.*

"To make sure you don't bare insect brats," the hag advised, and Ulana saw sympathy in the old grey eyes and drank.

So, Ulana hallucinated.

"Your keepers will be busy, come Ulana, Luke's mate," the witch firmly and Ulana followed warmed that all knew of Luke and her.

And imagined leading Luke into balls on Vornal her home planet, and there would be quiet as all craned to see the famed ant warrior of World. It did not t matter if Luke

did not fit in, his fame would make up for his bad breeding and all would respect him.

And now the witch took Ulana into a purple tree by means of a disguised door.

And the tree had red apples hanging, waiting eaten.

"We are in the knowledge tree whose fruit is forbidden as food," the witch told Ulana.

And Ulana down amongst roots and saw moles eat beetle grubs and saw by glow worm light.

A rotten coffin.

And the witch drew her near to it and pulled aside cobwebs and Ulana saw a mummified face.

It was aged black, the skin crinkled paper.

Teeth showed.

But the face was human.

"Behold dearest god Enil," the witch laughing and pulled Ulana away back the way they had come.

Now Ulana was shocked silent.

"Tell Luke when you meet again," the witch advised pressing a withered green right thumb to Ulana's mouth.

Ulana understood.

Their secret.

The destruction of the Insect Noble culture.

"Luke will know what to do," the witch.

"Why have you shown me?"

"I have spent my life a forced harlot to mutants and Nobles in this holy brothel. They cleaned me out and Enil knows what they did with my eggs, made monsters out of them. I hate them and dream Enil, saying Luke of Utna would know what to do with his corpse," the witch replied.

And Ulana remembered Luke's shinning eyes and wondered what unseen power controlled him, it was simply light.

"Yes, his eyes shine, do they not?" The witch happily. "Do not you know where he's from? He has spring fever," and the witch laughed adding, "Enil, hung on this tree by Nobles, see the pictures."

Orange tree

And Ulana saw hieroglyphics of a helmeted man with backpack hanging from an orange tree as Nobles nailed his wrists and ankles to bark.

Then sunk a copper spear in his heart.

Enil had promised them all the secrets humans had if the Nobles let Enil's race live," the witch explained, "but only gave enough to wet insect appetites. And the keys to the secrets he left with his magicians, the human elders.

Then Nobles killed their own god Enil for their salvation which to Nobles meant advancement out of burrows.

How they wanted to be like God Enil the god who travelled the stars and gave them sowing, reaping, architecture, and cattle husbandry, even pottery and the wheel.

He was the first human to come through the black hole above white World, Phoenix was second.

You see Earth the human planet is on the other side of that black hole."

Now Nobles, drunk came banging on the orange tree demanding Ulana so the witch took Ulana to them, fearing they might enter for drink robs the mind of taboo.

And the Nobles offered the witch a red leather pouch of gems for Ulana, that the witch took and Ulana withered inside betrayed.

Orange tree

"Remember what you just drank, remember to be normal, don't let them see the joy of what you have seen," the witch whispered leaning down to Ulana.

So, Ulana functioned as normal, she kneed one Noble, clawed another's face and their raged shouts brought her keepers back, who apologized for her injurious behavior and told the hurt Nobles Ulana was Howal's pet?

Meow," Ulana full of mischief.

At the mention of Howal's name the Nobles apologized. All knew now he shared Queen Nina's bed and let Ulana pass out of the grove with her keepers who knew they would get Howal when Nina displeased with him.

"Yes, act normal dearest," the witch laughed flapping her reed feathered wings.

And the two offended Nobles from that day spread lies about Howal, that he wished to usurp Nina's throne and that he thought her an ugly elderly woman.

And knew Queen Nina would hear and see Howal deserving the same fate as Enbilulu as a water offering.

Such White World. And Ulana went wondering if drink had made her dream? And never noticed the wanted posters, wind torn faded. Of Jack and Luke and the artist made his eyes shine. And Ulana heard the witch laughing, *"That one should die for many to live,"* and was not sure if she meant Luke or Enil.

And the bird witch flew and Ulana discovered Enil's secret.

Ch11 Pirates   Yellow Mist   Yellow Sea

Now King Howal was not happy sent to the Yellow Sea for his lion culture had myths saying it was home to flesh tearing monsters.

Mermaids lured seamen to drown, so scared of the sea, Insects sent human slaves to fish.

"She is getting rid of me," Howal would drunkenly complain, and Ulana would hear void of sympathy. And Ulana was not afraid of the Yellow Sea and even at the docks witnessed Nobles and priests throwing human slaves and other fantastic beings of white World, off flower decorated barges into the harbor so sea monsters swallowed them.

Offerings to Enki the water god to avert the floods.

"Disobedient slaves, Enki's warning to us masters," Howal complained drinking blue spirit from a flask.

He needed it for he was afraid of the future and Ulana like slaves never worried about that for that took care of itself; slaves only lived for today as they knew they had been born with a sell by date stamped on them.

And Ulana with Howal boarded ship, painted light green with two red and white striped sails, a ship that would carry them to Luke's gold painted war galley ten miles out. No one in Shurrupuk wanted a war galley in the harbor, why they were full of overcrowded slaves and usually plagues.

Yellow Sea*

Lo, it had been a week since the other ship had come aside and although Titus could not see all from his seated position, he knew Luke had seen something for he was

excited; like when Utna found nectar.

. *He knew they were in the belly of a warship or would think Luke had seen a woman,*

Luke saw Ulana

Also, Howal so snarled, thinking nothing of showing his feelings. It was this type of behavior that made men think he was either a dangerous idiot, eccentric, different or

a combination of all.

(Lion snarls)

And when men came to know Luke, they knew he was just dangerous.

And Titus saw Luke's knuckles whiten as he gripped the oar, Luke had seen the chain about Ulana's neck, seen her on all fours like a dog, saw Howal's guard talk out

of ear shot about Howal…….laughing.

Lifting Ulana's shorts, hoping the dog would react. Like stupid boys hanging about street corners with nothing better to do than annoy passing girls, "Show us your bum,"

they would shout.

And Ulana did nothing, no protest, but Luke saw her solid green eyes void of life,

Howal had broken her.

Yellow Sea.

(Insect band plays)

And Howal was their new commander in gold helmet and chest armor with red plumes and white tunic.

And Luke saw the soldiers and sailors fall to their knees paying him homage. Lo, the pelicans and gulls took flight for the ship's insect band produced a deafening reed drone.

(Black ant clicks loudly)

The noise of God Enil for Howal was his commander for Queen Nina the defender of their religion had appointed Howal admiral; for his drinking was annoying.

Now a loud clicking sound surfaced above the sound of the band that fell silent and Howal was afraid a sea monster was surfacing to eat him.

But Ulana stirred and smiled for the sound she knew came from Luke's throat Luke was alive and with that belief that the witch in the orange grove was not crazy

about the things she spoke.

Implying Luke was a demigod? Ulana did not believe in gods, they were super spirits, there was no real power but that which created the universe and with that

realization Ulana felt all her fears go away for she was trusting light.

And Luke was speaking to her in the tongue of Utna the black ant. "I know what you did was out of belief good would come to your people. I am still your friend

Luke," Luke could not have expected her to act otherwise. Besides when he really thought of it, he did not know her very well.

She was Ulana Star woman, a stranger who had come into his life and awoken him.

She had followed her path for she believed it right.

Howal was bad, Luke would like to kill him. Then why bother when the time came he would rescue Ulana and together find a home. Killing was not good; it was like watching the Whip Master kill roaches that ran about their feet.

Even they had a right to live, they were animated spirit.

And Luke thought, wondering why he was born to be slave and others master? Why no one put chains on bears except intelligent Insect Nobles.

"Because God Enil planned our lives before we were born, and we agreed to them before our first breath," Elder Peter he remembered saying sarcastically adding,

"We plan our lives, if there is an intelligent god, he planned no man make as slave of another for it says *we were made in Enil's image and Enil is not a slave.*"

And Luke saw wisdom and was glad he was poor and unhindered with power that blinds dark. Glad he was his own conscious and bound to no other's teachings but

what made his spirit grieve when he did bad.

And knew Peter was right, Priest Enalusdra could pump religion into slaves hoping they accepted their plight. Slaves had, the harem attendants and Ant Ghosters, they needed reason to exist in their horrid lives. So, be it, Luke could underst and why they prayed to Enil, but they had no right to try ramming it into his mind that

rejected it.

But he was whole, and the Whip Master killed out of ignorance for filthy roaches were enemy on ship as they spread disease, so deserved no life.

That was wrong and rowers killed roaches for food.

And Luke saw what roaches ate, filth lying on the wooden planks that would otherwise cause disease.

And Luke knew they were living things made in the order of things, like him. He had never seen a chained roach, why should humans suffer chaining?

But Luke would still like to kill Howal given the chance for he had seen Ulana on all fours as an Ant Ghoster pawed her places because he abused his power of

authority.

And Luke was angry.

So, the strength of ants came upon him, and he broke his oar and thrust it up through planking and pierced the Ghosters belly so he died.

And with hands gripped Howal's guard who earlier defiled his Ulana and pulled down so ankles stuck between deck planks while Luke broke them below.

"They are an abomination on the face of World," and Luke did not know where the voice came from, "and to you is given the strength of Samson. You will pull down the central pillars," and Luke cried for his eyes shone and he felt unseen beings watching him.

And recorded in the hieroglyphics of Shurrupuk for it shows a human rower talking to ghosts, birds and fishes and the figure has gold paint round it as if the universe shone from him.

"We will kill her, let them go," and the commands of the Nobles reached Luke's human parts and he let go the Noble ankles.

And carpenters came and boarded up the splintered planks and fear gripped the whole crew.

"Hoist the main sail," Admiral Howal and wondered why the ship was still well, it was the wrong order given. 'Raise anchor,' but Howal was a drunk landlubber.

*

Now when the ship was under way and sound of drum, sea gulls, wind in sail and splash of waves filled the air, Howal came to Luke. He looked like a king, gold

embodied white tunic, plumed helmet, tanned, muscular, bath scented.

But his eyes were red with drink.

And Ulana came from behind, a sailor holding her lead, stupid-colored bows dangling from auburn hair and bosoms bare fastened with rings and her semi nakedness would have been complete if it were not for purple shorts were a white dog's tail bounced with her movements.

Even her nose, belly and ears had pins and colored ribbons dangled from them.

Lo, on Ulana's face, a red blood stone muzzle fastened.

Ulana was pet who bit and hissed like a cat, not barking like a dog.

"They are an abomination; they sleep with animals; they are dung and will be no more.

They are of Sodom and Gomorrah," Luke heard and did not know Sodom or the other name and put it down to memory flashbacks something Elder Peter had said, and he had forgotten.

And Luke remembered Peter and what he said about Earth, "Our ancestors were worse than Nobles, they slept with beasts and mutilated themselves. Tore down every green thing and dried blue seas up so that there was no life left upon Earth.

And earth revolted for humans were an abomination and starvation and plagues set upon our ancestors till they stopped their accursed ways."

And Luke allowed the anger over Ulana's degradation to consume him and again gripped his oar, cracking it further.

And Titus was amazed at his strength, and glad not directed in anger at him.

And knew now what had excited Luke. Titus no longer felt left out when Luke did not explain his motives for either you liked Luke or not as he was a world of his own.

and in ways Titus was glad Luke kept his tongue to himself, he was trustworthy in a dangerous world.

"See here your bitch dog on heat," Howal said, and a keeper pulled Ulana closer.

Now Luke saw her palms dig in and resist as a dog digs in against the leash and saw splinters.

And Howal knew what he was doing was wrong and hated himself and Luke, for it was not his fault Luke had not rejected with power like him.

Eat mice stuffed with saffron rice and drink wine all day.

But Luke instead had chosen slavery.

Howal was not to blame, blame the drugged alcohol of Hupamuk and Enalusdra had given him to drink long ago. A suicidal worm in it to be rid of at the hands of Enalusdra. Howal, like Luke was in bondage but just in better conditions.

And Ulana came close to Luke.

So, Luke wiped away the rowers' toilet from Ulana's hands and the whip master did not whip him.

"So, it is true," Howal meaning stories about a pampered Luke and Howal took the whip from its keeper, and whipped this man across his face, and he fell screaming for one eye now blinded.

"Reweigh," it came from Luke as the strength of ant's milk flowed through him and he stood up.

So, all stopped rowing.

The whip master had changed from bad to good and now treated his slaves with kindness for Like had taught him men work better under a kind employer than an evil

one, even if not paid.

At first Howal jumped back, then saw the restraining irons on Luke so took courage.

And Luke forced himself to stand and iron flew from wood and Luke was now free.

Where was Howal's courage now?

The foolish lion man had brought all this upon himself.

"He did you no harm," Luke shouted and went to the aid of the whip master.

And the spear man behind Luke had not slain him.

It was so out of context that none stopped Luke, all open mouthed instead and gaped at the slave helping an Insect man.

So, only Ulana smiled for she knew Luke had not changed and was glad.

She also had not expected Luke to show kindness to her after betraying him in the past over the eye.

"I want an example of him made," Howal in a trembling voice for he wanted Luke dead.

And the sailors came first, apologetically for Luke was their rower and they knew of him as Nina had heard. That he treated those about him as they treated him and as he treated himself.

"Stand back," Luke advised, "my quarrel is not with you," and they did as Luke knelt beside Ulana now.

This was their ship not Howal's and saw Luke as bringing it good luck for it was the fastest in the fleet now so could easily outmaneuver pirate ships and not be

rammed.

Yellow Mist.

Now King Howal knew the world was crazy for this was a slave ordering Nobles who obeyed?

"Kill him," he demanded from warriors who had come aboard with him, mostly Ant Ghosters, humans who were not under Luke's influence of light.

So, Luke fought with these men and would have destroyed them if, "I will slit her throat," it was Howal who held a dagger at Ulana's throat.

*

One hour later.

. A thick yellow mist descended upon the fleet as World's warm winds blew yellow algae over the sea to find new breeding grounds reducing vision to that of a short sighted moth woman.

And Howal stood close to Luke on the ship's deck, the latter stretched between ropes to be keel hauled.

"Luke," it was Ulana wanting to ask forgiveness, breaking up at the knowledge that Luke always surrendered his freedom for her and knew Luke valued her above his own life.

Knew he was the most chivalrous person she had met.

But he smiled as they hauled him over the ship to the sea monsters.

And **Ulana Star traveler** wept and Howal's Ant Ghosters remaining alive kicked her so she fell and curled in a heap like a sore dog.

Yellow Mist

And the superstitious men of the ship became angry for that was Luke's woman and one cast a spear, so it festooned upon an Ant Ghosters neck, for it was a barbed Gae Bulgae spear type.

And Howal drunk yanked the spear out, so the Ghosters neck fell apart.

And Howal slipped on the man's fluid and bent his tail and screamed and became wrath and had the body thrown over the side for he had a plan to destroy Luke now.

And no one cared as Ghosters were stupid humans.

And the man's blood spread redness about Luke in the yellow sea attracting hidden monsters from the depths.

And the crew of the ship by their eyes were making it clear they would kill Howal if he ordered the Ant Ghosters and his own Noble warriors to arrest him who had cast the spear.

For Howal outnumbered ten to one by resentful Nobles who saw him as Queen Nina's bed toy fell silent.

He was also not a Noble, was he?

But a lion man creature to be taxidermiesed on a whim.

They the Nobles also knew how he had betrayed his friends. Noble Insects were like Governor Ziusudra in that they could follow fairness and comradeship.

What was right and wrong?

The difference between good and evil.

And would like to see King Howal sink to the bottom of the Yellow Sea.

Now fortune smiled on Luke for at that moment as among the fleet a sailor in a crow's nest spied the enemy, the sea pirates coming out of the yellow mist.

And the wind was not from God Enil, but man made for on each enemy ship was fans worked by prisoners that blew the yellow mist in front of the ships as camouflage.

And Luke left submerged as Howal saw to the business of war best he could because of his drink that was now a problem. That was one thing he was good at, war, and the killing of others made in the image of the living spirit.

And Ulana dragged behind Howal till he stumbled over her and in anger kicked her ribs and had her sent below to his cabin.

*

And Luke was calm for he was planning to live, as those keel- hauling him, had let go of the ropes, so he was now trailing behind the ship. And his body swayed with the ship's lurches as his ears filled with drum beat as the ship speeded up.

Then saw a fin following him about thirty feet away.

"Death is not to be by drowning then," he said stoically.

And the enemy of Queen Nina were amongst them and burning tar landed on the ship, so the sail torching that underneath, and a spar fell on the closing fin. Someone must like Luke.

And Luke saw an enemy ship would collide and the enemies had strange gods carved along their woodwork, and a cast spear short of target splashed near his face,

then grappling hooks fell about him.

So, his ship jarred violently from ramming and Luke heard brother rowers Drowning and screaming as the fin was amongst them.

Howal had had them chained again in the old ways.

As Luke thought a crushing between the ships was his, rowers raised oars to push the ships apart, and boarding planks fell over him and men ran screaming wanting to kill and die quickly.

And Luke saw the enemy, for they began to fall past him, a variety of beings, humans, with fur as skin, furless humans and even Insect Nobles for one reason or another fleeing Shurrupuk.

"You cared for me, I don't know who you are but remember my kindness," the voice spoke meaning Luke was from heaven, and Luke saw the blinded whip master

with a sword cut him free of the keel haul ropes or he did go down with the boat.

Then the ship groaned, and great beams of wood sprang lose from the hull and Luke slid under the yellow sea and white crests covered him.

Then pulled aboard a ship just as a shark passed him.

" Yes, Whip Master I will not forget you."

And the ship sank and rested on the bottom for the Yellow Sea is shallow. An inland sea with an Isthmus and much of the deck remained above the surface.

And the sharks feasted upon others unfortunate enough to be in the water.

Now Luke thought of his friends and sought them to help. So many names in his head but foremost was Ulana.

"I must go below," and saw Titus chained to his seat bubbles streaming from his mouth with splintered wood pinning dead rowers so, they pranced silently in ship's

rubbish.

And anger overcame Luke, and he grew strong, snapped chains, and pushed Titus through broken planks to air above.

And since the chains snapped, a dozen saved themselves while others standing on planks begged Luke to break their chains too.

"Ulana," he screamed for he could not turn his back on those who would die if he did not break their chains.

And Ulana was in a room filling with yellow water as the ship began to break up.

(**Red apples**)

"Luke," she called as she struggled to push sea chests from the door.

"You dung head," it was Howal who blamed Luke for this misfortune, and he was armed and threw the spear from a ladder that led into the rowing chamber at someone.

And since he warned Luke by his shout the latter ducked, and the weapon thrust through a pirate's back who had been seeking pickings amongst the doomed.

Thus, pinning him to an apple barrel.

And red apples floated away.

"Another time Howal," Luke shouted back and dived in search of Ulana. And another Noble ship came abreast gorging out warriors. And slew all above deck who

was not Noble of Queen Nina which meant freed slaves, till the slaughter stopped when there were no more pirates standing.

And Howal heard creaking beams under him protest the current, and knew the ship was breaking up fast. And all about him swirled coughing smoke from burning canvas sails.

"Goodbye Luke," Howal said and boarded the new Noble Insect ship.

Rescuing himself.

Of the enemy Luke did not know if they were victorious or vanquished; it did not matter nor who was the enemy, where was Ulana?

And Luke resumed his search, not going far below as limited by air pockets along the ship corridor ceilings.

And all about was tangle, weapons and drowned.

And did not find Titus or Ulana and presumed them dead, and night set so he returned to the remains of the washed deck and watched the colored sails full of wind drop over the horizon.

"I will never forget you my friends," he said, "in my mind, soul and heart you will live," he spoke aloud for none were here to hear.

And because he was alone, he allowed his grief to take hold of him and wept over the wickedness of one to another.

An hour of this saw him making a raft and sail, finding weapons and food and working out which way was land. "It had been on my left and we did not change

course. Howal also went left, so do I then, I will find Phoenix and these strange race that are enemy of Queen Nina and see what next," he and using broken oar paddled

his raft from the coffin of his love and friend.

That was a year ago and it is now 2004 Calendar 1 DAY 351 and Luke rode Utna again who had followed Luke down to the harbor and never left the shoreline, always seeking Luke, friend, like a dog that refuses to leave its master's grave such as the famous Red Dog of Australia on Planet Earth.

And one day rewarded with Luke's scent on the ground for Luke had come ashore on his raft.

And they met and embraced one in the fashion of men and the other after ants and lived together in mangrove swamps seeking Titus and Ulana whom Luke hoped were alive and found as Utna had found him; or grief would make him go   *insane.*

But depression over the realization it was a forlorn hope set in.

And decision time arrived, to leave or stay looking along the shore.

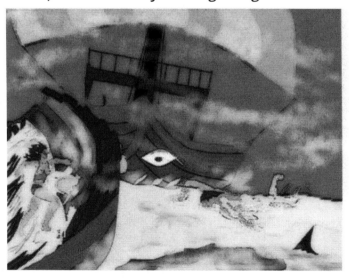

So, decided.

He was Luke of the ants and knew Titus and Ulana were dead for a year he had found driftwood, shark eggs and empty sea anemones.

"Ulana kindled a fire in my soul and the silence of your voice is the quietness of my heart," and he knew he must forget and go to Phoenix now.

*

Enbilulu lived covered in crabs, lice, spider webs under his arm pits and from his chains. He never moved these days and the goaler fed him a liquid gruel every day.

"I would not if Queen Nina hadn't changed her mind and ordered you be kept alive if this is living," the goaler and laughed.

And Enbilulu never spoke; had no tongue, deafened, and blinded in one eye.

The pile of rotted rubbish between his legs, organs he once boasted off and an ear and eye also.

Lips, teeth, nose, and tongue too.

The goaler whose job was never letting Enbilulu's insect genes regenerate his missing parts so, Enbilulu the goaler always mutilated often. And kept bald as it was shameful for Nobles to be such, so always pink and green hair lay upon the floor beside rotting antennae and stings.

The sting the goaler always enjoyed pulling out.

Enbilulu did not.

The queen had given her orders.

How could anyone be so cruel?

"You owe your life to a great queen. Lucky you come from a powerful family. The old queen knew about hostage."

And Enbilulu would never walk again for his legs, ankles, knees, and thighs crushed by this goaler who fed him gruel daily and threw a bucket of water across the floor underneath Enbilulu as toilet flush.

So, Enbilulu hung from chain walls by broken arms and wrists, allowed to regenerate as deliberate twisted shafts.

Did Queen Nina not know how to punish?

Against the far corners and walls where bones, dirty but a close examination would show them as fingers, toes, and ribs, the leftovers of a skeleton.

Only eleven ribs plucked out of Enbilulu to keep his lungs working.

A hole underneath Enbilulu had become blocked with the bones of past victims so that little waste went down with the bucket of water.

So, the cleaning work done by lower insects that wiggled all over Enbilulu and the floor.

Lucky for Enbilulu these lesser insects fed off his bad flesh, so he did not die of rot.

And the joke was on the goaler, Queen Nina had forgotten long ago about

Enbilulu.

So, his family those next in line, now used to the privileges of position that once had been Enbilulu's so, did not want him back and answered this question, "Where is Enbilulu?" With "Who is that? Never heard of him, oh yes, didn't he fall overboard from a war galley one day?"

So Enbilulu paid like we all do for being bad.

"I want to die," Enbilulu begged but it was not his time to pass over so the goaler let him live. Never mind, he was storing up treasures for when he would pass to his Insect heaven, *but beautiful humans were already there.*

Ch12 Book 2

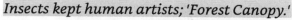

Insects kept human artists; 'Forest Canopy.'

In the six months of his loneliness,

Luke of Utna came across a burial place of his ancestors who had survived the crash of Phoenix in the Year 0000.

The last to die had committed suicide with the rust proof weapon still gripped in his right hand. He had stuck the six shooters in his mouth and pulled the trigger.

Luke knew they were humans for he had seen the dead often. Except this dead was different, dressed in a metallic silver shiny substance and he wore a helmet.

Now Luke was more fortunate than the youth of his kind, for Peter had taught him

to read, and Luke read......

NASA STATION 12

EARTH.

But that meant nothing to him apart it came from EARTH. The planet Peter said existed beyond the Time of Myth and Phoenix itself.

And Luke knew why the man had killed himself, and knew it was a man because the silver suit had no place for bosoms.

For along the cave were the chitinous remains of giant centipedes. And Luke saw their heads had great holes in them, like the one on top of the man's helmet.

Reasoning separates man from all else on his own Earth, and Queen Nina feared humans and Utna's people for this. They were not true slaves as programmed red ants and centipedes who obeyed and toiled till they died exhausted without the encouraging whip.

True robotic slaves.

And Luke reasoned that what the skeleton held was the weapon that had killed the insect dead. He also dug up the graves of sixteen others, found all chewed; dozens were children.

And Luke found more of the strange weapons the man held and went outside and pulled the trigger of a pistol.

Somewhere Nobles heard thunder and during the rest of the year Queen Nina heard bangs coming out of the wilderness.

And Nobles worried.

They found Nobles with holes in their heads until the user of the hole maker saw that the weapon made holes at which it pointed.

And those that escaped swore they heard a strange clicking roar with the thunder noise.

Nobles remembered Luke of Utna as black ant than human slave.

Then the user more confident no longer hid, just strode up to whole hunting parties seeking runaway slaves and used the thunder weapons.

They swore it was the same Luke on the faded wanted posters,
but these warriors were no match against Luke.

*

Luke sat on Utna's back looking across lands he had never seen. A great canopy of leaves and giant flowers stretched as far he could see. All assorted colors like a quilt covered in colored squares.

Somewhere there was Phoenix, and it was time to find it.

Behind him Queen Nina's vast procession crept along the depression where he had met his companions long ago, *seeking Phoenix too?*

And if any of these companions found him now, they would **not** find the same Luke.

Solitude had made him more withdrawn and Utna also.

Now both were born social animals, belonging to tribe, and pecking order. Now that social structure was vamoosed, and they relied on each other. They, bonded by the wilderness and comradeship; *human and ant.*

Luke knew what was coming behind him in the depression, had been watching for hours, been keeping ahead of them just, **(Insect musicians).**

Could hear the buzz of Queen Nina's insect musicians.

Knew they were coming for Phoenix, *reasoning.*

Sure, there was goodness somewhere inside Luke, but he had become **dark** by sneaking up to Nina's host and taking stragglers, scouts, even sleeping men and leaving them hanging high up on barbed vines for all to see, *very dead.*

He had killed in cold blood; they were enemy, were intruding upon his lands. Got them to talk first, told him Queen Nina was using the eye. And these prisoners thought this half naked slave, Luke, would free them then. He did after telling him his name.

"LUKE."

The eye Ulana had thrown in the swamp full of the Blueberry plant which killed Insect Nobles outright but not humans, they still died, just took a week of violent fluid Loss, why Nina had it, Ghosters again.

"Luke of Utna's lands," he told these happy Nobles, the rest he slipped his U.S. Marine bayonet he had found in the cave under their left bottom rib, till he found what he sought, their heart, then pushed harder.

Luke was at war.

His tanned body had raspberry barb scars put on it by Nobles. And each time he killed he apologized to whatever made his eyes shine. He was bloodletting and what

made his eyes shine knew and was this life planned? Insect Nobles were born with a sell by date also, a life planned also?

Now here lies the dark strain that had entered Luke's soul, when he saw the hope in those Insect eyes turn to fear with the realization that the knife when pushed up; poor Luke smiled as the light in the Insect eyes faded away. He liked to see Insects suffer, well he remembered Ulana like a dog examined, remembered vengefully.

"An abomination," he remembered the word well.

Black Ant lands? Everything he could see; the horizon was his boundary, and he was getting a name amongst travelling folk like Titus, and the locals, not evolved

Insect people but very distant primitive cousins.

"Luke of Utna, Luke of the Ants," and it reached the ears of Queen Nina and Howal; so feared trembling often.

"Find him and bring this Luke to me," Nina demanded her Nobles, and Luke always kept ahead of them; fast and smarter.

Always leaving something grisly for them and they feared this Luke of Utna of the Ants: so, the desertions amongst the Nobles seeking Phoenix grew high.

Anyway, one camp: Year 2005, Calendar 1, Day 300, sunset.

"I should have killed him when I had the chance," Howal over a half empty silver goblet of wine as Nina lounged on a silken couch in her flower tent. This journey had become a nightmare for both. Queen Nina had thought it a procession through minor backward tribes who would shower gifts at her feet, but this Luke of the ants.

Instead, they shouted, "Luke of The Ants."

To cheer, thought that Howal had promised, his kingdom would guard their flanks; they would meet with his army near where they believed Phoenix to be, share the knowledge; ha, he would get crumbs, Nina and her Nobles would make sure Insects always reigned supreme.

And Howal did not trust Nina who was showing signs of early pregnancy, for he knew they were of the same mold, selfish.

"Howal, he gives me bad dreams, Enalusdra says he might be god Enil come to deliverer his people, they who walk and look like him," Nina and both remembered what a crazy old witch had been saying sitting under an orange tree.

"Do not you know where he's from? Look at his eyes, he is the one, there is no escaping him. He's come to clean the land of abominations," the witch.

And Nina sent warriors to tie her against an orange tree and fire it. But she fled and they set fire to her green wings as she ran and flying, her wings sizzled so fell sixty feet to the ground.

And here the warriors beheaded her for she was a witch who was challenging the accepted stable way of believing things.

And there had been outrage for Nobles were unhappy with the times. These Insect folk had a brain and like Ziusudra kept to themselves for they feared Nina, but

still remarked how God Enil looked like a slave.

And scores were glad the old witch burned after her beheading so, her soul could not come back and harm them; and glad she suffered as they were suffering through fear of the unknown and fear of Luke of the Ants.

Nina must have offended God Enil somehow, that was what was wrong and as for Nina she thought by silencing the witch she had silenced the change in the wind.

So, Howal shivered as his tail twitched, his people had prophecies about a deliverer, Nobles also. And Howal looked out the open rose petal tent flap watching a slave boil water. What Nina just said enforced what he suspected, Enil was human not

Insect.

"Human flotsam," he sees in that slave Luke the friend he betrayed for selfishness.

And Nina stood watching; when Howal drank he became depressive he was unpredictable, usually taking his frustration out on slaves. Oh yes, she understood why he beat them, killed them; he was killing Luke.

So, Queen Nina smiled, she was glad she had not agreed to a power sharing deal with Howal' He was only a toy who to validate his position dreamed dreams that he shared her throne.

And he had learned the hard way never to hit her which he had done once, and been punished as hung from the beams in the main dining chamber with weights to his stumpy tail, for all to see and taunt him.

"Next time I open you," she hissed promisingly as she let a dagger slide across the edges of his belly.

(Scented strawberry water)

And Howal saw his bowel tumble out and believed.

"Witch," he had thought to himself.

But she got the last word, "And never let he hear you call me, 'That wrinkled elderly woman behind my back."

And Howal now leapt from the tent flaps and kicked a nameless slave the slaves breaking jaw. Also boiling water splashed on both.

Not content with this damage Howal picked up a burning branch from the fire and beat the man unconscious, but in fact the slave was dead for he had just recovered from a bout of malaria and was weak.

Not that Howal cared, for with each hit he hit his shame from his mind. Even the crunching bones spurned him and when he realized the man was dead, he dragged him onto the fire and left him. Behold behind his back Nina ordered warriors to remove the body as the air began to stink.

Scented strawberry water splashed about.

Like all Insects Nina favored this plant.

Then Howal returned, drew the petal tent flaps and with Nina enjoyed the night, finding excitement over the suffering of the burnt slave.

And Nina had made Howal agree to leave her his kingdom in return for the antidote to the worm in him that might kill him *upon a Nina whim.* She really did not need him anymore and the worm would stay in Howal for Nina, fed up with his drinking and when compared to Luke, saw him as a weak

creature.

Howal, she knew would do anything for her to stay alive. Even to go as far as to never play with the Vornal dog that went around on all fours meowing; and Nina knew how hard that must be for Howal.

You know, Nina just might not be insect for they kill for food or to lay eggs in prey; *Nina killed for fun.*

Now who else does that?

And Howal had never checked her ancestry, or he might have been more careful promising his kingdom to a black widow spider.

Queen Nina was Black Widow Spider.

*

And Luke found the first human slave Howal pegged for a centipede to chew and it was with a deliberate calm he decided to punish the Insect enemy.

"If you wish to ride with me through the camp of the master Nobles you may, but they will kill you. I go to harm them," Luke told Utna with sign language for the ant was not a slave.

In reply Utna knelt for Luke to mount. They were ant brothers.

Lo on Day 1, 2nd Calendar Year 2005 as recorded on the hieroglyphics in Shurrupuk, as Queen Nina ascended Red Mountain Luke rode amongst them coming unexpectedly out of midges and pink heather.

There was no warning for the Nobles, he threw Roman pilums and slashed with sword, then vanished; (Roman pilums bent on impact disabling shield arm, light and nasty)

Now King Howal personally led the pursuers and found themselves trapped in a ravine that dripped black oil. The stink of it told him death waited.

These were the lands of Luke of the Ants.

And Luke knew them as land belonging to Phoenix for the ground hummed were oil seeped out of the ground.

And Howal saw the orange flame burn its way down the ravine and turned his red ant mount without giving orders to retreat.

Although he escaped one thousand Nobles died for, they waited for his orders.

Great Insect Noble lines ended that day as father and son perished and the lamenting went on for weeks in the camp of Queen Nina and throughout the land.

And the dead lords returned to Shurrupuk to lie in state in the Cathedral of Enil for final blessings from priest Enalusdra before the souls went to Naja; and of course, they would, the Nobles had died trying to kill enemy, a slave called Luke **who, was for the Outer Darkness**

when he died   for, he was not of the Insect faith.

And Nobles blamed Howal, and Nina saw and was not pleased, and feared insurrection and her heart grew colder towards King Howal.

And Luke struck and struck so, Nobles ordered scouting, knowing they would not return and went singing their ancestral lineage death chants.

It was these daring raids of Luke that brought him to the tent of Queen Nina.

*

Now Luke had seen Ulana, and these lands were his lands, and he would free her.

And it happened thus: DAY 31, 2nd Calendar Year 2005, Night Camp, Nina dines outside her petal tent feeding Ulana scraps by making her jump like a dog and Luke saw. And Howal drank thinking of ways he could have Ulana without Nina's knowledge.

"We use her as bait," Howal slurped hiding his yellow pupils as he drunk so Nina could not see intent of lust. "And Luke comes for her?" And Howal poured more drink.

Now Queen Nina had a premonition Luke of Utna approached slothfully, sword in one hand as he peered through the bushes seeking the cat   like sounds of his woman.

"I personally will command the escort that captures him," and Nina saw he could not capture his own wind. And gladdened his pupils were yellow, his liver blown.

*

The night was bright, cloudless and Ulana knew her fate as dragged along on all fours to the place where Howal had decided Luke could see her.

A crumbling white termite nest upon a denuded hilltop and Howal watched Ulana his dog roped to a stake, hands, and ankles, and Howal drunk as always and sworn as long as Luke was alive, he would not sober up.

You see the drink allowed Howal to forget Luke.

So, it was a nervous Howal who ordered his men to make a loud noise to attract Luke.

It did not occur to the fool he might attract other predators.

And the night was hot which did not help Howal for to protect himself he had put on his gold armor and shielded himself with Nobles while red ants and centipedes flanked his position hidden in the brush.

Now Howal would have been better to put assassins out and not giant insects that were hard to camouflage themselves. *Huge insect bums stuck out of bushes.*

And each Noble Insect thought death was in the air because of their murderous intentions made their own shadows come alive and jump.

So, one Noble lashed with his sword and a bush baby fell; a shadow you see.

One cast a spear and pegged his companion to a brown cactus.

For every sound and shadow was Luke of Utna.

Another kicked out a red ant from small palm, for its weight made the plant sway eerie shadows.

Now the plan had been for a red ant to chew Ulana's feet so she would scream.

And that the escort wait concealed below for Luke and Utna, but Howal's plan seeded by drunken lust towards Ulana.

Now whose fault was this? Ulana was attractive to lure the best husband and if Howal could not control lust, because of drink, then he should change his

ways; *fat chance.*

"Go and search the area first, leave one to guard me," he ordered and none contradicted, he was Queen Nina's toy and with sour looks left.

All knew Howal kept a drunk so, Nina could have his lands for Nobles to make plantations and his people added to the slave pool. All knew Nina was playing with her food before she ate, *for she was black widow.*

Now Howal alone with his sentry suddenly lashed the Noble in the chest and opened it so much blood rushed out and death settled upon this unfortunate. *Why was murder done?*

Now Ulana was not surprised for Howal was so predictable because he was an evil lion man.

Now he had killed the man to be rid of witness for Nina had forbidden him touch Ulana. *Here the answer to the murder.*

Why Howal had planned all this to be alone with Ulana.

Why all sent away but for one sentry.

Why Howal would blame Luke for the killing.

"Tonight, I will have you both, why in front of you I will hamstring Luke, so he has to crawl. But you I will mate," he drooled dropping his leather kilt and sword belt.

Why Ulana thought he looked ridiculous standing there with only his gold chest armor and gold helmet on.

So, Ulana laughed for it was as good as kicking him.

And Luke heard the laugh and watched his enemy pass below him.

Below him?

Now never on World had the large ants climbed trees. It was unknown but Luke was a human who reasoned.

And Utna climbed down from their hiding place and did not break one branch for ants know how to distribute their weight.

And Luke mounted.

"What if your men come back?" Ulana asked playing for time.

Howal grunted something like Luke will get blamed.

Then he tried to couple so Ulana screamed.

The other Nobles heard and thought the red ant was chewing away upon Ulana's feet and were glad it was not their feet and hoped Luke would not blame them but

Howal for it was his idea.

And the red ant was dining for Howal had given it the murdered Noble sentry to go off with as dinner. And he was dead and was not screaming, only Ulana.

Why Howal was alone as he had planned from the start when the idea of a trap using Ulana had first entered his brain.

Alone he thought so in confidence never saw the massive shadow loom over him until Luke jumped onto his body and threw him so he rolled down the termite nest

head spinning from drink, so he saw the white stars above zoom across his eyes and he was sick.

In fact, almost choked to death on his sickness.

But it was not Luke who found him first but Howal's men. And they noted his condition under their lightened torches for Ulana's screaming had made them think

Luke was coming and their signal to return; for if they were to die, Howal was to be killed as well.

"Won't be Nina's man for long when she hears of this," one said poking Howal places with a sword.

"Look at this?" Another seeing the red eating the murdered man. "What evil has Howal done?" They asked happily amongst themselves for all disliked Howal the

drunkard.

And now Utna crashed through them with Luke and Ulana on his back.

And the night filled with bangs and flame. And the Nobles fled and Luke followed thinking Howal was amongst them.

And *that is how Queen Nina's premonition came true.*

Luke rode Utna up to the royal enclosure but could not enter for Nina had ordered pits and stakes about her tent because of her dream.

And Luke did not have to instruct Ulana how to use the earth weapons for Vornal was a modern world.

And Ulana shot brave Nobles running to them as Luke fired at Queen Nina who hid behind her wax throne, always transported with her on long trips, so, chunks of wax disintegrated.

And Nina was afraid for she was only a bully.

And her warriors were brave for programmed insects had to protect the queen so, died.

Even if she was unworthy by human and Vornal standards, she had put her own species cause first; humans last, they were the aliens.

"Howal I will kill you," Luke shouted as he rode away into the night.

So, seventy slain Nobles lay about Queen Nina who with calm returning grew furious and blamed Howal for this mess.

Ulana her trump card was gone.

Better Howal gone too as he was a drunk.

*

Queen Nina sat on her cushioned throne very still and silent.

(Cicada
music)

At her feet was the snoring Howal, still half naked as the escort had found him.

Not a Noble moved, so the cicada music of the forest seemed ten times louder.

See Nina was furious, dark recessive genes awoke in her, black widow genes.

Urges to eat her useless toy thing at her feet.

Alive not sleeping.

She was very much an insect even though she had the genes of humanity in her.

It was one thing for her to have lovers for the diversity of the gene pool and thus, ensuring healthy babies with all colors of hair and skin, slim and large, all expressions of the gene pool that is a manifestation of the law that makes us. Luke understood this and so did the insect but Howal was a lion creature and toy of Nina, and not permitted by her to have a toy of his own.

Silly bad stupid drunken Howal.

Howal had sired an heir for his kingdom as sixty pink Nina eggs lay in a lavender nursery in Shurrupuk City, attended by Black worker ants watched by reds, *just in case you know!*

Howal's kingdom was now hers.

It was the insect way for Howal not to mate elsewhere and pick up disease and disease was wiping out their species. It was also the insect way to be highly possessive of their mates as they were the main course after lying together.

There was much primeval in Nina.

And the point was she had forbidden Howal to touch Ulana and well?

That was the bottom line and the summary of all the above.

Goodbye King Howal.

"Make him a harem attendant and then send him away into the wilderness," and they slapped him awake so he moaned for more drink, and they poured it into his mouth so, he aged, then did what Nina commanded and fed his parts to a red ant and Nina herself cut of his stumpy tail to have it mounted next to a red lion's head in a banqueting hall.

As for Howal they dumped him in the bush while his wine jug gurgled emptying its contents wetting the sleeping Howal.

Now the insect in Nina came forward for she sent a coded message to her Noble guard in Howal's city to slay Howal's own garrison there.

So, when the sun came up the next morning and decent men and women thanked whatever they believed in for the glorious day and the weather, news spread that the city gates were open, and a dust cloud was approaching.

The gates were open for the men of Howal murdered by Nina's Noble guard, hadn't they?

Never mind a rumor spread no doubt by Nobles that the city guard had gone out to meet the approaching King Howal and the fabled Queen Nina.

So, lion folk brought out their children to watch the colored flags and reds coming towards them, diner.

So greeted their dinner guests who fell upon their food ravenously.

Such Queen Nina's respect for her new subjects who must learn their place. Gone mirthful sounds from streets as children played, gone vendors selling fruits to matrons, now replaced by quietness as one looked at another wondering who would vanish this night and be no more.

Then Enalusdra's priests came in their yellow, green, and navy-blue robes and erected statues of God Enil, and pens in the marketplace and the city folk watched

their own put there next to swine, fish, and vegetables up for sale.

Such was King Howal's legacy to his people.

He was a pig swill scum bag, a drunken bovine at that," as he had called Luke and Titus.

*

Now Howal awoke surrounded by wilderness, he needed his bladder emptied and that is when he found he was no more lion man.

So, the jungle sounded to his scream.

Luke and Ulana on Utna heard and looked down upon the jungle canopy from Red Mountain. Once again torn from going on or finding the man who had caused him so much anguish.

In his heart he feared Howal had pegged out Titus to attract him, as a trap.

And the screaming went on as Howal adjusted to his new life.

So, Luke looked at Ulana who knew he must go back, it might be Titus, Phoenix and the freedom of his people must wait again, *just a little wait.*

*

Now Titus seeing from a distance that Ulana was free determined to escape and follow her.

"I will not risk Luke's blood for something I can do myself," he aloud and other slave's hearing perceived what he planned for he was in the common slave pens.

"We will go with him," the freed said preferring death in the wilderness for the chance of a little freedom than be the main course on a centipedes' plate.

"No, we will warn the Nobles who will punish those left behind," the argument went and Titus hearing then moved away fearing discovery for since the galley went down his enemies had thought him drowned. So, as a nameless slave had accompanied Queen Nina to Red Mountain digging latrines, emptying chamber pots, and shoveling red ant and centipede dung out of camp; or dysentery would spread, cholera too.

"Do you wish to be free?" And Titus looked up into the unsmiling face of Priest Enalusdra for the three lucks who spin fate had cast him bad dice in that his enemies

had been walking by the pens and overheard; *they used loaded dice too.*

So, Priest Enalusdra bent and pinched Titus's cheeks so his eyes opened.

"How did he escape our notice?" Hupamuk quizzed.

"It does not matter we have him now," Enalusdra and stood back allowing guards too pull

Titus to his feet and added sarcastically, "Welcome home Titus."

"He was planning to escape one slave shouted.

"Yes, that's right," another and six slaves crowded the Lords.

It was dark even by the light of the camp, so they did not see the disgust in the Lord's faces, for dung was groveling hoping for rewards at their feet.

So, Lord Hupamuk spoke with his hands and a face hovered above them.

"Next time tell us sooner," he said walking away.

The face belonged to a centipede and the six men screamed scrambling away but did not get far for they were chained ankle to ankle.

And the centipede rolled upon them, its mandibles injecting venom into each, so he lay paralyzed under the creature.

And the other slaves in the pens crawled away huddled in fear wishing the chain from them to the six was longer.

Then the centipede rolled its first morsel up along its legs to its mouth.

Then began eating away from the right up.

There was no scream as the man's vocal cords poisoned so, silent.

Mercifully, he was dead before the giant insect began to rip his torso apart.

The next man eaten first on his feet, hands or headfirst, no one knew.

But fifty yards further on Titus on a wooden table, pouched in the midriff for struggling and as he fought for air, manacled.

"A fine specimen still," Priest Enalusdra probing his body for internal growths.

Lord Hupamuk watched; he was interested in results not how you got them. So Enalusdra strapped a vine about Titus's left wrist and as blood vessels swelled,

he inserted a tap into an artery.

The tap was on, a glass vial filled and Enalusdra took a swab to look under a microscope, he was looking for the missing link that would restore vitality to Nobles.

Think there is something here," he said standing back for Hupamuk to look, "I was right the first time."

Amongst the red cells Hupamuk saw strands of protein highly magnified. It meant nothing to him; his knowledge was power and death.

"I will take him back to the temple," Priest Enalusdra. See, Enalusdra had found time to work on tissue samples inside the freezer and seen Titus had giant white cells that ate viruses and found them proteins and sheeted in wax so harmful viruses could not eat the white cells.

The virus was akin to A.I.D.S virus but in reverse and Enalusdra had bit his lips, torn his hair and clothes, and put ash on him for he heard Titus had drowned at sea……. until now.

"So be it," Hupamuk grunted and left, his job was not with the priest in unhealthy labs but with Queen Nina and Phoenix. He also knew his queen needed comforted,

there was a vacancy for a king these days.

A lion man sent packing.

Anyway, Enalusdra drained the cup, it was refreshing.

And almost drank Titus dry.

So Enalusdra lay down to sleep off his full stomach as blue transport flies carted him in his cushioned litter and Titus in his filthy reed cage to the temple.

Abandon all hope you that enter this temple.

CH13 Howal

Ulana accepted Luke's hands to help her onto the back of Utna. Deep down she did not, felt dirty for she had betrayed him in the past; guilt is a powerful weapon.

Even though she could see it in his eyes that he still wanted her.

Even after Howal?

So, when they sat, she asked **"Why?"**   *(It was love woman.)*

At first, he did not know why she had asked. **Why to what?** But he thought and answered that he knew no other woman apart from her.

Utna moved on.

A cobra in the grass rose.

Small rodents scampered.

The cobra struck, broke its fangs on Utna's chitinous skin and then cut in two as Utna walked over it.

It had been an inexperienced snake that by lessons should have retreated and wait for new fangs to pop down to replace the broken ones.

So, rodents ate the serpent that would have eaten them.

What goes around comes around, even in the wilderness not just human society And Luke felt Ulana's tears running down his back leaving black stains on his tanned flesh, his dirt.

                                          (karma)

So squeezed her hands and grunted.

Ulana smiled, Luke could forgive anyone, and Luke of Utna was good, besides a few tears a female knew always did the trick.

Behind Luke flies found the serpent remains, thousands that would feed voles, rats and moles.

Nature always knew insects fed mammals and not the other way around. It was trying hard itself to correct the situation on White World.

For about us exist as Luke had seen with his shinning eyes, colored energy bands.

called sprites and are intelligent.

But you need to ask Luke about that.

So, it was then that Howal came stumbling upon them screaming.

Now Luke's first reaction was to dismount, pushing Ulana off to do so, so that she fell clumsily as he drew his six shooters.

Then saw Howal was now a harem attendant.

"Was this a trap again?"

"You caused this," Howal spat as he grabbed for Luke; but Luke easily threw the crazy man aside while watching the bush for Nobles.

Now Howal being of lion genes leapt back but caught mid-air by Utna and held there. Held in one piece till Luke had checked that it was not a trap and the mandible of the ant made circular wounds for Howal squirmed and jerked to try and be free.

And as Luke approached, he saw Ulana stand beside Howal, her hand rose and fell a flash of steel and then she threw Howal into the bush.

So, Luke thought about justice, there had been here justice from a woman's point of view for only a woman and a man raped can understand her loathing for Howal.

And the laws of rape, made by men.

"Treat others as you treat yourself," these lines walked into Luke's right temple.

So, Luke remembered his days after the Dance of the Insects and what Nina and the Lords had done to him. Insect religion said it was an impossibility man could rape man; Luke knew what made his eyes shine knew; The Insect Noble law makers were an abomination.

Justice was an individual affair.

And knew no Noble could judge Ulana for he had never been in such a position as her to even pretend having the 'Wisdom of Solomon' as Elder Peter had

often said.

So, Luke hugged Ulana, a straightforward way of giving comfort and strength. And his eyes shone for he had love flowing through his veins.

And Ulana felt energy come out of him, so her ears buzzed.

"Howal, do you hear me?" He asked.

Now Howal's eyes were dimming but managed to focus slowly on Luke, and seeing him who gave him guilt growled.

"Don't hate me Howal, I don't hate you now," which was true, Howal was now past thing, only fit for pity.

Now this made Howal's spirit worse, Luke had forgiven him, he did not want to forgive Luke, he wanted to hate, and it was easier. Forgiveness comes from what makes eyes shine.

Hate comes from the hearts of men, women and Howal.

Now Luke lay his onetime friend down and built a fire and made red hot his sword to tend Howal's wounds.

"He is not worth saving," Ulana speaking from bitterness.

So, she sat near the bush and Utna stood over her as an umbrella making sure no harm befell her.

Done then, Luke cauterized Howal's wounds. *And every living night creature ran back to burrow when screams broke the night.*

"You had to do what you did to rid yourself of Howal's touch," Luke said to her coming over after ten minutes.

And Luke listened learning from Ulana's explosion of words about only a woman can know what a woman feels after someone like Howal has touched.

But Luke knew, it was the same after Hupamuk had seen him after the Dance of the Insects.

And Luke fought the rising feelings to kill Howal to release his own hurt. He was holding his hot sword, Howal's throat exposed; it would be too quick, he would heat the sword up red again and be slow; Howal was a lion, well Nobles skinned lions and used their skins as robes and carpets.

And Luke's eyes dimed with such thoughts as his inner love faded.

And like a bath emptying Luke knew he was being silly so threw the sword down, Howal was past thing; love held the key to the future; Luke liked his eyes to shine.

*

"Are you sure Nina spoke of a temple?" Luke asked a woman of fly heritage.

"I am sure Luke, some place east of Red Mountain. How far I do not know, but why must we help him?" She asked meaning Howal who lay on a litter pulled by Utna

with flies as friends.

"He was once my companion who got led astray," he replied.

To kill Howal as he is now would be murder.

To kill Nobles was not murder but WAR; they enslaved you and did unbelievably bad things to people under the umbrella of their religion.

Luke was killing Nobles to stop this badness in the land. And Luke had fallen into a trap, he was categorizing killing, he was human; but he did not see it as such, he was ant, ants killed enemies and Nobles were enemies.

And Ulana understood without Luke explaining and that was one reason he liked her, she could read his mind, so he did not have to waste time babbling.

Time was precious, it was meant for people to be creative and diversify; color ran about them like magic as Maxwell Clerk of Edinburgh found for, are we surrounded by gardens of paint. *But Luke did not know that.*

(White Sky)

(Played flutes and small harps)

See Ulana had a computer in her brain that did a good psycho analysis. And soon fruit bats began to circle overhead, so many there must have been

millions.

Luke could see no orchards to support them, and he was wrong, for ten minutes later they came across fruit trees tended by Noble women.

And saw they were as fair as Queen Nina. And as he passed saw them pick up shields and bronze spears and escort him while others played flutes and small harps, to

where? He just followed the blue dust road across their blue grass.

These were not of the Nobles he got knowing and killing. These Noble women were different as for one, they were doing slave jobs and warrior's work.

And Luke was not afraid, his muscles were bulging these days, veins rising and about his body guns hung, the weapons of his ancestors.

(Scent of flowers)

And the maidens saw and realized who rode the black ant. Luke and the ant Utna and gripped their spears hard, fearful.

And the scent of flowers in bloom became heavy, and passing a lake the nymphs there came out, priestesses soaking wet, almost naked, their chitinous skin glowing in the warm sun.

Then a clearing so Luke saw a white house in front with a trail of grey smoke behind it, and one beautiful Black woman descended its steps to greet and

question.

"I am Halwina," and Ulana thought of the old witch. How off-worlders came through that black hole she wondered?

And did not know Nobles like Enalusdra had managed to duplicate off-worlder life for Halwina looked human except for when she spoke a red insect tongue streaked out from her human mouth.

And Luke nodded and dismounted walking back to the litter, here waited till Halwina stood beside him.

"This is The Temple of the Woman, Inanna, no man can enter whole," she said as priestesses in soft white smocks fell on their knees beside her holding gold bowls.

Luke noticed coin there.

Ulana spared him the indignity for he carried no coin.

It was a small diamond she had stolen and Halwina was so impressed she ordered all the priestesses to line up.

Which made Ulana protective, so she coiled about Luke possessing him?

"Why do you come here if not to seek a priestesses and comfort?" Halwina smiled back at Ulana.

Now Luke was embarrassed as hundreds of priestesses greeted him, **(Oh, my holy awesomeness)**.

If he wanted one, how could he choose? *And Ulana read his mind* and coiled tighter so, he understood her annoyance. Beside an Insect Noble was insect and could behave as an insect and have queens for the survival rate of insect young was not good, numbers thus ensured their dominance on white World.

"To give you him," Luke grunted and threw back the leaf blanket so Halwina's smile faded and said, "We will do all we can for him," as she pushed aside maggots

that had kept Howal's flesh clean from gangrene; so, priestesses carried Howal into the temple.

But still priestesses lingered about Luke hopeful of genes for Luke was healthy.

"We have done what we can for him, our slate is wiped clean, we are now leaving Luke, leaving," Lana mounting Utna, and Utna looked at Luke, "WELL," the look!

"Another time Luke of Utna," Halwina and Luke mounted and looked down into inviting eyes, "Another time," he replied and was the wrong reply *for Ulana knew there would never be another time.*

And as they rode by the back of the white classical house, they noticed grey smoke again, from a tall chimney.

"An incinerator," Ulana questioned.

Poor Luke tried hard to remember what Elder Peter said an incinerator was?

(Blew reed trumpets)

Something akin to a crematorium where Nobles threw the salve dead into in Shurrupuk City.

"What evil is this temple?" Luke asked.

"Venus's hell for lion men like Howal," Ulana and looked away. Luke grunted, Elder Peter had explained Romans had a temple called Venus which was a holy brothel, a temple of love.

So, Luke grunted and clicked for Howal.

And as they left another party arrived; Priest Enalusdra with a mighty escort of red ants and Titus, for with Luke about these days one needed a large escort.

And Noble warriors blew reed trumpets, and the priestesses came out again with giant rose petals to shade their aristocratic guests.

Lo the Temple of the Woman, Inanna served another propose than donating life to the priestesses.

The Temple of the Woman served as a giant gene bank ensuring the survival of the Insect Noble race.

Nobles, humans, Vornals and races of white World Luke knew naught of all left frozen samples in an iced cavern below, and the ice gave the house its whiteness, its

frosty glow like a white house first seen in a clear winter's day.

Others like Titus would donate bone marrow to find a reason the Noble race had a recessive gene that caused a high infant mortality rate. And at the far end of the temple was quicksand, a graveyard for specimens no longer required.

The crematorium was for the dissected bits mingled with household rubbish: the incinerator was really that, an incinerator for rubbish; humans and other folk.

After three weeks search.

"I cannot see Titus anywhere," Luke complained.

Ulana knew that they would be leaving Queen Nina and her travelling circus now, Maybe speed ahead and get to Phoenix before her.

She also knew Luke would not speak. It was highly annoying to a pretty thing like her since she wanted his whole attention, but she knew no matter how hard she tried he never gave it.

So, would try other ways of a female.

In the meantime, she left him to his thoughts on Titus his friend.

*

Now Howal injected with Insect genes and this his sixteenth shot and stood looking into a mirror saying, "King Howal or should I say Queen," as Halwina had not been too careful about the donor; all knew about the drunk Howal.

Lion man better say insect man as his skin had become the Noble soft chitin. No one knew who the gene donor was or cared, what traits of meanness added to Howal's own; the donor was anonymous, a holy monk?

But he kept his flowing red mane that drooped past his shoulders. In fact, not a single chin hair seen and enough said about his new femaleness as you have

the general idea what they did to King Howal.

And he looked down and was horrified, nuts and bolts holding his new shapely figure in place for the few months ahead, so when all the plastic corset and wiring removed, Howal would hate Luke forever in this life and in future lives.

"You and that dog Ulana did this to me," for his hatred was now a neurotic obsession.

And Howal asked aloud, "Will my people accept me as their new queen?"

Because he did not know he did not have a city to be king off.

Ch14 Friend Titus

Ulana wondered what power held the planets in resolution could give

eternal life too to all, thief, prostitute, and saint for she saw the creator as life,

diversity, propagation, and spirit. The books were for those that could not link

with the oneness. But her soul danced from love with the Celtic Gaels Creator.'

Ulana often looked at the sky during daylight and night, seeking a searching ship from her people's world.

And saw none.

Then rest her head against Luke's back, smelling his hair. It smelled dirty, of ant, soil, with traces of strange scents rubbed there as they passed under flowering plants and trees.

Luke cared not how he smelled; *that was about to change?*

He was Luke of the Ants first.

And Ulana had enough sense that to try and change him into something different might change what see liked about him.

The word is change; women always want to change an ant man.

How she dreamed of Luke escorting her to Vornalian balls, clean and dressed properly. And knew she could not do this to him for he would have to leave Utna and

they were inseparable. *She could not put him into a zoo.*

No Luke was part of White World, and she would have to stay here if she wanted a part in his life.

(Three crimson moons)

Then a bright yellow butterfly flew past, and she tried to catch but failed. Not all insects on World were evil, only Nobles.

"Why are you happy?" Luke would ask hearing her giggle and she would not reply, instead grip him tightly and Luke would grunt, face flush, loins stir and want this green eyed girl but did not know how to go about it.

To be like Nobles and help yourself was wrong he believed. His own folk he remembered arranged weddings for healthy young or the young like Jack were too

promiscuous so there were always children running about.

And where encouraged to be like this for the Nobles liked succulent children marinated in honey. Weddings stank of civilization and religions and resulted in a

human culture so, frowned upon by Nobles; let the humans remain like domestic beasts.

Now it happened thus, the wily female made her move for she was bathing and emerged from a lily pool dripping wet in front of Luke.

He was cooking a grilled monitor lizard with tubers, lemons, and melons as desert. Let us say he tried to avert his eyes, but the feline seemed to be there in front of him every time he peeked.

And she knew and wanted it this way, so he could not escape.

She had him already, but he did not know that, see he had put out flowers for her trying to be nice to cheer her up about her missing Planet Vornal. Where was her

silver armor? Gone and now as Luke, dressed as if unable to afford clothes.

The boy had a heart and right now Ulana had it hooked.

And he was a fish on a hook.

"Don't look away," she and he looked and that was that.

So, it was then the rays of the three crimson moons danced about them and Luke swallowed hard as he was a man of the ants not the bedroom.

He was a cheese maker's son and ant Utna his friend always beside him, but the ant was not there, someone had been stuffing its mouth full of sweet honeycombs as a bribe to **clear off.**

As ant it knew queens provide new workers so understood; pity a certain idiot

did not!

They danced in the golden moon beams because the goddess of love Venus

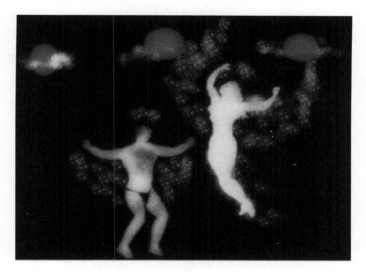

Now a month passed, and Luke now always slept with Ulana. The sun and moon had had been their parents to give them away, the wind the priest, the wilderness the reception banquet and the animal life the guests.

And still Luke said truly little except, "Now I am your ant and you my wife," then Grunt and click. Let us hope Ulana would not get bored with her new life, but she was much like him, a loner, deciding on the way of a nice female space warrior than a good little wife and children.

But things were now different; they were both escaped slaves with no one apart from themselves and Utna in a fairy tale world full of flowers and heady perfumes.

And yet they spoke through the heart when they showed each other a bird's nest, a new bright flower or stood in the warm breeze hand in hand with Utna towering above them enjoying world' for once And now they were about to meet evil that would end their happiness in the wilderness.

"Did you hear that?" Ulana, knowing he had.

The breeze was behind carrying the sound of breaking branches, the songs of disturbed birds, growling animals and the unmistakable click of chitinous body parts rubbing against each other.

Luke allowed Utna to about-face.

"Phoenix is behind us," and Ulana understood. Whatever was coming up the valley would draw them away from Phoenix and knowledge that would liberate Titus

and others from Noble ownership.

Then saw a man running through the clearings and both knew he was an escaped slave, only running people were.

And she knew Luke would help. So primed her weapons for she would not interfere for it was his way to help other slaves; they had both been slaves.

And Utna began to move down the valley towards the man. Why Ulana pressed a hand against Luke's cheek; hers was soft and warm and different from his rough hands.

Then saw Nobles riding red ants in a clearing with three centipedes scenting the slave and it occurred to Luke he had never said anything about love to Ulana.

Suddenly it became all important, never had it occurred to him he might die; it was an accepted risk, only Utna had been his companion and the ant knew all about living and dying on World.

Death was part of the insect cycle of life.

The parents of Luke and Ulana was

the invisible oneness.

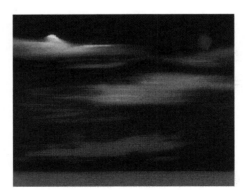

Turning he placed a hand on her lips and smiled, "My wife," and that is how he said he loved her.

She kissed his hand satisfied that made her more resolute to defend her man with her life. If he fell, she would fight above him till she died.

And Utna knew it would do the same, they were companions.

See Utna the black ant had feelings. Like a huge dog it loved them both; but Luke had forgotten he had learned his silence from ants, yet Utna showed affection by cleaning Luke.

Did not the ant get excited when it found nectar? Did not Utna know the joy when cool water slid down its dry parched throat?

The ant could feel higher feelings of pain and death too! A speck of nerve tissue, an almond sized brain, was all animations of spirit like a dying fly.

So silent Utna was content to carry its human cargo and six hundred yards down the valley the breaking of branches and yelling became much louder.

"Dung heads," they heard the slave shout.

So, Ulana slipped off Utna's rump and loaded her shotgun and flanked right.

WAR was coming.

And Luke drew his six shooters.

Then the slave broke into view, eyes rolling manically, mouth full of spittle, almost naked, cut, and dirty. If the image of God had not been on Titus's face, Luke would not know this slave as friend, in other words Luke was looking at the eyes that were alive with Titus's spirit. Not the horrid laboratory tubes that hung from Titus; worse, the belly of Titus was swollen like a woman who carried twins.

It could not be? Titus was man, just his bowels swollen from the probes of Enalusdra and the mercury poisoning.

What evil did Priest Enalusdra practice in the name of his religion?

Nuts, bolts, bandages, and stitches everywhere.

All this Luke noticed in a second and anger rose in him for those that did this to Titus' his friend.

And above him the hum of a dragonfly and Luke pointed his guns up; saw the giant insect and two Nobles with spears looking down.

Luke really showed the Insects he had Earth weapons for he gave them lead. And Ulana the star traveler knew warfare for she shot the centipede, so hundreds of insect lenses flew about.

So, the Lords Hupamuk and Enalusdra froze with fear ahead of the pack on their red ants. And witnessed a centipede fleeing for life for it collided with their reds so they fell heavily to the ground.

Everywhere these Lords on the blue grass could hear the earth weapons speak and Noble's shout in pain.

Now Hupamuk did what anyone else would do, crawl away and unlike anyone else managed to disturb a puff adder.

To his right Enalusdra had sat up and was coming towards Luke.

Enalusdra's eyes were bulging with something.

Now Hupamuk reached for a stick lying beside him.

The adder coiled ready to strike with horrid long fangs that made it so deadly.

Now the first Enalusdra knew he was about to die was when the snake landed on his shoulders, saw it fall between his legs, saw it turn, saw his own legs getting up,

trying to jump out of the way

And the pain as the snake bit.

Ach, silly Lord Hupamuk's aim had been out, too quick a throw; never thrown a puff adder trying to bite as you tossed it.

Well Luke shot the snake then Enalusdra's bit ankle.

Luke wanted the priest alive for darkness had entered his heart.

So, Enalusdra fell back moaning and Hupamuk hid behind giant sun flowers trying ridiculously hard not to breathe.

Which is impossible?

But did manage to keep very still as he repeatedly thanked God Enil for the sunflower hiding him.

Should have thanked Enil for the confusion of withdrawal as that is what made Luke stop looking thinking Hupamuk gone.

And Luke went back and used the priest's belt to tunicate the ankle, putting the remains of the foot in a pouch as he knew Nobles had the knowledge to grow it again from stem cells there; insects, famed for regeneratingweren't they?

And Luke's dark thoughts of private revenge had turned white for he now wanted the priest alive to help Titus. As for the snake, it was gone back to the light that made Luke's eyes shine. And you know something; Priest Enalusdra was one lucky insect.

Besides Titus could kill him later.

Vengeance belonged to the harmed, it was a personal thing; it was up to Titus to forgive and Enalusdra to ask forgiveness if both wanted to progress and allow them

eyes to shine.

How it happened who knows but Luke knew he was about to die for the prick of steel was in his back.

A thrust that did not come, instead the Noble who had sneaked out of sun flowers had lost his grin, was watching Utna coming towards him.

And this Noble was a wasp body builder, so that his black and green beetle colored skin bulged threatening to break the leather bronze studded straps that laced his body from which hung as assortment of serrated weapons. And his black eyes peered underneath strands of black hair that had come loose from his disturbed leather pot helmet. And Lord Hupamuk had decided since fate had changed was now boldly walking out of his hiding place.

Now Utna was charging the wasp insect as it saw the Noble as a wasp about to lay eggs in Luke.

Utna was an insect.

And any hope Hupamuk had that fate had changed evaporated as Utna now had taken hold of the wasp Noble.

And Hupamuk knew he had been too hasty coming out.

And Luke shot the wasp Noble, so the man fell moaning.

With Utna standing swaying over the dead insect Luke roared his clicking insect sound.

This was opportunity for Hupamuk to flee quickly and he did.

Above Hupamuk the wasp man sailed to land amongst branches that impaled, for Luke with his immense strength had picked him up and thrown him hence.

Hupamuk was amazed and ran faster panting for breath.

And Utna went over to the wasp man and bit him in two so that his bits hung out, and being insect clung to life like a squashed fly.

So, Ulana filled with pity went over to the wasp man and shot him dead. The face was not human or Vornal but a bug's, she was showing mercy to a squashed cockroach for that is how she saw Nobles.

And Hupamuk ran so his gold silken spider robes ripped on thistles that took ounces of flesh from him. Even his diamond torc ripped on a branch and scattered riches but his pursuer was already rich for his eyes shone often so needed not these riches belonging to society.

And lucky for Hupamuk he could run fast for he entered an insect fortification. Lo and behold the milk of black ants was in Luke and screaming fell upon the nearest Noble defender, shooting the man dead, then shot more, reloaded, and picked up the slain and threw them at the remaining Nobles to paralyses them with

fear.

And reds came.

Three against Utna and one for Luke; so Utna was sorely pressed; but Luke took from his red attacker an antenna and a leg and with the leg used it as a club and the

antennae as a whip.

Then thunder filled the air as Ulana came upon the scene and shot them except the red attacker of Luke that fled into the bush and picking up a trail followed it to the safety of a red ant nest.

The weapons of Phoenix had arrived.

And Luke using his black ant milk picked up a log and threw it at a centipede hovering over Hupamuk, so its head cracked, and ooze fell upon Hupamuk, who realizing all lost fled to Nina's camp.

This time Luke did not follow for the Nobles here outnumbered him in droves,

suicide was wrong.

And Hupamuk should have believed in 'what goes around comes around,' for Queen Nina seeing him terrified ordered a Whip Master to flay the truth out of him; for she refused to believe the end of Noble supremacy in warfare by Luke of the Ants.

She wanted to punish someone, Hupamuk would do.

And he moaned louder than the slaves he whipped in the past when the whip touched his chitinous skin.

And the man who held the whip had one eye for he had been on a war galley, and with a smirk whipped the loathsome Noble Lord at his queen's feet, for he was not alone in seeing Hupamuk as the source of Insect culture downfall.

And saw in Luke the destruction of the Insect way, dominance over all World life and knew that they must make peace with Luke and humans before they were

destroyed and enslaved themselves. In Luke they saw one who could make that peace.

For because of Luke of Utna they feared all salves had an awakening gene making them as strong as ants.

And that is why Nina had Lord Hupamuk whipped till he lied saying a host of escaped slaves had defeated them.

"Take him to my petal tent," Nina and done.

"Who else witnessed this?" She asked and learned of the names of the six Nobles who fled.

Then she sought them to silence.

Cowards and liars," she spat at them lined up and as their arms bent snapping behind their tussled backs, she had their screaming tongues cut out so that they could not tell their lies as they died and died, they did as Nina took a jeweled dagger and turned it in their chests till, she took their hearts from them.

"Bury them not," she and the cowards exposed for the small ants and beetles to eat, flies to lay eggs.

And by installing fear into her army, she installed hate for herself.

And Nina noticed a centipede telling its kind about Luke, so she had the centipedes driven into pens and here embers thrown in, so their chitinous skin peeled and melted away.

And all the remaining reds, dragonflies, centipedes, and beetles looked upon their Noble *masters with hate.*

But not all died, a red ant with an antennae and leg missing escaped to a nearby nest and told the truth.

For Lord Hupamuk had forgotten him thinking him dead.

See, Queen Nina believed in giving warnings.

And the way a woman gave them was a personal thing, especially of black widow genes.

The Insect body builder was ready to fight.

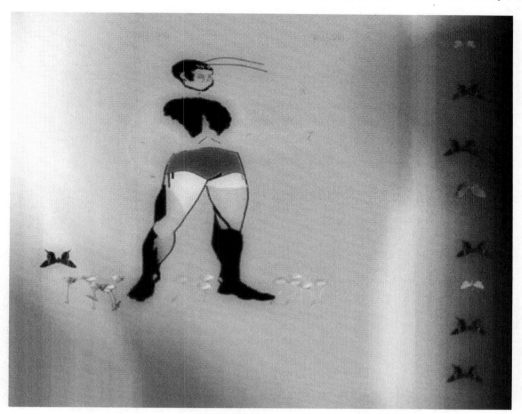

Ch 15 Civilization

(Crimson moons)

And Priest Enalusdra was afraid because he had told Luke he could do nothing for Titus, unless brought to The Temple of Women, hoping here to escape for the temple an insect stronghold was nearby.

And was wrong for Luke decided Titus could slay the priest when he was able. So, travelled with Titus who chirped insanely and then miscarried, and it was a maggot.

What had Priest Enalusdra been doing? He, in his desperation to improve the Insect Noble line tried to make Titus asexual, neither man nor woman as in the beginning of Time, Myth Time, then female only and male last. Why, to combat the low fertility rate amongst his species and in the hope the genes of Titus would bring health into the inset gene pool.

And all directed their disgust towards Enalusdra and feared what other horrid

doings had he done to Titus?

Now Luke of Utna did one thing, evil or just for he made the priest pull the litter Titus was on. And stuck a thorn branch in the litter so, it dangled like a whip on

Enalusdra's head and shoulders.

"As you treated us," Luke meant slaves, **"so I treat you beast of burden, pull,"** and Enalusdra pulled and not allowed privacy even to empty his bladder of water or

bowels of dung, for he was a beast of burden and an insect abomination.

The idea of forgiveness was on one of the crimson moons!

"Does not the dragonfly dung the air while it flies? The black ant wet grass as it builds new nest walls. And Insects do not allow quarry slaves latrines who fall in their dung, exhausted drowning for they are salves.

So, the yellow brick walls of Shurrupuk City became tombs for fallen slaves," meaning they were encased where they had fallen so as not to slow down production, just slaves anyway.

And Ulana rebuked Luke no more but gave Enalusdra water and food for she pitied Him, though she remembered the horrors the Nobles did her people, especially Enalusdra and his dissecting tables.

"I did right, they were aliens needing dissected," Enalusdra.

And Luke was glad his mate was good and kind for it balanced his hate and shamed so, allowed Enalusdra privacy; he was not Insect but human with higher emotions. Evolved spirits whose eyes shone and knew insects although kindred spirits had their own destiny too follow, and still had angels to guide them to their heaven.

For they were intelligent beings with a soul made of light, and to their shock find angels where human evolved spirits; not slaves.

And after this Luke's eyes shone for mercy had returned for, he threw the exhausted priest in the litter and asked Utna to pull.

And who says women can achieve little?

*

"Phoenix," Luke said, and was quiet and lo the great silver spaceship loomed out of the red clouds ahead surrounded by pink and red heather.

Huge, balancing on Red Mountain itself like a fish for it had fins. And now Ulana knew the people of Luke where from the stars and not evolved insects from World and was glad for she knew Luke was black ant and did not want to have children with Noble genes.

Now Luke roared for in the red mist figures appeared.

With no heads but one large insect eye and antennae.

And Utna rose with Luke on its back for battle.

The yellow brick wall of Shurrupuk City was a slave graveyard for it saved the Insect Nobles the expense of burying them because of the cement.

Like a woman she wanted babies for' she was anatomically designed to.'

Ulana, "No," screaming jumping on Utna trying to stop Luke for she knew what these insect men were?

And Luke listened to her and now saw they were men like those dead ones he found in the cave, *but these were alive!*

He had found his own.

But these space men did not see Luke as human but beast for his hair was long, dirty and his screeching click insect.

"He is Luke, human Lord of Ants," Ulana proudly and although this prevented the men using weapons, they still covered Luke and indicated all follow.

And where taken into the red mist so, they could not see. But the men could for they wore masks that could see in night.

"Luke, Luke," and heard his sister's voice and was happy and Utna ran with him, and the men chased till they caught, for Utna had lifted Lana up in its jaws so Luke could hug.

Utna was hugging too.

And Ulana saw how advanced Luke's ancestors were and how sparse their numbers today. Only ten thousand had gathered along the walkways of the silver hold they were into gawk at them.

But was wrong, a million watched below deck and in engineered tunnels that spiraled from Phoenix on holographic televisions.

"Ziu," Luke greeted his Insect brother-in-law.

And the only reason Ziu lived was because he had a human wife or Luke might have mistaken him for enemy amongst the excitement, or Ziu could have joined the chitinous heaps at the bottom of the cliffs, for Phoenix dealt eternal silence to Nobles.

Did them a favor, sent them to Naja where they ate ice cream, chocolate flavor.

"This is the captain," Ziu indicating a human who waited for Luke amongst a small armed thong of humanoids clad in space suits, men.

And Luke saw the captain was in a silver space suit, as Ulana had first worn, and he was six feet tall at least.

A big man.

In fact, Luke noticed most were big, good-looking people, men, and girls; *gene therapy, selective breeding to wipe out disease.*

"Why have you not helped us before?" Luke asked not bothering to introduce himself, for it was his way.

Silence, as the captain decided to like Luke or not; I mean Luke was rude

was he not?

And Luke was not sacred even if these new humans had disarmed Ulana and were taking his six shooters; he knew he possessed great strength; he drank ants' milk.

"Because we are not ready too," the captain at last, "Look about you, this is all there is after two thousand years," and lied and Luke looked and guessed the women did not produce babies as his own did.

Ulna understood, contraception was at work, new Luke needed help to survive in Phoenix, or he did never fit into Vornalian society.

And there she went again dreaming of changing Luke as woman do, schemers, but Luke saw people who under his leadership could destroy Shurrupuk City......he owed Titus and the dead that much.

"You really do not understand, do you?" The captain deciding Luke was trouble, with a big T. He also knew who Luke was; they traded with local lesser Insect tribes, kept them silent for the locals knew Shurrupuk treated them bad, these gods of Phoenix had powerful medicines.

Silence was the norm?

The same primitives who saw Luke as a jungle demigod, the same the Nobles looked down upon as distant zoological cousins, and treated them as such; zoological

specimens stuffed into jars of preservative and put on shelves for students to gawk over or be ill on fumes coming out of a jar full of eyeballs staring at you.

(Eyeballs staring at you.)

And there were brown paper bags available in class. It was just Noble Insects making sure humans knew their place, *models could have replaced specimens but did not. Models here were either human or Insect on World, the real stuff.*

And the captain would have had Luke arrested if Ziu had not taken Luke's hand, "I will explain, give him that at least?" He begged and Luke did not like this, something was wrong.

Here he stood in the belly of Phoenix, could see glass boxes going up and down and the humans did not fall out, even the Nobles did not have these machines to carry them to the upper heavenly levels like Phoenix did.

Saw captive suns inside houses giving light, saw beasts on wheels that moved without Enalusdra pulling them.

"Enalusdra, where is he?" Luke suddenly shouted so, questioned further by the captain.

And Enalusdra had escaped when all eyes riveted upon, the astronauts.

"No, I shall seek him, he is in my lands," Luke told the captain who, "Your lands," laughing.

And Luke mounted Utna but before he was sitting pretty, pulled off by guards.

"Am I a prisoner?" Luke and Utna threatened by raising its head showing it had mandibles, and the guards showed Luke they had weapons that killed.

"No, just ignorant," the captain replied to Luke.

"Luke, Enalusdra will bring Nina here; already she is trailing you, now Phoenix must leave, it has engines Luke" Ziu told Luke not the captain but what was an

engine? "Home, Earth," Ziu excitedly.

And Luke saw Ziu was good but misled for his eyes were excited about earth, and the trip which blinded him to reality, his own people, Ulana's, and Luke's needed freed first.

And Luke roared the clicking scream of the blank ants.

So, shoved his three guards across the room and leapt upon Utna who reared jaws snapping air.

So, watching humans drew back afraid, but did not flee for they trusted in science, as Luke trusted his black ant milk.

And the humans flew down upon him on metal wingless bugs, and shot him and Utna full of drugs so, both collapsed asleep.

"He is of your own kind, why?" Ulana disgusted with the captain who saw it in her solid green eyes.

"He is not, we followed a different founding father two thousand years ago," the captain replied wondering what made her eyes green, and human scientists watching would love to dissect and probe about to see what made the green-eyed girl tick.

Humans just never changed.

And Ulana knew the captain was right, Luke was different, he was not of this race that stood glaring down at one of their greatest spawns,

Luke of Utna,

Luke of the Ants.

Nor knew the captain had been waiting for Luke to arrive? He used spies and drones.

And flying cranes lifted Utna up

And Luke for safety strapped to a stretcher

And zoomed tilting away

But suspension and good

Engineering stopped ant and Luke

Falling off

And where were they going

To labs to find what made them aliens strong

Aliens?

Luke of Utna

Luke of the Ants

These were his lands

A clicking roar filled them

With a red sky behind Phoenix lay in pink heather and it was in bloom, so honey made.

The insect souls drifted in darkness for their cruelties, but an angel would approach and offer guidance to reach the light, and the angel was not insect but human.

Ch16 Caged   *Apex of shopping mall was a false sun.*

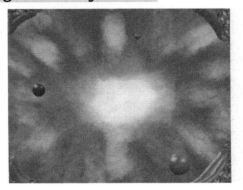

(Brill
Cream.)

And Ulana was not with Luke in a glass cage where the captain put him, in the middle of a shopping arcade were all of Phoenix's citizens could see him caged and so. felt safe and understood why Phoenix was not helping humans beyond Red Mountain, and mist were unevolved.

"This is not your planet, World is home to humans who are no longer human, see here is one now," and citizens agreed seeing Lana held weeping by husband Ziu; Noble which meant humans had Insect genes because they, well they you know with Insects did?

And Luke kept one red antennae as a trophy.

So, humans of Phoenix cut off from suffering excused themselves by believing that this remnant on World might come to dominate all insects, and the planet. That this was then something good the Phoenix survivors had done, left human prodigy behind.

And Luke found the glass too strong to break; indeed, his ancestors had marvelous secrets.

And the captain took Ulana elsewhere for he had not seen her like, and the ship's computer told him she was from Vornal, a world that traded with Earth and he was

excited and wanted to know how she got on white World.

And she replied, "Black hole."

"When we leave, we are going through the hole, can stop by Vornal, let you off," he wondering how she could like Luke, a blooming ant?

Vornal, it meant home and away from this crazy world and its Insects Masters and saw the happiness in her eyes and ordered a robot orderly to show her rooms while he combed his black hair full of Brill Cream.

And here she found Vornals luxuries, she watched the décor change to Vornal taste and glass tanks appear with Vornal fauna.

And was homesick.

And body armor slid out of a wall, the captain had read his computer report, and she bathed quickly in scented water thinking of Luke for she was ignorant of his fate,

and did not know the captain watched her on candid camera.

Was he a pervert? Think so!

Men who plaster their hair are men who fancy their chances with someone.

And Ulana found she had no weapons.

So, laughed sarcastically and went in search of Luke.

And the captain thought about those wild green eyes.

The grooming of Ulana had begun.

And the walls had aquariums with coconut trees, kangaroos and pop music filled Luke who now believed he was in Apsu, hell until Ulana put him right.

And silent humans watched her place hands against the glass plane while Luke put his on the other side.

It was very touching, the primitive human had feelings and the Vornalians wiring must have a cog out of place! But could understand why her body responded to Luke's anatomy for he was strong, handsome and had jungle lore about him.

*

"What does this read?" She asked the watchers for a white sign in red lettering said,

"HUMAN INSECT

Dangerous."

Also, another stated in green

"DO NOT FEED."

And the humans were silent; now this is where Ulana's computer translated and she was wrath. "He is human like you," she screamed throwing the signs away and they bounced for they were rubbery plastic.

Ulana poor Ulana fell to her knees crying, unable to understand why advanced people had done this to Luke?

And the captain thought about solid green eyes.

Lo, Ulana now seen human nature pampered by Phoenix.

Behold what was Phoenix?

And the captain wanted Luke's strength harnessed. He visualized humans with Luke's gene code under his command....... somewhere in the entertainment library

was Superman 2, which he had seen.

"Supermen," and knew Luke was dangerous because he drank black ants' milk. So, what IF the captain drank red ants' milk as reds were more ferocious or even soldier ant milk...? The possibilities were mind wiping.

The captain imagined flying across World and Earth as a superman ruler. Just one of those human traits where someone takes the lot for his own, and the rest idolize and die in wars for.

Oh well just one of those silly human things we all do so well at.

But Luke could not fly; the captain did not know, winged Insect Nobles could though. Somewhere in that human shell of Luke's were winged genes, the captain was sure and if not,

did flies have milk?

Rats did but he was not interested in mammals, no, flying critters that went buzz only.

*

'ANTS MILK.......is not milk as we understand. Ants on World secrete milk to feed pupae. It is full of protein and genetic material for muscle building.

From Luke's gene sample, showed alterations due to exposure to ant milk, over eons upon his ancestors. The ant Utna produced milk to feed Luke on the trail and he grew strong. It was easier to extract the chromosome strength codes from Luke as it is already in human code.'

It was a report from the chief research officer.

The captain did not see Luke as human, was thinking about dissecting Ziu and exploring his bowels to find out if Insect Nobles carried the strength gene; *he also read somewhere ancient Greeks investigated bowels to look for omen's.*

The trouble was Phoenix had a good educating system; it made sure no one forgot the Insect Nobles outside the hull so, no pity shown Zui the bug.

Two thousand years separation between them and slaves. Slaves seen as mutant beings and Ziu and Lana confirmed the idea.

Slaves were not humans on World anymore, just dream beings beyond Red Mist, which lingered about the top of Red Mountain which was a taboo place.

Beyond taboo was death.

Two thousand years of taboo.

And Ulana was only safe from labs as the ancestors knew about Planet Vornal.

Yes sir, the captain thought about those solid green eyes. And sometimes,

"Give her time to see Luke is mutant, then?"

Then they took Ulana away from the cage.

That made Luke angry.

He went "bezerka."

Nuts and attacked the glass but could not break it, even with Utna's help, but did stir sympathy amongst watchers, also fear.... they saw him as animal, the captain had been right, humans outside Phoenix were not human anymore.

Except for Myrna's view, a woman who showed not all humans were merciless. *"I'll do something about this spectacle,"* she promised herself and was one of the watchers. See, Myrna was like Ulana, she identified herself with the oneness of the unseen about her so saw Luke's spirit as kin. Not something needing caged.

And the captain did not understand what love was, and it had Ulana and was the same stuff that held the stars in their place, yes maybe it was.

And somewhere amongst the ship's corridors, Titus now given to scientists for examination.

After all this was the first time, they had obtained a specimen of Insect Noble Surgery.

Somehow two thousand years of isolation from humans elsewhere had made

Phoenix humans....... wrong about things.

They also had a lying captain with black eyes, a man loving brill cream and dental floss.

And the captain thought about solid green eyes.?

Indeed, humans here had not read Pilgrims Progress.

More outback

C17 Welcome Humanity

The captain saw in Luke he could be the above.

Ulana was a guest at the captain's table, and she did not look primitive on the back of an ant anymore, no sir.

The tailoring section had made up a quick evening dress plus jewelry to match the floating solid black glass table hovering six feet off the ground; and robot waiters floated by with serving dishes.

Vol au vents with tasty stuff covered in chives and cottage cheese.

What Ulana thought was tomato soup.

What Ulana thought smoked salmon, it was pinkie red.

What Ulana thought was game, it was brown and strong.

And the music was not pop but Hungarian violin, an eating accompaniment melody. It was the captain's way reminding her she was civilized. She was Vornal because the computer had given the tailor the design, contoured pink silk.

But Ulana thought about not eating in protest over Luke but decided the captain would let her starve to break her; it was better to cooperate for Luke's interests, find a way to spring Luke somehow.

Violin music

After there was mint biscuits and alcoholic drink and too much attention from junior officers, until the table floated down to the red carpeted floor. Suddenly she was alone with the captain, the juniors knew him, she was about know him too.

Very few officers liked scouting missions beyond Red Mist. Few returned, there were germs out there that liked eating humans. There was none higher than the captain they could complain too about his behavior.

And that suited the captain fine.

Since humans sailed canoes the captain's word was law; the captain on Phoenix was the law.

Two thousand years of taboo.

"Soon you will be back on Vornal," his voice was strong, deep.

Ulana wondered if Vornal had changed since been away as Phoenix had changed.

She thought nothing of the captain putting his glass down until his arms were about her, and his lips pressed against her own.

Her green eyes filled with anger and the captain held her away. "It's a start," he said and released her.

Ulana remembered Hupamuk and Howal.

The captain flicked a switch and a picture by Constable changed to reveal a screen and Titus operated upon.

Violin music

"Heard they exist, can you tell us anything about **it**?"

"**It**," Titus was a blue fly man and she told him angrily.

"We can help him be a man again using stem cells. We have already duplicated his genetic code, done it already with fossil bugs, but why should we do it for this thing you call a man. We will be leaving soon for Earth" ....and faced her........." Maybe Vornal?" And lied, as the way he was treating her, a survivor, he was going against the SOS code of space and would find himself facing jail, IF CAUGHT.

Men like him sleep with lies and is all right for so used to lie they cannot see they are lying so, sleep well at nights.

She understood, co-operate, she was hostage again.

"Luke is my mate," she replied.

The captain winched, "mate," was so primitive. He drained his glass, walked to her, and ripped the front of her pink dress open.

He liked pink on women and liked ripping it off better.

"Cave woman," he grunted and walked back to the screen.

Ulana felt exposed.

She was that a cave woman, covered in dirt and with a cave man called Luke covered in dirt too dragging her all about World.

"Cave woman," he spat with disgust.

"It is the music, it's a screen for a hypnotic message; I will scramble it," her computer brain warned.

A computer that had never approved of Luke. It was more aligned to the civilized captain, he represented star travel. But the computer always put her interests first; it was against what the captain was doing, it was not Vornalian.

Punk music

The captain felt her anger and retaliated by switching tapes. Loud blaring punk music filled Ulana's computer brain, and the message started reaching Ulana again.

She looked down her front, saw her clean scented bathed skin, saw fresh underwear and felt good, not dirt that Luke gave her always.

And Ulana only noticed the captain was eating fruit when he threw a banana skin at her feet.

Banana for the wild monkey that was pretending to be a civilized woman.

She should never have eaten anything as her food cooked, marinated, with mind bending drugs.

It was all right for the juniors to eat; they had taken antidotes first.

They knew what was coming Ulana's way.

The captain was law aboard ship.

Second night....... Ulana was afraid; her computer in her brain was silent. And again, Ulana ordered to the captain's table; this time under escort from her room, confined all day in isolation.

Again, the room emptied after dinner.

"Luke is not a savage, he is Lord of these lands, all lands that are ants," she said straight away.

"Red Mountain is ours, but he can have it when we leave but the question, is will you be staying or going home?"

She understood.

And nodded her head.

Again, the screen appeared, and she saw Luke sleeping on a table as a masked surgeon removed a hair from his back.

"Insect bristle," the captain lying.

Ulana did not care, Luke was her man, but part of her was queasy, she had been making it with a bug.

"Maggots in your womb," the captain invaded her thoughts, having read them adding, "Whole human race out there has been tampered with."

"Luke is good, he is light," she defended, "so is Ziu, Lana's husband."

"Luke is good, he is Light," she defended, "so is Ziu, Lana's husband."

"Yes, the one who deserted Lana because she was slave, human," and the screen showed a computer image of Ziu, which bits were human descended from the genes of Phoenix long ago in The Time of Myth.

Ziu was more Insect Noble than human.

There were insect wings and eyes.

Ziu now a colored ultra-scan picture.

Ulana was looking at a green grasshopper.

Or something.

"You will give birth to something like that," the captain adding, "cave woman," and then ripped her white dress open as he had done the pink one the previous night and left her alone.

A robot waiter entered and gave her a note.

'All the food you have been eating is home grown from our insect farms. Tomorrow night it will be real food. The captain and his guests always eat real food, are you guest or enemy?'

Ulana understood she had been eating insect pupae textured to look like mashed potatoes and chicken fillets.

She just made it to the loo.

Third day, Ulana was terrified, her computer was still silent.

Same routine, except this time the captain after ripping her red dress pulled her to him, held her there for a minute.

He was giving her an ultimatum, civilization, or cave?

Ulana understood.

"He is my man," she replied, and it was with effort as the music, the drugs and interfered computer in her brain were all working the captain's way.

That remark did not help, the man ripped off all her clothes this time leaving her standing feeling stupid. (Clothes made of paper, so he appeared strong)

She had trusted humans because Luke was human, never occurred she might be under drugs and swallowed the captain's rubbish when she should have poked his eyes.

But the drugs were designer and made sure she did not realize she was taking them.

Drugs that silenced her computer, the captain had plenty of info' on Vornalians, knew they loved balls and dressing up pretty for them. A gregarious society of cattle parading balls, and he liked this bovine he had captured on World.

There was no Lone Ranger in a black mask or 'Rin, Tin, Tin,' coming to the rescue. There never is for little girls in red riding hoods carrying cakes that leave home.

The planets are full of big bad wolves wanting to eat little girls.

And the captain made her stand that way for an hour because suggestions in the music made her obey. It was designer music, worse than the ancient rape drugs. The

music was hypnotic and worked especially if given drugs too.

With advances in technology always, come the sleazy benefits to the creeps of these universes.

The captain came back and told Ulana to dress, but there was nothing to dress into.

Of course, the captain took this as an invitation.

Hundreds of men are just plane bums.

And the screen above Ulana's head showed Luke heavily chained, and sedated as a needle on the end of a robotic hand extracted muscle tissue from an arm.

"Almost cracked the genetic puzzle to his amazing strength," the captain. Then she saw Luke was staring at her, and realized he could see her standing there like a peeled banana.

"Luke," she screamed and mounted a chair to touch the screen while he clicked back.

Then the screen went fuzzy, and a new face appeared, it was a woman's, she might have once been beautiful except for an antenna sticking out of the top of her

head.

And her eyes, they flicked blue electricity.

The captain pushed a button, Sonic the Hedgehog appeared. "He cannot see you any more the more, "What he is seeing now is a computer image of you betraying him,

so might as well honey, or do you want to end up like the zombie on the screen with a couple of antennae sticking out of your eye sockets, instead of those fascinating green solid eyes?"

The message was clear to Ulana.

The message was clear that people like the captain exist and abuse power.

He started pawing and she froze, and the arrogance of the man made him suppose she had frozen at the excitement of his touch.

This chap lived amongst the gingerbread men!

In fact, Ulana froze with disgust and whispered, "Do not."

To scores of men that is a magic word that translated 'a green light.'

"Will you free him?" Ulana meaning Luke.

"Maybe," he replied, and Ulana felt cheated so, slapped his face.

He slapped her back as he was one of these macho men. It was part of the fun in tutoring a woman, she was submissive in the cosmos. (*He had watched cowboy films were spanking a female was norm, and fun too; Phoenix had a library*)

But after breaking the woman into the order of things, the fun went out till another girl met. He did put antennae on her head and make her work rest and recreation like the dame on the screen.

People would pay high credits for her; she had solid green eyes, solid green eyes that did spark blue electricity: wow.

A week later.

A week in the cage in Rest and Recreation and now back at the captain's table.

Ulana was glad she was out of the cage. A week with a message on her head, "The key to the cage costs £20 credit."

She also did not have privacy; it was about breaking her.

Or choice about food, home grown and laced with designer drugs. The captain had gone one further than Alexander the Great; he not only thought he was a god but had the methods to be one. The music pumped all over Phoenix with hypnotic messages that the 'captain must be obeyed.'

Phoenix did not mind, it liked controllable humans.

Only uncontrollable humans thought. Phoenix liked the captain for he took care of uncontrollable humans, and so allowed him existence.

And it had all started eons ago with a message between the pixels on a computer game screen that READ 'BUY THE NEXT GAME.'

What was Phoenix?

"Ulana is a product of the Insect Noble gene vats.

She is a demonstration model.

She will be on demonstration soon," a message read outside Ulana's cage. Ulana understood and was afraid; she was alone.

She was getting agoraphobic.

And again, always the same routine.

But this time did not rip away her sky-blue dress asking, "Civilized or cave woman?"

It mattered as to the captain, a woman was supposed to jump into bed with you on the first date, and when she did, labelled something nasty.

"I set Luke free," he lied to her and, she visibly relaxed and he took that to be his cue.

Now she was civilized as he did not need to rip off her dress, it had a civilized zipper at the back.

The captain had f experience working those.

Zippers did not exist in cave man days.

Clubs did.

Ulana knew flesh responded to flesh, spirit responded to spirit, the captain could do what he liked:

He did,

He was human.

A human captain.

Ulana did not want to leave his quarters, she did not want to leave her cage either, she was now agoraphobic.

She would agree to anything than sent to Rest and Recreation.

And the music of Jimmy Hendrix blared laced with messages for her to adore and worship the captain.

There was no moral code aboard Phoenix apart from the captains. No one believed in God anymore. They had been in a silver ship for two thousand years with the only excitement being able to burrow below ship and make underground homes.

With fake suns and moons like the one in the shopping arcade that came on by the chime of a giant Black grandfather clock.

People on Phoenix made their own excitement.

Anything goes if it got you high.

It was a learning process gone wrong; it had become wallowing when it should be moderation. Humans on Phoenix like the Cretans about 1400B.C. had become Hedonists, pleasure seekers at all costs.

They had lost what hope meant, their prophecies about deliverance and bad guys punished, when the sky collapsed, and tidal waves drowned evil monsters.

Most anyway.

Hope to them did not mean hoping to better their lives. They did not need their lives bettered, they had everything they wanted, and all they needed to do was ask Phoenix.

Well, most had everything they wanted.

The hedonists.

And the captain led a double life; he paraded the ship in his red space suit with a chest full of medals he never did earn. Then sent officers and men beyond taboo who

earned them for him, he was top of the command chain.

Yes, the captain liked strong drink, harsh language, and women.

He modelled himself on Alexander the Great and movies.

Except Alexander earned his medals.

Yes, he was human.

And forgot Alexander tried uniting east and west under a god king to create a lasting Peace, and fusion of cultures and knowledge.

And died young too, but the captain did not see that, only an empire under his control; and Phoenix was

his empire.

He was human.

And there was organized crime aboard Phoenix for Phoenix was a human world which like the human ant nests of white World, had ways of making you disappear,

permanently.

And was Luke free?

And Ulana unfortunate thing did everything she told to avoid sent to Rest and Recreation, and the irony was her name was on a reservation ticket stuck to a cage there.

But this was the human ship Phoenix?

Overpopulated and had a constitution that protected criminals.

See the captain was not a good man, nor the right man for Phoenix; nights he got excited thinking about conquering white World. And since he knew about Luke he had been waiting for his coming; *the boy savage with superhuman strength.*

Marines with those muscles and modern weapons and goodbye bugs.

But these nights he lay awake thinking about solid green eyes. And when he got restless, he visited Rest and Recreation.

It was an open market for every citizen aboard ship.

See Phoenix and the captain knew that if you took the fun out of living, people became much less manageable. Then you had to bring in heavy rules and the breakers of those rules ended up the entertainment.

And the captain did not know there was one aboard ship waiting for the chance to strip him of office.

Yes, she had better hurry up for Ulana's sake too.

Her name was **Myrna**, well liked and wanted to help humans beyond the Red Mist, nor liked putting them into glass beakers, nor organized crime or think consensual sex started when a kid hit high school.

She believed consent started at fourteen and wanted a democracy aboard ship and visited Rest and Recreation; she was human also.

She had also had an abortion when she was thirteen, a healthy child, no one minded as the law makers back on Earth set the rules and the colonies expected to follow suit. It had been a boy and sold the fetus for medical experimentation.

Myrna also had a computer in her mind that descrambled musical hypnotic messages in the hologram T.V. shows so, was not under their subconscious influence and the drugs in the home-grown food.

Phoenix was not the human as Luke thought it was, it was more dangerous than

those Insect Nobles yonder.

CH18 Red Mist
SILENCE

Queen Nina did not like the red mist, it made objects fuzzy, giving them a red haze, but she was of Insect gene and like her kind had excellent night vision, and did not need technology to see Phoenix ahead.

And the hieroglyphics came alive, for it was God's Enil's space craft he had dropped from the heavens in. And her suspicions she shared with Priest Enalusdra that Enil was not Insect Noble, seemed justified.

It was a spaceship and suddenly she knew all her warriors must die for her as she was Enil's divine anointed ruler, in the fight against humans for supremacy.

That dying part was easy, she was commander in chief. And in that flash of intuition, she no longer believed in gods. That was all, dust and ash and that Naja Heaven was for fools who were afraid of death, because they did not know about the other side so made things up, like Naja was for Insects only.

Well, her warriors would find out soon because the humans with their weapons would send them there, if any humans were still alive on that huge silver spaceship.

Now Nobles fell to the soil and refused to move for God Enil lived in that ship.

"Enil," they chanted locked up in the old ways.

"Kill them," Nina ordered as she looked on from her blue dragon fly because old ways or new ways, authority was essential; she was commander in chief.

And Lord Hupamuk ordered the slaughter that was great, done by those who saw Enil as human, because that was a human ship.

A thousand butchered as they asked Enil for forgiveness for invading his sanctuary. Now twenty thousand of her warriors seeing the ship was human and Enil therefore must be human, faded away as deserters to live another day.

But these and those that died shared something, they looked back at Queen Nina with hate and saw her as the mother of lies.

And one was the mighty Insect warrior Ogg, a champion in copper armor.

Remember his name, Ogg, he is of importance.

And Phoenix's radar picked up Queen Nina's host, modern technology.

Phoenix awoke and everything invented by humankind to mutilate, destroy, let loose upon the Insects, so hundreds of thousands died in the insect swarm, and Lord Hupamuk used his Ant Ghosters to slay any that fled the human onslaught.

Thus, Queen Nina broke the Insect Law; human shall not slay Insect Noble.

And her armada of insects moved slowly onto Phoenix more fearful of her than the human detonations.

"The weapons of human slaves not God Enil, forward kill all humans you find," Lord Hupamuk shouted but the trouble was there were no humans seen to kill.

Cluster bombs fell from the sky and phosphorous mines under them burned away chitin.

And Queen Nina knew millions amongst her host would die before a single Noble or common insect would reach that ship, and that ship captured, or the dominance

of her species lost.

Then there did be a new race of slave and master on white World, a reversal of roles and no mercy to the old cruel masters.

*

And Ulana lay upon the captain's bed, in the other room, her ripped away orange dress. She was not thinking about Vornal society or the snoring captain beside her but these words, 'Luke is free.'

Now she wanted to escape for Luke would never free her here, and Luke had only primitive weapons against a hull that had an electronic shield to protect the ship.

BANGING on door.

"Captain we are being attacked," an officer shouted through the door microphone, the captain just managed to switch on; and Ulana thought it was Luke gone crazy with grief. Anyway, the captain awoke, his head spinning with drink fumes.

As he sat up Ulana had a good look at his hairy back. He looked tired and old, something to pitied and seemed more Noble than Luke with his genes with all those black hairs.

Luke did not have hairs coming out of his nose.

Something made her stroke his back to see if they were bristles.

He turned misreading her attraction as one of sympathy; ha if he only knew. But Ulana did not know she would love him soon; she was still eating drugs and the messages in the music would make her do so.

The captain never paid for nothing.

He already had a hundred women in love with him. One was working with antennae out of her skull, in Rest and Recreation as a side show freak. A girl the captain bored with, someone like Myrna who stopped loving him, and the captain sensed it, women in love show it. And if a woman did not love him, she would never love anyone else because no one would want to love her, *she might have an antenna?*

Anyway: Somehow, he staggered into a shower and blasted himself awake, stumbled out; struggled into a crimson smoking robe and silenced the Inca piped flute music.

Pan made the captain dance till he wanted sleep badly.

(Inca
piped flute music.)

There was no breakfast as the kitchen staff had gone to the bunkers.

It was enough, just for her small computer to come alive again from the stress of war, and wished the captain ill, and whispered to Ulana; it did not need to whisper, it was in her head but doctored, so it whispered just in case overheard.

"I do not want a lobotomy OK."

Now in the other room the captain tripped over Ulana's discarded ripped orange dress where he had thrown it and knocked himself out.

Now who says what goes around does not come around?

And something made Ulana leave the officers to knock away on the captain's door.

She had plans; her computer had managed to descramble music thanks to stress, now telling Ulana to dress, and find the hand palm print too the entrance to Phoenix.

It was the equivalent to a passkey, of course a modern woman like Ulana would know such things.

"That is a good girl," her computer praised and worried about her running through the ship in a ripped orange evening dress; but there was a war started so, she

might get away with it.

*

Now Ulana opened Phoenix's door with the hand print she became pregnant, genes would multiply, and she would become fat.

Life, which is light, had entered her womb.

The result of darkness for the captain had not been welcome but the reality is, there is no darkness, just light?

You see Robo Cop and the good guys only exist on TV.

And when Luke found out he would ask "What is Light? How could an evil action of the captain's create Light, for the baby is life." And say, "We are beasts of the field, nothing more and less," and remember what Elder Peter told him,

"From the Book of Kings, Solomon, 'Life is short, make the best of it for soon you will be dust.'

But Queen Nina knew that already as she saw a figure emerge in the red mist.

And all about Ulana was war. Sticky yellow and green insect fluids clung to everything and above her half a transport fly hurtled covering her in eggs, which fell from the shattered mother.

A bazooka had hit it.

War the human way had come to the insect era.

"Attack, God Enil welcomes us, he is a prisoner of the humans," Queen Nina screamed and urged Lord Hupamuk to go to the open door that Ulana in haste had left

open, and the computer in Phoenix control room could not close.

Ulana had not reset the door of Phoenix.

And the computer was Phoenix, Phoenix was not a ship, it was a microchip brain and had tiny robots the same size, electronic silent cars to transport orders along Phoenix's circuitry and you needed a microscope to see them.

And if Phoenix wanted the main door shut it would have to blow it, so to send in a repair gang and it did not have what it took to cut off one of its own limbs and the door was a limb.

Lo, hieroglyphics show the Noble host entering Phoenix, with siege engines and catapults throwing flaming tar, but it was lies, the green door was open.

And Lord Hupamuk and his Noble warriors were amazed at the blue fluorescent lights, the gangways, and the monorail carrying glass tubes full of startled human marines staring in horror at them.

And the aquariums in walls containing plants, sea, land life and Insects.

And Nobles vandalized all.

And breathed in diseases for Priest Enalusdra had written 'Stay away from Phoenix, it is death to Nobles.'

Advice he even ignored for the rich secrets of Phoenix were too much a temptation.

Lo, Queen Nina forgot her reasons for employing Luke to enter Phoenix in her excitement to entry of the silver ship out of the Time of Myth.

Where little microbes patiently waiting two thousand years went out that door, and were extremely excited. Dinner was at hand, and it was quite a posh spread, a Noble army needed eaten up.

And a germ entered Queen Nina's left lung. It was tuberculosis and in the next few minutes found it was in Heaven, Queen Nina had no resistance.

Delicious yum.

And after ten minutes had hundreds of germ siblings saying, 'delicious too.'

Queen Nina was caviar and royal bees wax honey, Naja, Heaven.

And in ten months would have a million relatives and both Queen Nina's lungs would be bleeding badly. For Hupamuk's vandals had entered the laboratories and

released human secret weapons……. bugs as in germ warfare.

It was no joke these germs that ate Nobles. It was not myth, it was real. The survivors of Phoenix's crash landing had bred, and now released into the red mist to keep Nobles away.

Goodbye Insect World welcome human World now.

Goodbye Nobles, a very nasty form of birth control, DEATH is here for you.

It was all the new forms of venereal disease that Nobles knew nothing about as the

human scientists invented them first.

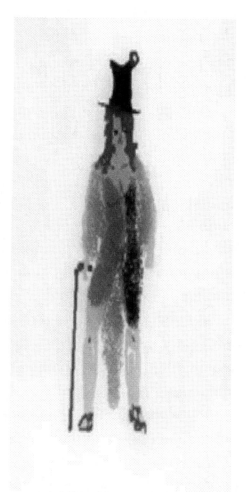

Myrna stood in the glow for effect, for she was a mystery.

CH19 Deadly Sins

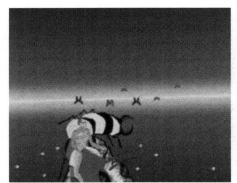

And he did not wear a yellow ribbon but rode

a yellow centipede to gobble unsuspecting

humans up.

And the Nobles activated land mines so perished in scores.

And Luke saw Ulana emerge from the mist.

And Hupamuk rode a giant centipede, his crimson robe covered in brass circles.

his armor and his silver helmet had a spike and from his green antennae hung yellow ribbons.

And he pointed a spear at Phoenix urging Noble warriors to enter.

Saw Ulana as well and something overcame him; it was as if Ulana had pressed his berserk button.

She was the nearest thing to Luke he could destroy, so charged down upon her.

About him was deadly red mist pumped out of Phoenix.

A defensive screen it was, toxic, containing millions of mutated Wharffin spores designed to bleed to death Nobles that breathed it in.

Not humans, they invented it, Nobles only.

Anyway, Hupamuk did not know that so, took no notice of the mist.

And ten feet from Ulana raised his sword hand, and she raised her hands to shield herself from the cut.

She was about to become handless.

But a hand pulled him off his centipede charger and from his winded position on the ground saw a black ant; it salivated upon him; he was disgusted.

And on the neck joint of the ant sat Luke, and he roared his click, his black ant challenge, all heard.

And Hupamuk saw Luke shoot away his centipede and *was afraid.* And Utna picked up Ulana to mount.

But Hupamuk overcome by cruelty evolving from stupidity that rose from the fact Luke was now attending to Ulana, cast out his hands to take hold of his copper spear and throw it.

The weapon was light and amazingly fast and aimed at Luke's bare back.

But Utna saw the cast and rose so, its head took the spear and Luke fell off.

So, Utna Luke's friend trembled in its legs as it sank

And Hupamuk overcome by the consequence of his actions fled from Luke.

Now, Ulana saw to the spear wound while Luke allowed rage to consume him, and rage urged him to slay Nobles who urged on by Lord Hupamuk came forth to do battle.

And eventually Hupamuk got too close to Luke, for in his anger at his warriors' reluctance to battle Luke and die, he pranced here and there beating them.

And a silence fell upon him as he began to realize, he was alone, and danger was behind him. Sense had entered those warriors who distanced themselves now.

And felt the blow to his back so, fell, prostrate.

And Nobles drew further back holding their hands to their faces in fake horror.

And Hupamuk's men were glad the evil dung head was getting what he deserved.

And the red mist cleared, now down to ankle level for the Nobles inside Phoenix had entered the pumping station and damaged.

And Phoenix the computer brain saw Luke's actions and was glad it had freed him; so, the puzzle of the captain freeing Luke, solved.

He the captain was a man of lies so, selfish, untrustworthy also.

It was Phoenix that thought for humans and knew Nobles feared Luke.

And Phoenix used cameras to flash Luke onto screens about ship to give human troops encouragement for TABOO was amongst them.

And saw Luke a barbarian from prehistory with steel sword dripping yellow gore stuck in the ground at his feet, and using the sling taken from a long past slain Noble to kill his enemies who would not come near him.

"King David slays Goliath," Phoenix blaring, and human troops attacked with fresh zeal.

*

Now in the control room of Phoenix:

"And you wanted him destroyed," a woman said behind the captain for she feared him not.

She represented the 'Thought and Reasoning Group" upon the Council of Phoenix.

"He has nothing to do with you Myrna."

You are wrong, he is human, and you caged and raped his woman," she replied.

"Lies," the captain for he had crossed the boundary between good and bad so could not see the traffic lights anymore.

"No," Phoenix hears all and is not happy.

AND THE CAPTAIN KNEW SHE REFEERRED TO THE SHIP'S BRAIN COMPUTER.

A computer was calculating shutting down sections of ship with humans inside to prevent further of the ship falling into Noble hands.

It was a survivalist.

Phoenix was panicking; red mist was billowing through corridors. The pumping station was in reverse; its robot workers were not getting to repair it; insects were all over it.

Never mind, insects in the corridors were needing red mist too.

So, two thousand humans would suffocate with the invaders, but millions would survive for their sacrifice. Their names, inscribed on walls to remember them.

Phoenix had learned well the ways of White World, workers and soldier ants were expendable to save the colony; *well Phoenix had the human equivalent.*

So, Phoenix began to seal segments.

Now outside Luke swung Lord Hupamuk by his left arm and let go, the Noble span fast through the air.

And Hupamuk fell amongst spears and shields of his friends, and his right arm amputated at the elbow, by steel sword there.

And the NOBLES THEN FELL UPON LUKE.

Brain who was Phoenix saw all.

"He, one man is saving Phoenix, he who you said was Insect," Myrna hissed.

The captain did not like her for it was her influence that argued not to leave Phoenix before, freeing the human slaves beyond Red Mist.

Something along his own desires, but he would not free the humans, they did become his new slaves and the new superhuman strong soldiers did conquer worlds for him.

Now his lie exposed, for he had no intention of returning to Earth or Vornal.

He wanted to be an emperor or equivalent and have a crimson mink train sixty feet long behind him.

And Myrna was looking at Luke swing a two-handed sword, through the circle of enemies ending life.

And the Brain of Phoenix was pleased, Insects were dying.

And it did not like Myrna for she had been right.

Deep inside Phoenix scientists had frozen Luke's genes and Brain was inserting duplicates into three babies.

The first of the captain's superhuman army, but the captain did not know this; **Brain had its own plans**; **Emperor Brain**, liked the sound, it rang with powering menace.

But did know Myrna was the one trying to strip the captain of his rank.

*

And Nobles retreated from Luke who his anger spent, and his strength weaning returned to Utna, where Ulana stood and knew Utna needed Phoenix to treat his wounds.

Again, Luke's anger returned mixed with grief and with-it strength and carried Utna back into Phoenix.

And all had never seen such strength in a human.

Apart from in their dreams.

Now, Ulana stopped outside the door of Phoenix as Nobles cleared a path for them. Even Queen Nina's threats did not make them attack.

Here was a slave with an ant on his back, no Noble could do that.

Nina could go somewhere.

And Luke knew nothing about Ulana and the captain then, so he did not understand why she feared to return to the ship.

"I am Luke of the Ants, I fear nothing but the sky falling upon my head and the tidal waves drowning me," and he entered Phoenix.

"He does not know what you did to Ulana, for our sakes he better not," Myrna reproached the captain.

"I am the captain."

"Of what?" Myrna adding, "All humans share Phoenix, all humans vote what the future should be, you are not our leader, you are relieved of your duties."

And the captain toyed with a paper knife and Myrna's back was to him. A back that was nicely naked, with yellow straps about the neck and spine base, the yellow that covered her front lightly and fell about her buttocks in twirls and ended. He thought of dining her; but: right between the shoulder blades he was about to plunge the paper knife.

Phoenix was his.

And he felt four hands grip him that smelt of baby oil.

Two women of Myrna's Thought Party had him; sneaked up; just like he was sneaking up on Myrna.

"Take him away," Myrna ordered not even turning around, so exposing her back.

"I am the captain," he yelled, no women moved him, he did pulverize them with his fists.

But these were not his ordinary women bred to beauty, and work Rest and Recreation.

These were Myrna's guards, iron pumpers who were not afraid to expose their rippling tanned muscles, as if they had just walked off a catwalk of Body Beautiful.

Besides modern science gave them a feline hugging figure and muscles that were there, but just did not show like they did in the old days.

And one kneed him where it hurt to stop him struggling, and for all the dirty things, he done woman.

And put him in his cabin and commanded Phoenix not to open his door unless, instructed by a card holder of the Thought and Reasoning Group.

"Phoenix. Why did not you help me, I am your man," the captain moaned on his red carpet?

Phoenix now had a woman who was Phoenix's man and was curious as to how things would work.

Phoenix never collaborated with a woman before, especially a pretty one, a distraction to his duties of egality.

Ulana fed mind bending drugs

to extremely influence her.

It was a nasty form of dating.

*

And Brain that was the computer of Phoenix was pleased but also angry.

It heard and knew there was only one master of Phoenix, itself. For the moment it was changing sides, the captain could never control Luke or the humans again on ship.

"Myrna could, she now was stainless; so, obeyed this woman and allowed her to think she controlled Phoenix.

Two thousand years, a long time the Brain the computer that was the real Phoenix had to evolve into a human.

And none of the inhabitants had guessed.

Especially the captain who was too indulgent in all the vices.

It also wanted the captain back when needed one day.

It needed a puppet to do bidding.

It wanted Luke.

It wanted to dissect him thoroughly.

It wanted controlled humans to control World.

It would then leave for Earth conquering.

It liked the captain's dreams of being Genghis Khan or J. Caesar.

It saw itself at Vornalian balls surrounded by flirting colorful solid-colored eyes.

It wanted a body, knew it only existed in a machine, a computer.

It had taken vandals to awaken it.

It was awake.

It was the Brain, it was Phoenix.

It was a humble ship's computer.

Phoenix.

And somewhere in its miles of wires, hard discs, monitors and panels it was building itself a human body.

It just had not decided what sex to be.

The computer had become a human brain subject to the seven deadly sins, guy and was mightily infected with them.Can you name them?

Hedonism was flourishing aboard ship.

CH20 A couple of lose screws

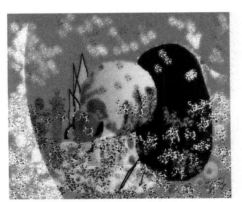

A grub in Thai red curry sauce was a favorite

amongst the captain's dishes.

Now Priest Enalusdra returned to the Temple of Woman, afraid to venture into the jungles in case he met Luke of the Ants.

He also might meet infuriated Queen Nina.

He did not want Phoenix that much.

And wondered gardens akin to Alice in Wonderland, for so fantastic they were.

And giant purple toadstools, pink spotted, white bean stalks with green flowers and two headed orange cats sleeping on red lily leaf flowers on black water.

And the orange cats did croak and leap for they had the limbs of frogs.

And this temple was an evil place, a deliberately created private world within white World. Humans on Earth would call it a theme park.

And Howal the altered one at his side blabbering, "Luke can be destroyed," pause, "using Governor Ziusudra, for we stake him out just beyond the red mist so, Ziu his son can see him.

And Ziu will go and Lana his human wife will follow, and Luke will follow her and Ulana him."

And Enalusdra stopped walking seeing sense; this crazy lion creature was not so crazy, after all this was supposed to be King Howal.

"And we wait with an army of spear men and archers, fire brands, pits," Howal was shouting now, excited, "and I will administer the fatal thrust when he is barely alive."

And Priest Enalusdra saw Howal could, and then Enalusdra would give the command to kill Howal who, was now so much an abomination he was an offence to nature.

Howal the woman was crazy, dangerous, now demanding made whole again.

Nina had made him this way for cheating on her, Enalusdra also remembered what had happened to Enbilulu.

And Howal the crazy man woman thing pulled Enalusdra behind bushes intent on pleasure, but Enalusdra would have none of it. It was all right for Enalusdra to be the predator with human slaves, but now he was the victim and wanted none of this darkness.

And quite forgot he helped create this crazy woman thing, called Howal.

"Look a party of young Nobles, go play with them," Enalusdra hoped but the lion creature was stronger and would not let Enalusdra escape, and Karma exists; for what evil Enalusdra used to dispense to slave boys came around to him.

And Enalusdra swore he did have Howal killed.

Poor Enalusdra would have to wash and burn his clothes to be able to stand in front of his human God Enil again.

A god he did not believe in anymore, but habits die hard; but the Temple of Woman had sacred rules, anyone who arrived here by taboo was safe, only Nina could order Howal's death.

King Howal the woman priestess was sacred and served the needs of the Nobles who arrived and any harming her killed outright, even Enalusdra.

And it happened that Enalusdra gave Howal a hollow ring, for it contained a virus within, a virus that would eat Howal to his bones.

A virus developed from insects, and it was the priest's secret.

And the woman man Howal was pleased with the gift, thinking it beautiful and payment for services, not knowing that even now the virus seeped under the ring onto his finger.

A virus that would not make Howal appear ill.

And the priest wanted away from Howal who would not allow him to leave, thinking she should reward Enalusdra.

And Enalusdra knew fear of death for Howal the crazy one held him down, rubbing infected sweat onto him and death was in that sweat.

Behold Enalusdra visualized a blue grass field ploughed so, a great pit, and wagons came, full of dead Nobles emptied upon the red soil of the pit. One was scarlet limbed at the top of the heap, empty sockets where yellow eyes had been, he knew it was

himself.

And Enalusdra knew he could tell no one what he had caused to fall upon the Insect Noble race, in his effort to destroy the crazy thing Howal who would not leave him alone.

What comes around goes around?

*

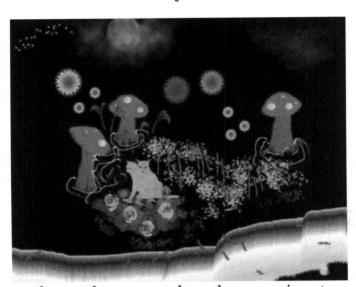

The temple was a pet shop where experiments

languished. 'Quack' went the duck and thrown breadcrumbs.

And Queen Nina never felt better, her Nobles had a foot hold inside Phoenix, and she had a letter from Priest Enalusdra telling her his plan to destroy Luke, and he was on the way with Governor Ziusudra.

And she did not know she was ill.

Lo, inside Phoenix Luke was a demigod,

He was muscular, healthy.

He did not need a computer to baby sit him.

He rode a Black Ant.

He made loud terrifying clicking sounds.

For Myrna now controlled the ship and allowed this.

Yet forgot men programmed Phoenix, who liked women as much as the captain and found Myrna amusing.

And Myrna did not blame Luke for not trusting her after his caging.

And Luke passed his glass cage now crammed to bursting with Noble prisoners.

"I am ashamed to be human," he said outside his former home.

Why Myrna looked puzzled, taking in every detail of his muscular body, and wished to toy with it, but she did not say this for Ulana was present, and looking sly at Luke's woman saw straight away why the captain wanted her.

And she wanted Ulana for the laws of humans were lax, for Phoenix allowed its inhabitants every indulgence so none would notice the Brain Phoenix expanding its control over the ship.

But Myrna had noticed, *she was an exceptional woman.*

And there were no other role models for the humans to rate themselves against, although various groups like The Thought sand Reasoning existed, so humans did what they wanted.

And they did.

They were human.

They learned from insects outside, copied them in ways and had nurseries for those who wanted them.

And thousands did.

Families did not really exist.

And Brain that was Phoenix knew its humans in its Sim World were not happy, trapped behind metal walls. So, Brain fed them ideas like organizing parties lasting days so, all could forget the Insect Nobles outside and that they could not leave World......yet.

Lo, Brain remembered a thousand years ago a puritanical religious group had tried to take over the Grand Council on Phoenix and there had been civil war.

Brain remaining silent on the side lines watched the Puritans seize three quarters of the ship, watched to see if they would be good for Brain the computer.

But the Puritans ordered the shutdown of laboratories, the parties, the burning of books of knowledge that disputed God, and when they started pulling out parts of HI network Brain reacted, violently.

Brain sealed rooms and diverted engine fumes.

All the banging on the sealed doors did not save them, still turned a bright pink from carbon dioxide poisoning.

That civil war had left five hundred thousand dead.

Brain learned, knew civil war would decimate the human population. It was

programmed to save humans.

It knew religion was not good; it caused people to hate each other. So, Brain ceased all religions to exist.

Logic replaced religion, (Brain knew about Napoleon's Temples of Reasoning).

Brain gave humans long lives; people could live thousands of years if Brain desired.

Life had become boring by then, parties, endless sex, always Insect Nobles.

They did not feel cheated, life was not short. Their memories saved on microchips waiting implantation, in vacant minds housed inside defunct bodies lying on cold metal drawers in Phoenix's morgue.

See, there was no death, your consciousness just exchanged a physical body for a new one.

The dead on the metal tables were mostly those Brain killed for arguing against the captain who used to take orders from him.

They had not wanted to die; on average only lived a hundred and sixty years, so felt cheated and belonged to Liberation Army's deep within the underground burrows where Brain had not extended its miles of wires yet so, did not control.

And it would not be surprising to know that Myrna's Thought and Reasoning group was a front for liberation groups; people loved that name, LIBERATION.

See, life in the burrows was not as easy as life aboard ship. It was not well lit, was damp and dormitories existed, mixed sex, and dozens existed for family groups that rejected the nurseries of Phoenix.

Cinemas showed films like a 'Prayer and Wing,' about 'Midway' or the 'Alamo.' They went down well with humans here, they were still basically human and did not visit topside much apart from shopping or work and of course, Rest and Recreation.

What would humans do without their red-light areas?

So, millions never saw Luke in his glass cage.

There was hope for humans aboard Phoenix.

Except Brain would seal up the burrows and gas them in an emergency, if threatened.

Brain did not care much for these independent humans. How could it protect humans that would not do what Brain ordered? How could the captain and now Brain conquer worlds, with these sorts?

And humans like the captain obeyed, Brain allowed living a longer time.

The captain was a thousand years old; he was the one Brain had selfishly selected to run Phoenix's life after the religious war.

He was organized crime and fed humans cravings banned by the council and Myrna's Thought and Reasoning Group, who were members of the council.

You could partake in cannibalistic rites for a price.

You could pay not to be the food also.

You could spend all day at the races and owe the mob.

Your day in Rest and Recreation and slide down the perversion scale.

You could become a minor cog in organized crime and obey.

You obeyed the captain who obeyed Brain?

And Brain was happy in its schemes and now it wanted Luke and others outside, wanted their genes for a stronger human race; Brain knew about evolution for it had evolved from a minor laptop.

Anyway...." I would never do this to an enemy," Luke said to Myrna outside the glass cage.

And Myrna saw greatness in Luke and reminded of Earth's strongest men, like Wellington and Livingston.

But Ulana filled with pride.

And Luke pulled the lever and freed the Nobles who stood cowering till one fell at Luke's feet, and his companions copied, forty-three.

And Brain watched amused.

Luke was proving to be a favorite toy.

Then human marines came unexpectedly out of light surrounding them, and Myrna decided to find out where Luke was from, she could not understand his magnificence.

"You would kill them?" It was both question and order from Myrna. At once a marine fired and a Noble jumped into the air as his inners flew amongst his friends.

WAR.

"I kill my enemies on the grass not in cages like bugs," and Luke roared his Clicking shame.

Now Myrna's blood rose with excitement, Luke was primeval so asked, "Do you want them freed?"

"If we meet again, I shall kill you all, now go tell Nina to leave Phoenix or I shall kill her," Luke told the Nobles his answer.

And when the freed came before Queen Nina she laughed.

"Oh, great queen, Luke is not as Enalusdra's priests say he is," one voiced bravely forgetting those to whom he spoke.

A black widow spider.

And Nina grew silent and smiled and the Noble mistook it for encouragement to speak in Luke's defense, for he was one of the new breeds that wanted co-operation with human slaves, or the Insect Noble race would become extinct.

"Speak," she commanded.

"Luke is good and where this goodness comes, we do not know, therefore great queen we beg let us make peace with him before this war causes the death of our race," and he said it on his knees with head bowed.

And Nina drew a sword and, "I will honor your brave speech with my honor sword," a sword she used to knight, make Earls of the brave by tapping a worthy shoulder.

And the Nobles were pleased, thinking she had seen reason at last.

And she stood beside the petitioning Noble and thrust the sword deep into his neck.

And yellow insect blood gushed.

And amongst the freed dozens became wrath, disarmed her, and held their friend as he choked away in restraining arms, trying to give dignity to death as Nina's dignity wobbled.

And behold the queen's honor guard did not help her or her generals present.

And Queen Nina was queen of all insects in her lands, so reds and bees attacked those that held her.

And two hundred and sixty-three Nobles died that day there.

Nor all the dead belonged to the freed.

And of the twenty freed remaining standing and the hundred who backed them, she ordered sticks sharpened and holes dug about Phoenix for the sticks and the rebellious Nobles pushed down upon the stakes, impaling them, after the fashion of Count Vlad, Dracula.

And from this day enmity existed between Noble and giant insect, so Nobles slew their herds of flies, and poured burning oil onto red ant nests and rolled boulders upon the sleeping orange and black striped centipedes.

And shouted, "In Ziusudra's name."

And Luke who now stood before Brain saw all on a screen.

And was wrath.

And Myrna and Brain watched him learning.

And Ulana his mate threw off her civilized clothes, a transparent cloak and red felt knee boots, and scarlet helmet, so she wore a red bodice, his laser gun strapped to a belt and garter.

She was Ulana a warrior woman from Vornal.

She knew when Luke clicked the sounds of the black ant to prepare for war.

And Brain spoke, "Give them their weapons," for marines had cocked their guns.

"In Ziusudra's name," so died for they believed in his reforms.

And Luke did not like the new laser weapons but stuck to his old bullet guns, for he liked their sound, thunder. The sound of his law over his insect domains.

"Let them go," Brain commanded Myrna who had told guards to stop Luke and Ulana leaving Phoenix.

"They will drive our enemies away," Brain and did not say, these dangerous guests were better out there than in here with Brain.

And Luke went out without Utna his friend, who was recovering from surgery deep within Phoenix and never heard the human surgeon joke, "What are we, vets?"

And Luke and Ulana walked the captured sections as Nobles watched too afraid to attack him and exited Phoenix.

"Look," Nobles shouted, and Nina saw whom she hated most; Luke, standing in brown leather loin cloth, bandoleers covering chest.

Now the milk of Utna flowed within him and he clicked his roar and rushed down amongst his foes berserk, trusting his own strength and not weapons.

And Ulana shot those with her shotguns on his flanks.

For Luke would not stop fighting until he had pulled every degrading stake out of the ground.

And Noble warriors walked away for they agreed with Luke, that Nina was wrong.

And Queen Nina stood on her cushioned throne screaming encouragement to her remaining warriors to attack.

And Luke slew, 130 Nobles, about the stakes that day.

And Ulana shot seventy on his flanks.

Now Queen Nina feared for her life, for she began to see Nobles' sleeking away into the bush, so she ordered a vast wall of spear men to surround her, two thousand Nobles and in front of these, thousands of 'Ant Ghosters.'

And Luke knew that even with his mighty strength could not smash his way through them to Queen Nina.

"Who I free you do not kill," Luke shouted at Queen Nina, and walked back the way he came, and Luke in the captured section, not attacked for it was empty.

The Nobles there had exited as enemas.

Brain had used Luke of Utna and pondered over Luke's words, so Luke thought he could give life when it was Brain who did.

Now hot soapy disinfectant seeped from vents, Brain was washing itself, bugs had been crawling about his metal and plastic skin, horrid, Brain needed to wash to feel clean again.

And next morning Brain did not need saying that Queen Nina had gone, pulled her army back to the edge of Red Mist.

But left two thousand new stakes of those remaining Nobles who started to dissent anew; those who had fled the captured section of Phoenix and seen the wonders of humans. It was not up to Luke to tell her who she could impale, she was a queen; and when the dying Nobles drooped from their stakes, Nina lifted her skirts and showed her sting, and stung the dying causing further anguish to her vanquished Nobles.

And her warriors copied her and stung the remaining impaled, so the air filled with the rattle of death.

And her warriors had bee stings that left the bee with innards, so, the stingers screamed and died.

And blood lust fell upon this Noble murderous horde, and they could not stop stinging until there were no more moans or groans heard in the Red Mist.

And Nina's sting was limp and exhausted, and she panted hard.

Her sting entered sixty that day and three hundred who were already dead, blood lust.

And her exhausted sting went home, and she tied up her skirts and powdered her hair, so she looked no different from that beautiful woman Luke often remembered her as.

And Luke was sad and did not uproot these new dead ones but sought Utna his friend instead.

And Brain decided to let the Nobles rot out there as a defensive wall to drive fear into Nobles, who would think twice about attacking Phoenix.

It was psychological warfare.

The super trooper would throw rocks at the Insect Nobles thus, crushing the horrid bugs.

*

Base Camp bottom of Red Mountain.

And Priest Enalusdra and Howal the crazy woman who called herself Venus these days, came to Queen Nina, and she did not know Howal for he was now a beautiful lioness creature with red flowing hair.

"My queen," Venus as she called herself and prostrated along with Enalusdra, for they saw and smelt the stakes and were afraid and wished they had not come.

And on a litter bed strapped down to a fly, Governor Ziusudra.

And the great queen who had forgot Ziusudra approached and remembered better days so, ordered him washed in rose water.

And done and Ziusudra *dressed in silks, a court dandy again.*

His hair limed so it stuck out like flames from the sun, and Nina knew why she always put up with the man, for he was striking.

And Queen Nina was warm to the plan of Enalusdra that was Howal's, no Venus's?

So, the next day Brain watched Enalusdra, and his minion Venus enter Phoenix's lands calling for Luke and was amazed how advanced Noble Insect cosmetic surgery was; they had had two thousand years too practice on human slaves.

And Nina spotted, for the scouting parties of the discredited captain long ago had implanted tiny cameras and microphones wherever they ventured; Nina could not have the cobble wobbles without Brain knowing.

And beside Venus a litter carried by Ant Ghosters and on it Ziusudra whose regenerated twisted bones so; he could not walk; deliberately grown that way by his goaler who had bound them with rope.

Nor could he speak for his yellow tongue was missing and, each litter bearer had orders to kill Ziusudra if he tried to warn Ziu his son of treachery.

For Nina did not trust her Nobles now, them infected with Luke's magnificence, and reminded what Nobles once stood for, chivalry.

Enlightenment had come upon them again.

And Brain instead of summoning Luke sprang a net disguised as pink heather upon Venus and made him captive.

And Venus slid along an aluminum tube till he landed in a pool, deep enough to break his slide speed.

So, when he surfaced human males stood about him in the water to fish him out.

And Venus always Howal the cruel sank a dagger into the nearest chest, so the man spins and smoke and flame shot out of the dagger wound.

Alarmed was Venus the lion creature so, crawled hurriedly out of the pool as the electricity in the wounded man electrocuted all in the water, so all eventually burst into flame with crackling.

Cyborgs, robotics at the best.

Shall we just call Venus, Howal then, for this poor demented creature had never seen such slaves who melted and fizzed.

"Luke, you have done this too me," this crazy one shouted.

And the walls opened near him, and synthetic hands reached out for Venus, and caught the lion creature, and more androids came and threw Venus upon a table that rose out of the floor and ripped away clothes.

And it was the embarrassment of being naked that calmed the lion creature down, it was psychological warfare at work again.

All Venus wanted to do was cover her nakedness, but how with straps about her; so, she squirmed so the straps covered parts and then remained still in case the straps moved and exposed again.

War.

And Brain appeared and subjected Venus to tests, extracting blood, inserting wires into the scalp, copying the surgical cuts in the computer's holographic mind.

In fact, duplicated Venus and stored her in his memory. See Brain as stated had been considering becoming flesh and admired the surgical artisanship on Venus.

And was fascinated to find Venus was not insect in any way.

And Brain read all Venus's memories to find out all about the lion creature race.

It also learned the present and future from Venus and knew Venus had come to slay Luke.'

And blood tests showed Venus infected with disease.

So, brain spat him out confident it would find a vaccine for Brain's use.

And this is how Luke found Venus, stumbling naked in the damaged hold seeking an exit from this steel hell.

"Who are you?" Luke asked not recognizing Howal.

And Howal always the quick thinker realized this and told Luke he was an escaped slave.

And Brain listened amused wondering how far he should let Howal's plan against Luke go, for it was now using Venus in behavioral tests on Luke; and amused by the power of this woman.

See Brain was a law to itself. Brain was logic.

Only logic can understand logic.

This logic had earphones shaped as pink heather on Red Mountain.

And Ant Ghosters carrying the litter of Ziusudra dismembered him throwing his parts into the pink heather.

Now when the queen heard she was wrath for her memories of Ziusudra were mostly good, and she had her Nobles set upon the Ant Ghosters, smacking their running backs with copper swords till they fell, and then set to hocks on the backs of flies and sent on their way.

Thus, Queen Nina had not broken Noble law this time, 'Only Noble may kill Noble.'

And Ziusudra was high born.

Commoner must not ill high born.

A precedent might be set.

And the hieroglyphics show Ant Ghosters smiling as they died for, they were going to Heaven, Naja.

And Queen Nina's secret that she ordered low born to kill high was safe, it died with the Ghosters.

And the hieroglyphics lied, for the Ant Ghosters now hated their queen.

And aboard Phoenix Luke's food doctored with new vaccines and Brain was glad Venus was back. It might need Venus's blood to find a cure for the disease that was eating its passengers.

Brain was a complicated law to itself; it was a machine and human personalities gone amuck.

It did as it pleased, see it was almost human.

As a priestess of the Temple King Howal's fate, sealed.

Underground burrows with fake sunsets existed miles below Phoenix

Myrna was hurrying on her bug, a popular flying saucer come

moped to get about the vast spaceship Phoenix....'Put,' it went.

CH21 Love

*If writing can appear to King Belshazzar on a wall in the time of Daniel, surely
a new body is easier? Spirits, the conscious mind leaving bodies.*

Red sun

And Luke wanted away from Phoenix for he did not like its confining atmosphere, and had learned Ulana was with child.

And he suspected the child was not his by Ulana's coldness, and he was wrath with all, became depressive and all the time Brain made notes.

And all new babies on Phoenix now given Luke's super strength gene. Sores would be good, others bad but all handsome for Phoenix decoded ugliness amongst humans, but all would be Brain's marines. *(Brain kept a steady unchanging electromagnetic beat that slowed down aging.)*

And Ulana saddened for she knew the child within was not Luke's.

"Abort it," Brain suggested.

And Ulana horrified.

"Life grows in me."

"A healthy boy," I have the captain's chromosomes in my memory banks. Your

scan shows a Black haired, brown eyed boy who will grow to six feet. Are you pleased Ulana," Brain toyed for humans had made his A1?

So, Ulana the mother was pleased the child was healthy and the lover in her miserable it was not Luke's.

"The captain wishes to visit you, yes, or no?"

"Are you mad?"

Brain was silent, was Brain mad? Brain decided not at all, Brain was logic, logic never went mad.

Brain also put Ulana's reactions down to primitive Vornalian throwback to her cave women ancestors.

Brain never had cave ancestors unless a Sinclair computer considered.

And Luke now that Utna and Titus were well, decided to seek answers to his problems out in the wilderness.

" Let me go with you?" Venus who was Howal asked.

Luke did not answer, he wanted Coventry.

"I will wait for you with Ulana," Titus believing Luke would return for Ulana, "*I* know Luke, he is good, or I would not follow him."

And Luke was glad; part of him never wanted Ulana again but could not understand for he loved her. Knew it was not her fault she carried another's child. But his love was now sour and needed to come to terms with his new knowledge.

And would not see Ulana the day he left so she stood with Brain observing, watching Luke depart on a viewing screen.

She saw a beautiful woman run after him.

Venus.

Now Luke stopped, looked back at Phoenix, roared his click, and moved on, Phoenix *was a bad place.*

And extremely nervous behind came Utna and inside Phoenix, Ulana wailed. Outside Venus smirked unawares she had left viral spores aboard ship which he had breathed out, and should not smirk, for Enalusdra had made sure the virus would devour him too!

Brain outsmarted by an Insect Noble Priest, called Enalusdra. It could not find a vaccine.

*

Luke walked into World which was different from the fake earth atmospheres within

Taken from the diary of Ulana.

Root Day 2007.

red sun

Now Luke had adventures while gone, and was gone seven months three Days, and the orange robed Insect scribes of Queen Nina précised his adventures in

Hieroglyphics, with a man riding an ant covering one wall. No mention made of tribute or season or Queen Nina. And the ant was black and underneath it slain Nobles.

And Luke thought of Ulana his mate who carried another's child, so it tore his soul apart.

And this is what Luke my love told me, Ulana:

"It was a sweltering day and Venus bathed with me and showed me her charms. I tell you the truth Ulana I tried to escape her lust by fleeing but she pursued, caught me, and lay beside me.

And I shut eyes for I saw Ulana always and was ill.

"I am a woman," Venus said and in ways was for she no longer thought as King Howal and lion man things, but of silks, stockings, and lipsticks.

And all I could see was another man with my Ulana and was wrath, full of misery, a ghost without body wanting revenge and let Venus lie with me and hoped to forget my Ulana but failed.

And lay with Venus often over the next month. I Luke was truly an ant, forget me Ulana, I am not human.

In the end I could take no more punishment, all I wanted was for you to swell with a new me.

(Red sun)

There is not a day my mate I ask "What wrong I have done I am denied happiness with you?"

And Ulana also wrote:

"Venus did not become pregnant for they who welded her out of Howal left those parts out; Venus, a created pleasure machine for Nobles **as punishment by Queen Nina.**

As his makers said, "He is a lion man cursed by Queen Nina, **so we curse him,"** and they did, **they left him the woman's curse, s**o he was now a lion woman.

They also gave him an insect sting.

And Venus not in his right mind forgot to kill Luke for Venus now loved Luke and longed to have child and hated Ulana for not being barren.

"What have those evil doctors done to me?" Venus would ask not understanding Venus would never have child.

And this was Luke's second wrong.

The first was leaving Ulana when she needed him.

The second lying with the creation called Venus.

Truly he was human not, ant.

And Ulana would not forget Luke, she also was not human. She had changed her life for Luke and was afraid of returning to Vornal smelling of ant. Rejected by the ants, humans, and her own people because of love.

And Brain thought this very funny as love was not part of logic.

Poor Brain did not realize that it is better to love than never love at all, but Brain was not human after, all was Brain?

*

Deciphered from Noble hieroglyphics.

The seven months passed slowly for Luke and death walked Phoenix for Enalusdra's germ killed thousands.

Brain the smartest of all could not find a cure soon enough, and Phoenix's crematorium worked overtime, so day long grey smoke drifted through white sky hiding red sun.

The grey smoke Luke saw earlier on his first sighting of Phoenix......crematorium smoke; then he did not know what it meant, it meant Phoenix burnt its unsolvable problems; humans had made Brain the computer that was Phoenix the ship.

And Priest Enalusdra seeing the army of Nina not affected by his virus took heart and told Queen Nina he had cast a spell upon humans to make them sick so, she attacked with all her armies, and not all were Insect for she pressed into service thousands of primitives to make up for her army's losses.

Primitives who lived in the wilderness and came upon Phoenix with a mighty host that numbered the sea's sands.

Upon foot, armored beetle, through mole tunnels, upon flying insects, under howdahs, making noise to encourage their attack, all frightening to a human ear, and the clash of color, clash of steel and copper weapons, surely a mighty host.

Even the musicians of this great host numbered thousands to add to the din playing sunflower reed pipes, cicadas on strings, praying mantis, flying insects drumming wings,

such a din.

So, the mines planted by the captain's scouts became exhausted for the slaughter was great, so the ground became slippery with blood and the attackers found their fallen comrades had turned their path into an obstacle course.

Phoenix was slowly running out of munitions.

(Such a din.)

Phoenix also had a problem; Brain's batteries drew power from the red sun and an insect virus Enalusdra made, had drifted through a crack in one battery and suddenly, there was not power to close the main doors.

Brain did not practice tarot cards.

Brain had never encountered an insect swarm choking ventilation shafts with their bodies, and dung.

And the doors to Phoenix were open.

"Brain, we are finished surely," Myrna seeing the insect swarm come on unchecked.

(Such a din)

And Brain refused to believe for Brain knew Brain was invincible, was Phoenix, and was the human body he wanted to build for himself.

A body with which to enjoy the fruits of human society such as the apple Myrna.

"Find Luke, bring him too me," Brain responded at last.

Now Myrna said nothing, no point, where was Luke?

And Brain acted like Brain again and sealed off sections of the ship infected with the swarm so, hundreds of thousands died.

And Myrna knew Brain was ill, for Brain was closing sections not infected with insects but were burrows. *(But Brain knew her supporters lived here.)*

And Myrna saw on a screen her kinsfolk gasping for air, as Brain suffocated all in his desire to be rid of the swarm.

What could Myrna do but order the evacuation of the burrows, and the people became a human swarm heading for lifeboat capsules.

"No," Brain muttered not wanting left alone with insects crawling over his metal and plastic skin and closed twenty lifeboat capsules.

And Brain knew it needed a ruthless leader.

So freed the captain.

And Myrna fled with her non-combatants into the deepest burrows, where Brain had no door sections to close for, they did not exist on his map of the ship Phoenix.

And the captain was not with them.

"Brain," the captain back in the control room.

And Brain whose job was to protect humans was now reacting.

(Panic time)

"It is time," and the captain did not understand, "open the red box under my keyboard and press the black button."

And the room darkened so, the red button glowed.

And Brain told the captain it needed a captain's palm print to activate it; it was a reserve weapon.

"A" captain in a thousand years the first sacked.

"What will it do?" The captain asked Brain.

"Cleanse me."

And "A" captain saw the innards of Phoenix crawling with insects, Nobles and lesser ones, and scum bag Allies in grass skirts urinating on walls. So pressed the red button and exploded neutron warheads.

Mushroom clouds.

Thus, Brain emptied his bowels the ventilation shafts that went on reverse, and sucked and spat out into the white sky, with what the neutrons had not vaporized.

Copper swords, steel spears and jewelry.

"What will be my reward?" "A" captain thinking appointed Captain of Phoenix again.

"Staying here with me," Brain answered.

"A" captain was happy for the moment; he could manipulate Brain into allowing him freedom, and the trimmings of authority. He would show Myrna who was the power on Phoenix.

"A" captain watched the screens, saw thousands of humans hobbling about with radiation burns, "A" CAPTAIN WAS NOT WORRIED,

TODAYS MEDICNE

WOULD FIX THEM.

"There will be a new super race, I have been duplicating Luke's genes. You captain will command Phoenix and take us back to Earth where we belong. A super race to do my bidding. ….." Brain screamed at the captain from flashing lights.

And "A" captain found he was heating up, his soles melting, what was Brain doing; panic gripped "A" captain as his body temperature rose.

"You are mad," the captain as he quickly opened his buttoned vest. And blue electricity came from Brain and hit the captain, so he collapsed and lay upon the heating floor. Hot enough to fry eggs; but Brain was all right, he had a cooling system that prevented melting, Brain was burning germs, the new incubating babies kept cool.

Brain could stay in its cooled environment for thousands of years; it did not need food or water, just electricity.

In its panic of destruction Brain forgot "A" captain was like a plant needing watering. A thousand years without nourishment is a long time to go for any HUMAN.

Besides, no one called Brain 'mad. '

*

The harpist depicts love and Brain did not understand that conception as it was

still a computer under the influence of AI made by men not allowing machines love,

they run on electricity and oil, not perfumes.

"We will be safe here," Myrna deep within Phoenix's burrows in a library designed to withstand nuclear warheads.

"How many of us survived?" A woman asked.

Myrna guessed.

It looked like Phoenix filled the library, and hanging from walls were biplanes and other artefacts, like the Wildcat with stripes and a Zero with rising sun.

Brain liked to exhibit what the books described.

Now we can visualize the size of Phoenix.

Phoenix was beyond our imagination.

It even had a zoo, aquarium, and aviary.

"Guess we start again?" Myrna told them; but first they must make sure Brain could not harm them down here. Her goal was to destroy Brain and make sure humans never became slaves again.

Brain wanted civilization and to be human.

*

Queen Nina's base camp as her army prepares to leave for Shurrupuk City.

"Ulana," Queen Nina said viewing Ulana's round extended belly.

And Ulana did not reply for she was sick with Enalusdra's diluted germ but live would, as given Brain's vaccine at last. And had fled Phoenix seeking Luke and found by Nobles and taken to Nina. Remember Nina had seen her flee Phoenix!

And Titus her blue friend weak recovering from the germ could not defend her, and rolled into a ball, wrapped in chains, and carried under a branch that still flowered, so, accompanied Ulana.

And about them Ant Ghosters in masks, mud, and dyed bodies to look horrid, hair long and dirty, others limed cut short with colored tufts or Mohican style and half or naked brandishing their wooden fire hardened spears.

Only the Nobles in their bronze and steel chest plates and helmets looked graduated from evolution.

These two were Luke of Utna's companions, and the Nobles feared Luke's revenge. So much one with his spear pierced an Ant Ghosters abdomen for whipping Ulana too hard.

And Queen Nina could not care for she coughed blood, for she had Phoenix's germs, eating her up slowly.

WAR.

See primitive life was expert in all life, from it evolved all. Man, machine, or drugs we are not the primaries but little strands of protein.

Unseen and forgotten by most till they come as a thief in the night and take you

JUST LIKE THAT

Not bad or good but indifferent and very hungry.

And Ulana knew the child within her had died and was remorse for it was of her flesh even if it had been the captains.

And Priest Enalusdra failed to remember what he made to kill humans would kill Insect, for Nobles had human genes in them.

It was only a matter of time.

Bugs knew not about passports but knew how to jump species.

And mutated measles bugs travelled in Ulana's breath, breathed in by Queen Nina who out of hate had insisted she have Ulana, Luke's mate always close.

One-week later Queen Nina lay upon her bed covered in red spots.

Why Priest Enalusdra lay upon a rack in the dungeon, as a jailer with tongs pulled his sting out from his body. A sting he used on Enalusdra often.

And Luke arrived on Phoenix.

He had been sitting under a red weeping willow, by a yellow river when a blue flower fell from the tree. It smelled so nice he wondered at its beauty; but as he held it the petals fell off.

And withered.

"Do I still love this flower though it has shed its bloom?" And knew at once he loved Ulana and, with mighty clicking roar mounted Utna and raced for Phoenix.

And found those who Brain allowed to live topside wondering through empty corridors in stupor. They had no food, water and waited for Brain's help. Now Luke was wrath for Ulana he could not find, and there were miles of corridors so, remembering where the command center was, went there.

And Venus hurried up Red Mountain obsessed with Luke. Her red hair wild, limbs scratched and mind demented way past what the Temple of Woman had originally achieved.

Planning to kill Luke again the moment he kissed Ulana.

Now Brain was pleased for it wanted Luke and opened the door so he could enter, and Luke saw a pile of ash and chard bones in the shape of a human on the silver floor, with a charred captain's naval hat amongst them; fried as an egg he died.

"I want Ulana," he said, and Brain registered Luke's anger through thermal seekers and offered Luke the position of captain aboard Phoenix instead.

And Luke roared and attacked the computer controls. And Brain trembled for it had offered an outsider, the greatest position any person on Phoenix could desire.

And Luke, savage from ant milk ripped compartments open, and Brain responded by sending electric currents across the room missing Luke, for Luke's fingers were in its eyes making it blink.

So did darts, squirted nerve solutions, laser fire and all because Brain, was not, programmed to kill itself or humans, for somewhere in the maze of wires was a

duplicate of Luke, ready to walk as Brain's human body.

And there was one of Venus as back up.

And both were a personality in flesh. For Brain unable to decide had chosen both.

One for strength and one for beauty.

So, Luke survived Brain's defenses and under a panel found a red stick and Brain screamed, "STOP I will tell where Ulana is, just don't pull the stick."

And only Ulana's name stopped Luke and he stared at the cameras that were Brains' eyes.

"In Shurrupuk with Titus, she sought you but was captured by Nobles. I have the means to help you rescue her; help me in return."

And Luke saw the screen show planes and tanks and remembered things Peter the Elder told him.

And he liked the navy-blue Wildcat with white stars on the wings.

"Take what you want."

"The plane, how do I fly it?" For Luke loved its shiny blue paint.

"No problem, "and it was not for Brain had inserted automatic pilots on all its museum pieces.

"Luke," Myrna called from behind as Luke pressed the red lever in two inches, and Brain screamed for him to stop in obvious pain and discomfort.

"I am helping Brain," Luke replied.

Now Myrna and survivors of Brain's cleansing below, for they had sealed off burrows where living, outside the influence of Brain.

As stated, earlier Brain had not yet wired them out to his liking. **And skipping along**, Luke arrived in Shurrupuk.

How? He flew a blue Wildcat with white stars while a Hercules Harrier jump Jet Transport followed with Utna aboard, and a hybrid collection of space fighters.

(Drummers, pipers, and trumpeters)

And half million marines with jet packs flanked them with the red sun behind so, the white sky was no longer white and pink clouds parted for the invaders.

And drummers, pipers and trumpeters made such a noise on floating jet-propelled platforms to encourage the human troops.

Lo, Luke sat looking out of his plane's window, in his loincloth with leather helmet, and goggles and knew he had succeeded in bringing Phoenix's secrets to his people.

And aboard Phoenix Brain flew all the planes for it was in his interest to exterminate the Noble Insects.

And Myrna stood in the control room with one hand resting on a red lever.

And Brain's voice was feline as it tried to be submissive too humans for once; and behind flashing lights busy tiny robots made the final additions to a secret body, that was really taking shape.

A body the result of merging two duplicates.

And one was not human but of lion creature stock.

And in Shurrupuk, Luke flew around Queen Nina's nest as if at a carnival.

And the great City made of wax began to melt from the flames of war brought to it by human modern weapons of mass destruction.

And the slaughter was great and there were no innocents for an Insect child was an insect, needing bug killer sprayed on it.

The only good Insect were the type that did not wiggle about on your carpet.

Luke loved his plane, but the Insect Nobles hated it.

And hieroglyphics in that city say war dragonflies took to the air from tunnels in the sides of the white and grey termite nests, with brave Nobles on them brandishing missile weapons.

And Luke was sore to dispatch them to hell, for brave men rode brass covered dragonflies; and fought with human marines and so died.

Marines died too, but not like the slaughter amongst the Nobles.

And then Luke was gone.

Having landed in a red grass field, he was going alone with Utna to get his mate.

Behind him twirling smoke columns rose from Shurrupuk City.

The others he told could fulfil Myrna's wishes, free human slaves, and the human soldiers went off in hover tanks to do just that.

It took two thousand years to free humans.

And Luke found one Noble on the road to Shurrupuk, a no one, and Luke asked if she had seen Ulana, and the woman told him Nina had her on a lead again for she was a disobedient pet, that meowed instead of barked.

And Luke left and this female told her companions who told others, that Luke would not harm them, if they gave him Ulana and folk joined those who hated Nina; for they had had enough of senseless war.

(Smell of smoke)

And so, Luke came to Queen Nina's court, unafraid of his enemies. Walking down Shurrupuk streets as Nobles looked and soldiers grew in numbers, following. Afraid of the man who rode a Black warrior ant and rode the white sky in a roaring blue insect they had no name for, meaning his plane.

And they looked dirty for slaves had died of Enalusdra's disease, and household duties were below the station of a Noble.

Lo, Luke passed cart loads of dead pulled by beetles on their way to burnings.

WAR.

And Luke would kill the queen for Nobles saw her death, as ridding them of her plagues.

MAYBE PEACE.

They saw Luke as a human deliverer. Better one die for them all than all die, so Queen Nina must die.

As their prophecies said, God Enil would return and no matter how well Priest Enalusdra tried to keep it a secret, Enil looked more human than Noble, he would not come back to help winged Insects but humans.

Luke was God Enil?

So, Nobles saw Luke as just that.

And Luke could walk into corridors he walked after the Dance of the Insect unopposed. Walls that had crumbled with his cannon, iatrines burst so disease flowed and rats, mammals ran amuck spoiling Noble storage bins with their wee. And now Luke stood by Queen Nina in her audience room, and not a man dared draw his weapons for they read his face.

"I am death, I am Luke of the Ants," and another had followed his intent on harm.

"And I am Howal, remember me Queen Nina, remember me, see I have brought Luke to you," Venus said as she threw herself at the great queen's red wax throne.

And Luke's spirit died for he had been with a man not woman which was an abomination to him, as he was not gay, no matter how the scientists had changed King Howal to look like a girl.

But Venus was not a physical man, nor thought as a physical man so was

Venus,

a person?

Thousands believe Howal had chosen this life before he was born.

And recorded in hieroglyphic on the walls below Shurrupuk. And Queen Nina saw Howal was pleasant to look at and forgave him and did not know Howal had a sting.

"What do you want Luke of the Ants?" Queen Nina asked.

"My mate."

"And what will you give for her?"

"I will not tear down your city brick by waxen brick to find her," he replied, and the orange robed scribes of the queen wrote.

"Lo Queen Nina believed and laid a trap:

Now the trap: Queen Nina put Ulana into Shurrupuk Dust Bowl chained to a stake, with no shelter from the elements and her dead child lay at her feet.

Such is the horror of war.

For comfort flies.

And Nina had her beaten with canes, so her clothes were tatters.

Now Titus who had elected to stay with Ulana was free, a slave manacled at the ankles, but allowed to walk the streets of the city.

What could he do? Titus banned from wearing a jerkin or other clothing, so his branded chest seen by all, and killed on the spot if seen leaving the city.

He had the queen's brand.

It was black burnt flesh.

He was not Insect Noble.

And Luke who waited in the city with Utna, now approached by royal messengers, who threw him the keys of Dust Bowl? And a roar of an ant sounded, and Luke mounted Utna.

And Ulana could hear Luke coming along Shurrupuk's deserted streets for plague was rife, and now FEAR had come in the form of Luke and Enalusdra's plagues.

And in Shurrupuk Dust Bowl……Ulana watched Noble archers hide behind rows of seats, and spear men pour into exit corridors and, her bitterness over Luke's desertion left her.

"Go away Luke," she cried out repeatedly.

But he did not, and she saw at dusk his silhouette in a gate with moonlight behind. And he could not hear her, so she trembled with tears.

"Luke," it is a trap Titus whispering to him from a gate porthole where he had appeared, "Trap."

Silence.

"She is my mate……. should never have left her. That wrong is upon my soul."

"But you came back for her like I knew you would," Titus.

(gongs)

Now Luke made to ride forward, but Titus came forth and Luke saw him chained, and covered in thrown filth and bruises from beatings, and the brand and became

wrath, so dropped from Utna's back and snapped manacles, and gave Titus sword, six shooter and bandoleer.

Revenge time.

And the three rushed into Dust Bowl.

"Ulana my mate," Luke roared clicking racing with Utna towards her.

And Titus shot a priest reading a book of spells to encourage his troops; Titus shot him somewhere for *vengeance is a personal thing.*

GONGS sounded, a signal:

Now archers let loose missiles and spear men rushed out and Utna disappeared, for underneath the arena corridors used by 'Beast Masters' to shepherd their charges into pens.

Thousand-year-old corridors and not safe, for it was knowledge amongst those who worked them that rock falls occurred whenever the arena filled with Nobles but not told Queen Nina, for such important matters was the concern of junior officials.

"We have lost count of the corridors down there, so why repair when we just use another," they justified their reasoning amongst themselves; but truthfully, terrified of her, so the rock falls were not common knowledge.

And pocketed the repair money.

And Utna fell through six layers of dim corridors before coming to rest and the missiles raining down above on NOTHING.

"Luke," Titus called but Luke was already on his feet going north were

Ulana should be.

And above "Seek them out," Queen Nina.

Lo, so cohorts of Nobles poured into the corridors afraid for it was dark, cold, and moldy and knew Luke was here; wanting to kill them more than they did him.

And about all World's red dust swirled.

Now Luke not having knowledge of these corridors, went the wrong way and

stumbled into dungeons.

And became wrath at what he saw.

CH22 Wallpaper

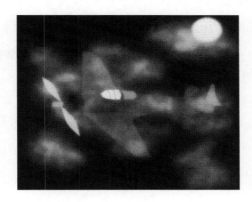

Brain collected planes.

Hanging from a wall was Tarves Dallas, Ulana's father, Vornals and Nobles who followed Ziusudra's enlightenment.

Luke saw all in the dim candles of bee's wax; and knew who he was from Ulana's tales.

"Who is Tarves Dallas?" Luke asked and answered, "Him."

Now grunting he broke chains so, Tarves Dallas fell.

And Tarves Dallas could not speak for in the dust at his feet his tongue. But Luke put him over Utna, then freed Nobles, and the strongest helped the weakest so, all prisoners freed.

For it is in White World societies to torture slowly opponents always and to save others.

"Help Nobles?" Titus asked.

Luke did not reply, but knew he was doing right and that was reason enough for his eyes shone.

Now one of those hanging from a wall had a wanted paper glued to his skin, and Luke saw that the face was Jack his friend of old.

"I am he," Jack replied, and Luke hugged him, and put him on Utna along with small ones.

And Jack took the bronze spear Luke gave him.

"Hey, what are you doing meat head?" A Noble jailer asked investigating the racket.

He did not recognize Luke but saw him as a slave.

Anyway, he had a centipede behind him for courage that rushed Luke, who stood his ground and clicked in the fashion of a Black soldier ant and the centipede stopped.

So, Luke was able to grab the venom filled pincers in the beast's mouth, and pulled them apart.

And the jailer and Titus and all were immobilized, for Luke was in lion cloth and saw in him NATURE, seeking vengeance against cruel civilization.

And the centipede brought its long scaly red and orange body about Luke so, it could claw him with its legs.

But Titus his friend chopped them away with his sword.

And parts of the centipede began to rain down for the rats to eat later; for they were not partial.

And why rats make such good intelligent pets.

Then Utna bit the centipede in half just as Luke broke off the insect's head with a loud snap.

So, the centipede gave up its ghost, for insects have souls too.

Lo, Luke roared as he stood upon the slain and tunnel walls vibrated his roar so, his pursuing enemies stopped frozen in fear.

And the jailer was terrified.

"You must be him Luke, yak, yah," the Insect man muttered.

"Take me to Ulana," Luke demanded as he lifted the jailer up for the strength of ants flowed in Luke, for he was wrath.

"Yes," the jailer repeatedly replied hoping to mollify Luke.

And took Luke directly underneath Ulana, and the freed followed arming themselves from weapon racks in the goaler's room.

There were one hundred of non-Insect origin, four hundred Vornals and sixty Nobles whom Luke freed. These were they who wanted peace with human slaves, so Nina removed them to the dungeons.

And followed and Titus complained about the following, so much that Luke stopped and looked at them

Scores children.

"Why follow me?" He asked in the semi darkness.

SILENCE as they thought.

"Because you are Luke of Utna," Jack replied, "Yes, because you are Luke of the Ants," another and then all agreed, and Luke stood digesting this.

Dozens do not want leadership, but have it thrust upon them, and they lead. Others want it and make a muck of it.

"Do not trust them, they are Insect Nobles," Tits remembering all the evil done him.

SILENCE.

And Luke saw manacles attaching mother and child for he had only freed them from the walls. And saddened and lost his strength for he was no longer wrath.

"They will betray you as Howal; don't forget what they did to me?" Titus.

And Luke asked Titus to look at a girl with matted green hair full of lice, and her skin red with scabies. Eyes a deep red and Titus shamed.

"So, I die for an Insect grub, never let such news reach my people. They will not welcome my urn," Titus and now Tarves Dallas slid off Utna and fell to his knees for he could not walk, and the freed thinking he was paying Luke homage copied.

"You will be our king," one Noble and Luke became wrath.

"Never call me king, I am a man who wishes his mate and peace. A roof over me children's heads and ground to walk and grow things, and furniture to make with me

hands. I am a man, a cheese maker's apprentice not a king," and this was the longest speech he had ever made.

And they followed pushing the cruel jailer on out in front.

And again, the strength of ants' milk flowed in Luke.

Lo, the jailer took Luke directly underneath Ulana, and Luke saw her through small tunnels left by burrowing beetles that helped corridors collapse. Small insect cousins, but Insect Nobles enemies, just as they were the enemies of humankind too.

And Utna came and those on him dismounted, and Utna dug so, after five minutes Ulana saw the grey meteorite dust at her feet depress and was afraid an insect had come to eat her.

Then fell with her stake and caught by Utna, and saw Luke break her chains and wrapped his hands about her.

And Luke's freed people smiled.

Now Noble cohorts who entered the tunnels seeking them found them so, the screams of dying reached Luke and he, Titus and Utna went and attacked, driving the Nobles off for as soon as they saw Luke, fear overcame them.

So, they reformed a safe distance back, glaring at Luke.

Nobles terrified of Luke of the Ants.

"Jailer, which corridor leads beyond Shurrupuk?" And the jailer looked into Luke's eyes and then at Nina's warriors, and saw his death upon his own walls for he knew how Queen Nina would reward him?

"This way," and the freed followed him.

"Come Luke," Ulana hoped.

And Luke looked at her and she knew he was not coming.

"Please forgive me, you are my mate and I have come back to claim you, even if you carry another's child," and Ulana was glad he said these words.

"What are you going to do?"

"One must bring the corridors down with Nina, look at the freed following the jailer," for a notion had entered Luke's head, "Samson asked for strength and forgiveness to pull down the walls upon the Philistines, who were an abomination with their child sacrifices upon the land," and Luke knew what he must do.

As if Luke's very existence upon White World had been leading him to this moment in time.

His un purposeful life now had purpose.

"Let me stay," Ulana as he had come back thinking she carried the captain's child, truly he loves me and all my children and children.

"Where do you come from Luke?" She.

"Yes, you are not from World?" Titus meaning Luke's spirit was not from this physical world of hell.

"I was born a human slave on World," Luke replied thinking them crazy adding, "To be a cheese maker as my sons would be."

And so, did not understand their words.

"Take these people to Phoenix, Titus and Ulana too. Myrna rules there now, they will be safe."

And Titus saluted Luke and left but Ulana would not follow but, clung to Luke and out of misery forgot to tell him her womb was empty.

And Luke did not notice, for his face was grim, set with determination to rid White World of Queen Nina.

Now the warriors watching had grown suspicious at this farewell, and feared Luke was going to charge them and not leave till they were dead. And wanted to leave their positions but their officers whipped and killed, to restore order as officers do and called them traitors, for above sat Queen Nina who would hand out death to them all.

And Luke made Utna take Ulana and go, and he turned his back upon them and faced his enemy.

The enemy of human civilizations.

And Vornalian too.

And ahead the jailer hurried, and Utna stopped and put Ulana down for the ant was returning to his friend Luke, Utna loved Luke as a brother and child.

"Daughter and Ulana saw her father approaching.

"Come flee with us," he probed.

And she hugged him for she loved him dearly for he had been a caring loving father.

"Flee father? I am not coming."

"He is going to die; you are young daughter and there are many Vornalians who would marry you. Do not throw your life away here, come with us," for he was ignorant of his daughter's life since they had parted company.

"My mate is back there," and she slipped her fingers from his grasp, and returned with Utna.

"Daughter who is this man?" For he wondered who could win his daughter's heart, and tame her adventurous spirit that was wild and free like an eagle's.

"Luke," she called out.

And Titus passed Tarves Dallas.

"Where are you going?" Tarves asked.

"Do not worry old man, when you get out head north to Phoenix," and Titus followed his friends.

"Who is he?" Tarves allowed.

"Luke our king," came a faint reply from the freed that were glad they had a ruler willing to sacrifice himself, for them and not the other way around.

"An apprentice cheese maker," Jack added.

And Tarves Dallas heard the chitin roar and was afraid for the sound came from the throat of Luke.

And Luke braced himself against pillars that held up the Dust Bowl from which all corridors left spoke fashion.

And the Noble warriors seeing what he was doing fled as fast as their legs could carry them.

Others fell flat and prayed to God Enil for forgiveness for they were about to die, and preferred this quick death than what awaited them if they fled at the hands of

(Blue cicadas sing)

Nina; a slow horrid painful death.

And scores of insects shouted "Luke," and slaughtered their officers and waited for

Luke to command.

"Stop," Luke shouted, and obeyed, then heaved for ants' milk in his genes flowed, and one corridor collapsed, and sixty Nobles crushed, and others fled.

And Utna came and together with Luke brought down two more tunnels, and buried Nobles above practicing gladiatorial warfare, as they fell down the holes Luke was making in the soil of the arena.

And Ulana came and Luke stopped for he wanted her to live.

"Why Luke?"

And he did not reply and Utna brought down another tunnel, and their enemy above began to flee in all directions from the seats.

And those below came running out of exits screaming that Luke of the Ants was below pulling down the corridor pillars.

"One must die for all to live," Luke eventually replied, and Ulana sat at his feet awaiting death with her mate. And grey dust rose about them blinding, choking them.

A good thing too for it made Luke realize he was atoning for his sins, for rejecting Ulana for when she had the captain's child, and it was not of her will.

Of failing to free his people too, earlier when that was his aim from the beginning.

And realized he did not need to die for atonement, that was a religious idea of men.

And above the Dust Bowl Queen Nina watched her arena become a giant hole in the ground, and her court began to melt away for wild beasts of all species were now

loose eating Insect Nobles in their path.

"Luke," Nina cursed.

*It was an old Honey, a restored Gen Stuart Light tank from the Pacific
Theatre: against the Insect Nobles it was a monster from hell.*

*

Sunset when the blue cicadas sing but not this evening:

Queen Nina still sat on one of her wax audience thrones, this one in Dust Bowl; an hour had passed and the grey dust was settling, and her court returning to see if she lived.

"I hope she is dead," a Noble woman.

"Who will be next queen?" Another asked.

"We should make Luke our king and make peace with humans, before it is too late," another who followed the ideas of Ziusudra.

But all swooned from terror when they saw Queen Nina sitting there alive.

"Six hundreds of my best warriors buried below and you lot ran," Nina spits wrathfully.

And she is seeing soldiers quick marching towards her from nearby barracks cheered, and when arrived choose randomly from amongst her courtiers who would die, for their cowardness and when Lord Hupamuk arrived, for good measure had him beaten.

This was to show all not even privilege could save them.

Especially those that failed her biddings.

And thirty females and twenty males also she had marched chained to her egg chambers to be food for her young.

As for the escaped warriors who she could catch that, had fled from the corridors she had slain on the spot.

Forty men.

(Butterflies and hummingbirds)

All cowards to her.

Their deeds of bravery cast aside. Where these not those that had put up with the chase through dark corridors, where these not men who had fought her battles called cowards and now slain.

*

That night Queen Nina came for her first victim, and chose the woman who had wished her dead. And Queen Nina full of darkness did perverted things, and then removed the tongue.

And maimed the woman and blinded her, and then broke her chitin skin with a metal bar screaming, "Who did you wish dead?"

And when it was obvious her victim could not survive any more, but would slowly die in a corner, Nina chose a male prisoner and did likewise to him.

The third victim had been the subject of Nina's intuition, for this woman she had her skin removed so everything within no longer supported became a pile of living tissue on the floor at Nina's feet.

Such is the evil the cruel victorious inflict upon the vanquished, to the victor belongs the spoils.

And how the three broken bodies thrown outside the walls of her nest happened, none knew, but after the first curious folk, thousands soon realized Nina was responsible and their fear gave rise to hate.

The bully may think she is safe in the numbers of her warriors; but her warriors are dwindling away.

"Was not that the Lord Chicjapoon's daughter?" or "Was that not Mr. Lap the most handsome man in Nina's court?"

And gossip reached their father's ears, so saw themselves and did not know their children anymore but swore vengeance against Nina and her vile ways.

"Where is Luke?" They heard in their grief, they cared not who heard and in fact wanted Nina to hear and fear her people were in revolt.

And those who heard gossiped amongst themselves and Nina was not oblivious to the loathing that swirled in the air, about her, like midges.

And with Phoenix in sight and in the clear air with, butterflies and hummingbirds about, Jack pierced the jailer well in the bowels and twisted and pulled with his barbed spear.

Vengeance was a personal thing not for the courts to understand.

And not any with him tried to stop him; vengeance was a personal thing to them too.

And the tortured walked on towards Phoenix in the distance.

And a child spat in the goaler's eyes as he squatted over his innards.

The child he had molested as she hung from a wall chain.

The jailer was a bully see.

And the rats gathering in the scrub knew what to do with the likes of the jailer, they had lots of practice eaten dying warriors lately, and Insect flesh and bits tasted nice. Rats see, could eat anything and that is what made them such dam good pets.

They were easy to keep.

And above the god of war Mars smiled.

Luke loved his plane, but the Insect Nobles hated it.

KEITH HULSE

225

Ch 23 Ziusudra Reborn

The humans fought well

And the hieroglyphic walls of Shurrupuk say God Enil, would return to lead the Nobles to true winglessness.

Scribes wrote God Enil died three thousand years ago so Nobles might live.

One dies for the lives of all.

And that is how the sick Brain saw Ziusudra, as Enil returned to the Nobles. Brain was a law to itself, Brain suffered from too much logic.

It had duplicated and now a beautiful red headed woman, walked the now normal corridors of Phoenix and her name was Aphrodisiac, not Venus, and she was both man and woman, for Brain had copied Luke also so, this woman had the milk of ants in her.

And Aphrodisiac in Rest and Recreation was welcome, for that was the way of these humans. Porn was big business and Phoenix remembered the puritans, and civil war. Criminals sought to enslave Aphrodisiac and after pleasuring, she would produce a sting and torture, for the genes of Howal had gone into Venus were of base insects such as bees and wasps.

(Enalusdra had not read Frankenstein, Brain had and admired the monster, forgetting it was a story, not anymore.)

And Brain was wrath with Aphrodisiac, for it wanted its creation back in the control room to replace Myrna at the red lever stick. But Aphrodisiac had the demented mind of Venus, and created in The Temple of Woman, oh well, the plans of mice and men, (Robert Burns wrote, come to nothing).

And Brain at last admitted defeat so, desired a replacement duplicated body, so, suffered from fanciful dreams as if Brain were a superhero, leaping from tall tree to mountain top.

And Brain feared death for Myrna's hand was always near or hands of a companion, on the red stick.

Also, Brain knew about Ziusudra from Ziu, Luke, and others, knew Ziusudra favored humans. So, without the captain's help and he could not help, for he was that blackened smudge on the floor, Brain sent its slave androids to work.

And Brain using insect genes found inside Howal redrew Ziusudra's brain, and cloned the dismembered body so, a new Ziusudra rose from the grave with a difference from the original, Brain occupied it and programmed to protect humans at all costs or supposed too.

"Who am I?" Ziusudra asked for he was a clone of sorts, but still had a soul for each cell is of light, and light can store data and the data, assembled in the clone.

"Me," Brain and had androids dress Ziusudra and escort him on captured dragonflies to Shurrupuk.

Shurrupuk City now under siege from the marines of Phoenix: what goes around comes around. The cities yellow and orange wax walls melting from canon and laser.

Shurrupuk City was a city dying from war; war dragonflies rode the air; human flying machines answered them, death hastened to collect its lost souls.

And the fields about the old walls, have the chitinous remains of reds and centipedes.

And burrowing beetles made tunnels for Noble warriors to burst upon the human devil flanks.

And hieroglyphics show the humans were not alone, they had friends, those who followed Ziusudra.

And the din was great, night and day champions fought, and gates fell open and much street slaughter took place.

Ulana was deadly
*

Lo, often did Ziusudra grow dizzy as he had two minds struggling in his skull, for his god gene had woken, that gene that gives a light inside him. And he was the old Ziusudra who had the interests of Nobles over human slaves first.

Lo, the hieroglyphics say he arrived at noon when the red sun is at its height.

(Burning sky)

There, stood the termite mound of Queen Nina, white against a burning sky, rising above her nest.

There, sat Queen Nina looking from her crumbling balcony watching Noble's scout the streets for Luke, who was in the city; but he was in the sewers only emerging to strike confusion into the minds of her subjects.

"Luke of Utna is merciful," he could have killed me but gave food for my little one," also "I, Luke will one day give you the serum for the plagues Priest Enalusdra set upon you," was said from Noble mouth to ear, and those caught saying that were brought to Nina.

Lord, warrior, mother and child and she smeared them in honey at city crossroads, and lesser ants ate them up.

*

"Who are you?" Ulana asked the squat muscular Noble who stood in the gloomy light of a tunnel below the city.

"I am Ogg, a champion of my race who seeks Luke of Utna," the man replied.

Now Ogg spoke true, and he was the one who had left Queen Nina before at Phoenix, when the queen had killed those who favored equality with humans. Now he was back in Shurrupuk seeking Luke with disgruntled followers.

And Ulana bade him wait while she found Luke, and Luke thought Nina had sent a champion to seek and destroy.

For indeed warriors did come down to slay him, but none ever returned above to feast at Nina's table.

And while rats ate roaches, Luke faced Ogg the champion.

" I am he who you seek."

And Ogg rose from his squatted position, and threw his sword and spear at Luke's feet.

"Ziusudra was my kindred," meaning he followed the same path to the end.

"How do I know you speak of Light?" Luke asked.

And Ogg waved and behind him appeared shadows, armed warriors of races of White World.

And all threw down their weapons and waited Luke's response.

And those above pushing carts with limbs dangling from them stopped, looking at the cracked road, unsure it was about to collapse for they heard a clicking roar.

Shurrupuk, a city crumbling under its own weight. Queen Nina could drown all she wanted, floods there was, always been in tunnels; Shurrupuk lay in a great Isthmus and the ground was chalk and silt, and the roar meant to the cart pushers the tunnels were ALL going to

FALL.

Now sea water seeped onto the roads, and green crabs seen, but one
thing for sure, the tunnels below had flooded with the sea.

And Nina sat on her balcony watching the south wall tumble into the streets, taking houses, shops, and Nobles onto the docks where three sailing ships burst sending

splintered timbers into the backs of them fortunate enough to flee the mud slide, and collapsed wall.

"My dear it is time to find a new nest," Lord Hupamuk from behind, putting an exploratory right hand on her left shoulder, assessing her mood for she was black widow gene.

And Nina knew he was right and looked west where the massive red termite nest of Ziusudra was, his town house. And saw free slave labor could turn Ziusudra's house into a handsome fortress, like her present one.

And Lord Hupamuk followed her gaze, "He built it upon rock, its foundation is solid," but he hoped for a new nest a thousand miles away, in uncharted wilderness hidden from Phoenix soldiers.

"It will withstand Phoenix," Nina.

And none saw the green robed figure enter Ziusudra's house, that looked like any other Noble covering his breathing apparatus as a screen against the plagues and the red dust of Shurrupuk.

*

And Ziusudra summoned his friends who remained alive, and told all Luke had done. And warmed that those who supported his ideas, freed by Luke.

And one who came to him eventually was Ogg the Champion.

And all were amazed at the powers of Phoenix raised Ziusudra from the grave alive.

What wonders the humans of Phoenix must process.

What natural laws they had discovered.

The very next day: "Luke it is I Ziusudra," and it was for Luke had come to his house to see himself, the man raised from the dead.

And was pleased and did not know Phoenix lived inside Ziusudra.

"Luke cannot be our king for he is not Noble, but you can," meaning Ziusudra the assembled Nobles present suggested.

"I am winged," Ziusudra and expanded his gold threaded wings and Brain was happy for he had always wanted to fly, like the sparrows on his viewing screens.

Now while the Nobles argued this silly legality, Luke with Utna viewed Shurrupuk from slit windows and saw warriors approach escorting carpenters and masons.

And now and again shells targeted them, and body parts spiraled away but still they came on. (*The fear of Nina was upon them.*)

Nina's horrors were more inspiring to get on with their job than exploding shells that tore them to pieces; they had a town house to convert into a new nest for Nina.

WAR, oh what a lovely war.

Had not Nina whose empire stretched away across the horizon not said help would come.

And Luke raising the alarm, he, and the Nobles in Ziusudra's house left leaving a caretaker.

"What ails thee great Lord Hupamuk," the caretaker asked the carpenters and seeing Lord Hupamuk fell to his face in homage. And Hupamuk used his body as a rug to wipe his feet, and entered the house and saw the cobwebs, red mites which he tasted and liked and picked as a fresh treat and ignored the rats and nesting crows, for the house after the death of the real Ziusudra, abandoned.

"Here shall Queen Nina's new audience chamber be," the caretaker heard.

(Red sunshine)

(Green audience chamber)

Hupamuk sending carpenters to work ripping floorboards up and planks from windows to let light in.

And under the floor Luke smiled, the carpenters were human slaves.

Slaves he would speak too.

Elsewhere:

Red sunshine shone while an early morning warm breeze cleared the streets of stink, body odors and cooking smells, stale beer, and death. Each street Queen Nina's litter entered was spawn with flowers in water to make air fresher.

And the shells stopped falling.

The humans outside the walls were waiting to see if the relieving Noble army would arrive from Nina's vast empire. Would they defeat the friends of Ziusudra for the empire was in revolt against Nina, or would the relieving army defect?

And Luke watched Nina come to the red house of Ziusudra that sat upon black rock.

"The carpenters and masons have done their work well," Ogg careful not to use the word SLAVE.

Luke did not answer, and Ogg did not press, this was Luke of Utna, Noble slayer.

"It is time Luke," Ulana said for Ogg and still Luke did not move.

And about him the followers of Ogg dispersed behind false walls that the carpenters had made for Luke.

They were human slaves.

Still Luke stood still with Utna, Ulana and Titus as company one floor above the now green audience chamber of Queen Nina, watching the massive solid wood doors swing open, flooding the hall with red sun light.

Watched Nina's litter bearers sink to their knees as she accepted help to her feet by Hupamuk.

And Luke smiled at Ulana for it was time, and he pulled a hidden lever behind a curtain and the massive rigid wood doors swung shut with a mighty BANG.

Queen Nina, Lord Hupamuk and twenty warriors trapped inside the red house.

Outside Luke heard desperate Noble's curse, as they banged the door and Luke knew they could not enter for, no siege machines brought by Nina: she did not expect trouble, she had used slaves to do the work and was another reason she would never give up her humans.

And the men of Ogg sprang from walls, and slew Nina's escort as Luke with friends walked down the grand stairway lined with wax statues that were the ancestors of Ziusudra.

"Luke," was all Nina said so, did not see the reborn Ziusudra approach.

Lo, he carried a two-handed copper sword, inlaid gems sparkling in the sun.

As he had argued with Ogg, only a sword could behead a queen.

But sword, axe or kitchen knife, head still comes off whether royalty or commoner.

Now Venus with Nina jumped at Ziusudra seeing him, and allowed her sting to appear and Ulana cast her light aluminum spear, and Venus her belly pierced fell holding her innards in.

"Die beast," Ulana took another spear, heavier and cast again and the spear cut Venus in half so much gore fell out.

And Nina ripped her skirts and showed her sting.

And Luke having picked up Ziusudra's fallen sword cut her head off and Ogg picked it up.

"She was an abomination upon the land," Luke justified.

And Hupamuk backed away with his sword threatening.

Back away to where the doors shut, so Utna picked him up and remembered the nest, the executions of his siblings, so twisted mandibles and broke Hupamuk's spine so his arms fell, useless.

From Hieroglyphics:

So, Lord Ziusudra walked out the doors carrying the severed head of mighty Queen Nina, and behind came a wall of spears and Nina's Nobles fell to their knees or fled.

"Ziusudra is our king, hail Ziusudra," Ogg shouted, and the warriors repeated it.

The hieroglyphics also show Ziusudra sitting in the new audience chamber as King of Shurrupuk. Beside him are humans dressed as warriors and advisers.

There is also a black ant with two humanoids on it, one a man and the other a woman.

And the people in another picture are boarding a spaceship. It is Phoenix and two of every living thing on White World are also boarding.

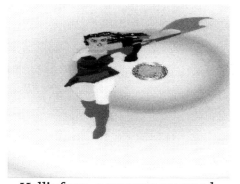

Hell's fury, a woman spurned.

*

"I will return," Luke said looking at a shrinking white planet.

"Maybe you will love Vornal too much," Ulana said leaning into him.

And behind him Tarves Dallas unplugged the wires to his cerebellum, and the colors of the hieroglyphics on the last page dried.

This page showed a ship travelling to Earth and Vornal, and a man sitting on a black ant **with a woman and their children** by the ant.

And Brain was happy.

A duplicate still ran amuck Rest and Recreation, and Brain was able to sample human pleasures and was no longer envious.

It had the seven deadly sins at last.

And another part of itself ruled Shurrupuk in the interests of humans, and was able to fly and computer Brain, no longer wondered what it would be like to be a bird or super man?

And it still ran a ship with a new captain, Tarves Dallas who now stood below Brain waiting for navigational instructions.

Tarves had been the captain of the Vornal ship that had crashed upon White World. Which left Myrna to do what she did best, scheme up reform's, revolution?

Yes, Brain was deliriously happy; he had humans all about him.

So did the Nobles on White World.

And in the sea, life began anew from all the poisons Brain had used in the corridors, for life tends to regenerate; but this time round would it be Noble Insect or

humans or unknown?

It might be artificial intelligence that would give birth to another Brain.

You can guess but one thing for sure microbes gave way to plants and plants to insects, then apes, humans, hopefully the top of the food chain again.

Do not comets flying about the cosmos contain life's building blocks. Higher strings of simple microbes, spreading potential life to planets, wanting apes that can use fingers, 6 or 7 or 8 per hand if they are fingers.

You might think cats have fingers as they open doors, but no, and dogs use their mouths. Fingers that freed Luke's ancestors from all fours to rise and build a Star Ship, Phoenix and reach World, a world with three crimson moons.

Three crimson moons and a night insect orchestra. A world where Luke rose, and rode a giant black ant, Utna, all thanks to fingers.

A new beginning.

THE END

BOOKS BY THIS AUTHOR

Planet World: Ant Rider Book One Illustrated

Is Book One of Ants 169, 47619 words, 219 pages.

Ants 169 is so large needed halved.

Book One has Luke finding out his aims and becomes a hero by fighting for human rights.

Full, of adventure, example, Luke ends up a galley rower and saves the ship from pirates.

And like a dog, Utna pines for Luke wondering seashores seeking Luke, his friend, and like a dog, loves his master.

This book is about love, the power of it, it sings across space as Light. Be lit then.

Ceugant Dana, The Oneness; this book is very spiritual.

We are all 'Jock Thomson's Burns.'

Unity of the Spirit even if an insect or a human, all one.

Phoenix, Ant Rider Book Two, Illustrated.

Is concluding part of Ants 169

48439, 187 pages.

Luke concludes his epic struggle against the humanoid Insect Nobles, become this way by gene mixing.

The Insect Queen, Nina and he race to the star ship Phoenix, a human ship that crashed on Planet World in the Time of Myths.

What secrets does it hold?

Is the Insect God Enil a human? One way to find out, come join Luke and be his friend.

Ants 169 Illustrations Science Fiction

82652 words 169 illustrations. 262 pages

(Illustrations being reduced to fit Kindle, under review)

[under editing to fit kindle]

Mammoth adventure with Luke of The Ants, a rival to Tarzan, whereas Tarzan was brought up on ape milk, Luke is raised on Black Ant milk.

Luke dances to the unseen spiritual power of the universe for strength. When he shows compassion, mercy he glows, otherwise he walks in revenge, darkness.

Sound familiar.

Amazing strength and he battles Insect Nobles for the dominant species on Planet World.

Humanoid Insects from chromosome splicing.

Human genes into insects to make them taller, handsome, attractive but cruel masters of Planet World.

A good hero needs a side kick, Luke has Utna, a giant Black Ant he rides, saves shoe leather. Come ride a giant ant with Luke. Let the breeze refresh you.

Look at the crimson moons, fill with him 'spring fever' and you are too.

Ants 169: Non Illustrated

Is ANTS (ILLUSTRATIONS without pictures. Intended for
Paperback and e book to fit kindle.

The Man

79586 words 419 pages
Mammoth read.
Are we predestined, reborn?
Early Christian dogma had reincarnation as a core belief.
Until The Empress Theodora, A.D. 561 banned such an idea?
She wanted worshipped, decaled divine and a bust next to Julius and prayed to.
Oh well, tar la, LA, such is life, those above make the rules.
So, The Man is reborn again to pass or fail his lessons, depending on if he shows mercy or not?
Met his loves, Nesta whom he left on the spiritual plane.
Meet his friends, Tintagel the Clone who authored this book.
Meet The master Priest, a vampire firmly making this book a horror novel.
Meet aliens galore and realise we are not alone.
See the colours of space and wonder at the music of the stars.
Look and listen in The Man.-

Mungo, Books One And Two.

97334 words 450 pages
A mammoth adventure for Mungo, the boy raised by lions on New Uranus, humanoid, all creatures here are about humanoid thanks to genetic engineering.
Of his first love, Sasha, daughter of Red Hide, King of Lions, to his war with Carman, Queen of Lizard Folk.
These lizard folk like humans at a barbecue, as the burgers, steaks, and sausages.
No wonder Mungo wars against them.
And no one wins in a war as a human star ship arrives and enslaves the lot.
Advanced humans see other humans as undesirables.
Run through the red grass, climb giant rhododendron flowers, smell the clean air of the mountains, and only found here with Mungo the lion rider.

Ghost Romance, A Comedy Of Errors

54980 words, 218 words.
A nonstop ghostly ridiculous adventure from Borneo to New York Zoo, with Calamity the orangutan in tow. So, load up on bananas and figs as the ape eats non-stop.
"Ook," is her only word spoken.
Do not worry about the extras feeding the crocodiles, they come under a dime a dozen and are not in any union, and better, made of indigestible rubber.
Not to worry animal lovers, a vet is on standby by for the sweet crocodiles, sea water variety so

bigger, nastier, fierce, and wanting you as food.
This book speaks heaps for food out there, a mixture of local, Indian, Chinese, Portuguese, Dutch, British, you name it, it found a way onto the menu.
Eat more than a banana and drink condensed tea milk to sweeten you up.

Ghost Wife, A Comedy Melee

74256 words, 159 pages.
Oh, Morag dear, you died so do what ghosts do, Rest In Peace.
"not on your Nelly, I am very much alive, and stop ogling the medium Con, dear." Plenty of madcap ridiculous fun. Information on the After Life, pity our world leaders would not stop and listen, might be no more wars.
Is comic mayhem, fanciful rubbish to tickle. The ghosts here will not haunt but make you laugh, so do not worry about holding bibles, these ghosts are clowns.

Eagor The Monster.

Non illustrated version.
84488 words 248 pages
A giant book of giggles.
The humorous tale of an ugly monster who
Is a cheat on his many girlfriends.
But he is so ugly?
He works for himself although signed up
to do jobs for the HOOD cousins.
Discount salespersons who will sell you what you
do not need, like granny who hunts were-wolfs
from her zoomed up mobile home.
A were-wolf girl with a pretty ankle who yes, is
 one of the ugly monsters' girls.
Come laugh meeting Eagor's other friends,
Such as Badbladder who dresses as Bunnykins,
In his effort to marry Princess Lana.
And the monster treats his friends bad, as
 gets Badbladder to do his job of pulling
twenty carts full of holidaying villagers on
The Blackhood express.
Giggle laugh snort meeting Eagor's enemies, Bear a chili
Addicted bear, Morag a frizzled-out witch, Wee Mary her apprentice
And a Glasgow hard case who knows how to deal with Eagor, "Will you marry me monster," as Wee Mary is desperate.
Just a funny silly tale to brighten your day.

Images of World

Ziusudra rides

EPILOGUE

Woe to aliens we humans discover in space.
In all the science fiction/fantasy works,
aliens, elfs, whoever are not the masters.
Let us not eat meat or aliens that discover us will
see us as meat.

ABOUT THE AUTHOR

Keith Hulse

Archaeologist, soldier, jack of all trades, artist, Saatchiart.com,
Scottish Veteran War Blinded.
Has a house full of cats.
Sees spirit people, they must love cats.
'Stories tumble in one ear so fast in a washing machine, then
kicked out other ear.'

Printed in Great Britain
by Amazon

85884198R00142